John Vine Hall

Hope for the Hopeless

An autobiography of John Vine Hall

John Vine Hall

Hope for the Hopeless
An autobiography of John Vine Hall

ISBN/EAN: 9783337087722

Printed in Europe, USA, Canada, Australia, Japan

Cover: Foto ©Raphael Reischuk / pixelio.de

More available books at **www.hansebooks.com**

HOPE FOR THE HOPELESS.

AN AUTOBIOGRAPHY

OF

JOHN VINE HALL,

AUTHOR OF "THE SINNER'S FRIEND."

EDITED BY

REV. NEWMAN HALL, LL.B.

OF SURREY CHAPEL, LONDON.

ABRIDGED WITH THE AUTHOR'S SANCTION

PUBLISHED BY THE

AMERICAN TRACT SOCIETY,

150 NASSAU-STREET, NEW YORK.

THE Rev. Newman Hall, successor of Rowland Hill in Surrey chapel, London, committed the English edition of this work, comprising nearly five hundred pages, to the American Tract Society, to be abridged as judged best for its widest usefulness. It has been curtailed by omitting Mr. Vine Hall's more extensive records of his labors for criminals and prisoners and of his applying Perkins' electric or "metallic tractors" for the relief of suffering, and by dropping many of his letters and sundry other details.

The vital aim to strengthen the great principles of the Temperance Reformation, in the origin of which he was indeed "a burning and a shining light," sometimes presenting himself to assembled thousands as one hopelessly lost, but rescued by Divine grace from the depths of ruin ; and his aim to magnify that grace in the writing and marvellous success of "The Sinner's Friend," have been scrupulously cherished and sacredly regarded.

TO THE AMERICAN READER.

On the lip of the Mediterranean, in an obscure street, stands a small, gloomy chapel. In itself uninteresting, it attracts multitudes of pilgrims from all quarters of the world, and of all sects. The secret of its attractiveness is, that it enshrines three pieces of unique and beautiful statuary, each of life size, and of exquisite workmanship. So highly are they esteemed as specimens of art, that their weight in silver coin, it is said, has been offered for their purchase.

The subject represented by one of these is a dead Christ, just taken from the cross. The anatomy of the figure perfect; the expression in the features of placid and grateful repose, blended strangely with the traces of recent agony, wonderfully impressive ; the whole covered with a veil, but figure and veil alike chiselled from the same block of marble.

Another figure, which is specially to the present purpose, and which is also created from an entire block, represents a young man enveloped by a net. Despair and hope are as mysteriously blended in this countenance as are repose and agony in the other. The captive is in the act of struggling for escape. Every nerve is strained. He has grappled frantically with his toils, and one or two of the meshes have given way. But behind him, away from his line of vision, stands his guardian angel, now acting as his *helper*. His agency is unsuspected, but real ; and every spectator, sympathizing with the captive of vice, exclaims unawares, " He *will* get free !"

What is thus beautifully symbolized in the sombre chapel of Naples, is shown as a reality in the book here presented. The pitiless tyranny of the giant vice of our day; the horror and desperation of one conscious at last of the power that enthralls him ; his wild struggles for deliverance ; his despair alternating with hope ; his sinking faintness; his rallying resolution, his discouragements, his relapses, his impotence, his helpers—are all depicted to the life in the marble group and in the written book.

But here the parallel ends. The emblem culminates in the *presence* of the angel and the *beginning* of emancipation. But the book portrays the *efficiency* of the angel : the success, the exultation, the clustering *fruits* of emancipation, perennial through a long and peaceful life. The emblem is rich ; the reality richer. The emblem, though touchingly suggestive, is mute ; the reality, eloquent. The one is marble ; the other, life. In that the artist bespeaks your pity and sympathy for *another;* in this, the freedman tells you of *himself.* You have the record of his *experience*, the burning words wrung from his own heart, his quivering notes of thanksgiving, his fervid ascriptions of "Grace, grace!" his sad analysis of the thraldom, his subdued rapture of deliverance. And he also tells you, modestly but truthfully, of the blessed *usefulness* to which one may be raised even from the very mire and impotence of hopeless degradation.

Many hints are incidentally given in these pages by which, if our Temperance Volunteers will seize upon and ponder them, they will be the better equipped and the better skilled for their heroic warfare. May God grant it ; for if any soldiery need discretion as well as valor, surely and eminently do they.

A word to those who are in the net. A word! No. Before him who though dead yet speaketh, the writer will be dumb. We only commend *his* words. They echo to your experience. They breathe the sympathy of a true heart for *your* sadness and *your* condition. They are big with hope. When you have read them, hope you *must,* hope you *will.* And then—and then ? *Act* on hope? Some angel—perhaps unseen—*will stand near* TO HELP. God *will* provide.

PREFACE.

THIS book is a genuine autobiography. The manuscript was so carefully written, that scarcely a word needed correction, and I have abstained from editorial comments. My work has been simply that of selecting, from fourteen closely written large quarto volumes, those portions which I thought most likely to interest the reader, to illustrate impartially the character of the autobiographer, and to accomplish his main object in writing.

If any reader should censure me for making the book too large, he might, could he see the quantity of material before me, give me some credit for self-restraint in publishing so little.

The repetition towards the end of the diary may appear tedious, but it is a faithful representation of the habitual character of the autobiographer's penitence, gratitude, and zeal, and may be a useful lesson of "patient continuance in well-doing."

I hope I shall be excused for having inserted a few out of many references to myself. To have excluded the whole would have been an affectation of modesty on my part, and would have implied an unnatural omission on that of my father.

If any reader is surprised that a son should publish a record of painful circumstances which half a century of godliness and philanthropy had obliterated from the memory of every one but the father who wrote it, my reply is, that the very love and reverence I cherish towards that father demand, at any cost of personal feeling, the fulfilment of his own long cherished purpose. He often spoke of his diary, intimating that after his death it would be made public. It bears internal evidence of this intention. On several occasions he solemnly intrusted the task to myself. Having undertaken it at all, I was bound to execute it so as to accomplish his own object. All who knew him and all who read his autobiography must feel that this object, during nearly fifty years, was, by his own history, to magnify the mercy of God in the salvation of sinners. Knowing him only after his great deliverance, I feel pained in perpetuating a record of what is so contrary to the idea of him with which alone I am familiar. But no personal considerations would have justified the omission, or even the softening down of his own language, in relation to his earlier life. Moreover, as with the biographies of the Bible, the record of the faults of God's saints is not the least profitable element in their history.

May he who during life was made so useful to multitudes, and who "being dead, yet speaketh," still, by the Divine blessing on this autobiography, encourage desponding sinners to trust in the sinner's Friend, and stimulate many professed Christians to a life of more fervent love to God and more habitual zeal in his service.

NEWMAN HALL.

HAMPSTEAD, (near London,) Feb. 1, 1865.

CONTENTS.

CHAPTER I.

INCIDENTS OF LIFE TILL HIS MARRIAGE.

CHAPTER II.

CONFLICT AND DEFEAT.

CHAPTER III.

CONFLICT AND VICTORY.

CHAPTER IV.

EMANCIPATION.

CHAPTER V.

"THE SINNER'S FRIEND."

CHAPTER VI.

"WISDOM'S PATHS PEACE."

CHAPTER VII.

"WHO MAKETH THEE TO DIFFER?"

CHAPTER VIII.

"BRINGING IN SHEAVES."

CHAPTER IX.

CONTENT.

CHAPTER X.

SERENE AGE.

CHAPTER XI.

FILIAL REMINISCENCES BY THE EDITOR.

JOHN VINE HALL.*

CHAPTER I.

INCIDENTS OF LIFE TILL HIS MARRIAGE.

A. D. 1774 TO 1806, AGE 32.

SURROUNDED now—1820—with every blessing, my mind is led to contrast present happiness with past trials, and to reflect on the manifold wisdom of God in his dealings towards me. The great scroll of Providence has been gradually unfolding from my birth to the present hour.

I am now seated as master of that house in which as a boy I occupied the lowest place. I was of a willing disposition, and desirous to please everybody. God blessed my endeavors, and in turn everybody became pleased with "little Jack." In the course of time I became more useful, and drudgery work was conferred on another. I con-

* John Vine Hall was born at Diss, in Norfolk, England, March 14, 1774, and died 1860, in his 87th year. His father failing in business, "Little Jack," at twelve years of age, was sent to earn his own bread as an errand-boy in the shop of Mr. M——, a stationer and wine-merchant at Maidstone. The body of the volume consists of his own records of his history, the closing chapter being a summary view of his life and character by the editor, Rev. Newman Hall.

tinued to rise step after step, but through scenes of
wickedness of every description, till my heart became changed and filled with desire to love and
honor that God whose laws I had set at defiance.
Oh the depths of the mercy of God to sinners, even
if their sins have been red as crimson, for mine
were surely such ; and yet I have been restored
through Jesus Christ, who has indeed "redeemed
my life from destruction, and crowned me with loving kindness and tender mercies."

Indeed I may well say that God himself hath
saved my life from absolute destruction, when I
record the following accidents which have already
happened to me, although I have doubtless been
preserved by the same invisible hand from a far
greater number of unseen dangers.

When about four years old, I fell through the
ice upon a small river, at Gissing, in Norfolk, but
was rescued from death. About the same time a
horse I was playing with in a field kicked me in the
stomach and threw me into the air, but did me no
other injury than a few bruises. When eight years
of age, I got a horse out of my father's stable,
mounted his bare back, and stood my brother Joseph up before me, he being only four years old.
In this manner we were suffered to proceed several
miles. When turning the horse to return home, he
set off at full gallop. My brother fell off first and
was taken up for dead, and I was pitched upon my
left shoulder and taken up with my left arm broken.

The next year—1783—I was playing with other
boys in a loft, and trying to jump across a large space

in the floor, I fell to the ground below, and my head was thrown with great violence against the edge of a sharp flint-stone, which sunk into my forehead close over my left eye, and made a dreadful wound. I was taken up for dead, but I recovered after a long illness, retaining a scar which forms a very prominent feature in my countenance, to keep me in remembrance of the mercy of God. But as I was a sadly wicked boy, these great escapes had no effect whatever to make me better. I was become so notoriously bad, that when any mischief was perpetrated, all the neighbors would cry out, "Ah, it is done by that wicked boy, Vine Hall."

When I had attained my eleventh year, my father put me apprentice to Mr. G——, a schoolmaster, who taught me to write the law hands, and by way of making the most of me, hired me to the then clerk of the peace. Going one morning to the office, my attention was attracted by some birds' nests in the elm-trees. I soon climbed up and made myself master of the eggs, which I placed in my mouth and began to descend; but a bough gave way, and I fell on some spiked palings below, which pressed hard into my loins, and I was suspended for a considerable time, till the agony I endured was so great, that by a violent effort I threw myself off the pales upon the ground, where I lay for half an hour unable to move.

While engaged in the office of Mr. P——, I was sent all kinds of errands, many of which were to the shop of Mr. M——, stationer and wine-merchant. It so happened that at Christmas, 1785, my master

failed, and in consequence I was sent home. Soon
after, a letter was received by my father from Mr.
M——, stating that he had before written two letters to know whether he would like his little boy to
be an errand-boy in his shop, and if so, to send him
down to Maidstone by the first coach. This third
letter being the first my father had received, he hurried me off in an instant, on Tuesday, January 24,
1786, and here commenced that good fortune which,
under the direction of heaven, has followed me ever
since. But to return to absolute accidents.

In the summer of 1798, I was one evening returning in a boat by myself from " Gibraltar," a tea-
drinking house on the Medway, about a mile below
Maidstone. I pushed the boat along by means of
a single oar. Coming to where the water was deeper, I put the oar into the water as before, leaning
upon it with all my might, supposing it would be
sure to reach the bottom; but here I was terribly
mistaken, and I plunged head foremost into fifteen
feet water. Down I went, and up I came again.
Down I went again, and the sudden effect of the
first plunge being a little over, I began to swim for
my life, and reached the shore in safety, with only
the loss of my hat.

About five years afterwards, two porters were
putting down a hogshead of wine into my cellar,
the steps of which were exceedingly steep. I desired them to stop till I had gone down to place
straw at the bottom in case of accidents. While
there, my leg being between the two sides of the
pulley, and an iron bar being close behind the calf

of my leg, a voice called out, "Take care." On looking up I saw the hogshead of wine descending with the utmost rapidity, the men having lost their hold. Through the mercy of God I extricated my leg in the twinkling of an eye, and before I had time to breathe, the cask passed close to my stomach and tore its way through the straw to the floor. Had my leg been in the least entangled, or had I been a single moment later in jumping from between the pulley, I should have been thrown upon my back, my leg torn to pieces, and the weight of the cask would have stripped my face completely off, from the chin to the forehead.

In the same year, riding in a gig from Worcester to Malvern Wells, the horse started at full gallop, overturning the chaise, by which I was thrown out with great velocity, but was preserved from broken bones or severe bruises. On the 15th of November, 1810, at Kidderminster, it being tremendously dark, I was walking in a proper direction towards the bridge, as I thought, but finding that the toe of my foot did not rest firmly on the ground, I bent forward to examine more closely into my situation, when I found that I had got to the very farthest edge of a dipping-place in the side of the river, which at that time was swollen to the edge of the bank, from the quantity of rain that had lately fallen. Had I stepped only six inches further, I should have been precipitated into a rapid stream, in total darkness, and lost for ever. But again that same invisible hand was stretched forth to give me renewed time for repentance.

On the 13th of March, 1811, I went to S——, to visit Mr. B——, and we drank so much wine, that I lost my recollection, and instead of returning into the house, I wandered down the hill amid the blazing fires of the iron works, and the frightful coalpits with which that country abounds. I wandered insensibly till I found myself rolling over and over down a precipice and was suddenly stopped by something. This brought me to a momentary recollection, and I was struck with the most inconceivable terror on finding myself close to the edge of a deep canal. I lay motionless to survey the danger and to study my escape, and I perceived that if I had rolled over only once more I should have been plunged into a very deep place, where the sides were bricked up perpendicularly, and thus my thirty-sixth birthday would have commenced in eternity. I now began to consider how I should reascend the sloping bank, and I had sense enough left to be aware that if I offered to stand upon my feet, I should in all probability fall backwards into the water. I therefore turned gently round, so as to get my heels towards the canal, and by fixing my hands one after the other firmly into the ground, I crawled gently up the steep, but more frightened than ever I had been in my life, for I saw death so very close that even the rolling of a stone might have brought on destruction. The night was exceedingly dark, and I began to recollect that I had passed the dangerous coal-pits in safety, but if I should attempt to return I might not be so fortunate. Next morning, on passing the place, I felt that nothing but an invisible hand had rescued me from death. When I arrived at Mr. B——'s, I found that their fears on my account had been so great that they had employed a vast number of persons to go among the coal-pits, and also to search the country round with lanterns, and had sat up all night with fearful apprehensions that I had fallen into one of the coal-mines, which are left so exposed that any straggling traveller, without being intoxicated, might unwarily fall into them. Some are five hundred feet deep.

I was so stung with remorse at the grief which had been occasioned, that I took a hasty leave and returned to Worcester, with one of my usual determinations never to drink any wine again as long as I lived. But this resolution, like all the others which had been formed in my own strength, gave way to the very next temptation that assailed me; and one evening, as I was attempting to go down the wine-vault stairs, I fell from top to bottom instantaneously. The steps were almost perpendicular, and I pitched upon my head in the midst of three or four dozen bottles of wine, which were broken in all directions. But most providentially my hat remained firm upon my head, and none of the splinters were permitted to wound me. I lay some minutes after the fall to consider whether I was or was not dreadfully cut by the glass bottles; and not feeling any pain or any moisture from the flowing of blood, I carefully extricated myself and regained the house. While I review these wonderful escapes, I would most humbly bow before that

almighty Being whose saving power alone has
effected these deliverances, and whose long suffering has preserved me to be a monument of his
great love.

In early life I made several attempts to quit
this house, but God overruled all my endeavors.
At the age of seventeen, I fancied that the situation
of a writer to an attorney would suit my purpose,
and therefore I waited on Mr. B—— of Wrotham,
but without success. I next turned my attention to
the navy, and was on the point of engaging myself
as clerk to Captain W—— of the *Majestic*, then fit-
ting out as part of the Channel-fleet, under Lord
Howe. But duty interposed. I found my mother
had been pacing the room all night in distraction.
She wept bitterly, and implored me not to leave
her, for then all her comfort would be gone. My
heart was melted, and the command, "Honor thy
father and thy mother," rushed upon my mind. My
resolution was immediately changed; for although
I was indifferent about religion, or rather, hated it,
yet this commandment had long been impressed
upon my mind so strongly, that I used to take hold
of it as a kind of anchor, and say to myself, "If I
honor my poor mother, I shall be sure to do well."
Thus I gave up all my airy schemes of becoming a
purser of a man-of-war, and acquiring wealth to
support my mother in her old age. But a gracious
God had appointed other means by which I should
perform that pleasing duty till her eyes were closed
in death.

Soon after, an anxious affair had very nearly

determined my fate. My mind had been so much harassed, that in an hour of phrensy I determined to enlist as a soldier. I packed up a small change of linen in a bundle, and putting a flute in my pocket, actually quitted the house without taking leave of any person, intending to go to Gravesend, where troops were embarking for India. Fully bent on my mad-brained scheme, I walked very rapidly till I began to ascend Boxley hill, when, becoming fatigued, I stopped to rest. I considered that I was flying from every prospect of doing well, and I was also deserting my poor mother, whose gray hairs would probably be brought with sorrow to the grave. While thus musing, the lines, "Turn again, Whittington," rushed forcibly on my mind, and although I thought it very foolish, yet I could not get rid of the impression. Blessed be God, I did turn again, and retracing my steps, reached home before my absence had been discovered. Thus was I again saved from inevitable ruin.

My restless spirit, however, soon broke forth again, and my next effort was to obtain the situation of quartermaster in the Fourteenth regiment of Dragoons. I qualified this attempt by thinking that I should be enabled to allow my mother something comfortable out of my pay; but my designs were frustrated by a new regulation, that the situation should be filled by old sergeants only. From the respectability of my application, I was almost certain of being appointed, and some stress was laid upon my belonging to the Coxheath troop of yeomanry cavalry, in which corps I had acquired a very expert use of the sword, so much so, that I frequently officiated as fugleman.

It appeared unaccountable that I should be so restless, when I had every thing comfortable around me and was highly respected. My employer kept a horse on purpose for my use in the cavalry, of which he himself was also a member; and so master and servant frequently rode together through the street armed at all points. He also felt pleasure in taking me with him to the weekly concerts, where I played principal flute, and sometimes exhibited my talents in performing a solo. But this talent was mischievous, as it filled me with pride, and also drew me into evil company. Indeed at this time I was living in all kinds of wickedness—a deist in principle and practice. Volney's "Law of Nature" and Paine's "Age of Reason" were my favorite pocket companions, and I followed their pernicious precepts most faithfully. I was a truly jolly fellow, sitting up late at nights, either at cards or dancing. I had not then become intemperate in drinking, but in every thing else I was sensual and devilish.

At this time I belonged to a spouting society, and we became so pleased with our own performances, that it was determined to fit up an old warehouse as a theatre, where it fell to my lot to perform the part of Robin in "No Song, No Supper," and of Justice Mittimus in "The Village Lawyer." All things being prepared, a representation was announced, and tickets issued gratis, which brought a crowded audience, and we received great applause,

particularly the female performers, who consisted of
mantua-makers and milliners. On this occasion I
began the folly by strutting through the prologue.
There being a company of comedians in the town,
performing at the public theatre, I was tempted by
my own vanity, of which I had a large stock, and
the entreaties of one of the performers, for his benefit, to undertake the part of Henry Woodville, in
the "Wheel of Fortune;" upon which occasion the
house was completely filled, and the applause award-
ed me induced me to repeat the same folly. Most
fortunately my theatrical mania now subsided, but
not so my disposition to wander.

A short time afterwards a new temptation assailed me, arising from a correspondence carried on
between myself and the daughter of a clergyman at
E——, where my uncle resided as an apothecary.
Nothing could serve my turn but to become a surgeon; and for this purpose I furnished myself with
a set of instruments, being resolved to reside with
my uncle, so that I might be constantly near the
object of my attentions. I now made sure of quitting a house where I had been fostered for eight
years; yet my attempts were again frustrated by
the lady herself giving me a formal notice to retreat,
and make way for a gentleman who would be more
attentive than I had latterly been.

My ardor had already been a little damped from
the following circumstance : A poor cottager, residing about two miles from E——, had, through sickness, been unable to make his payments in proper
time; so his only bed had been taken from him by

his creditors, and deposited for security in a farm-
house.   His wife and children had now no other
place for repose than a cold brick floor.   I happened at this time to be on a visit to my uncle, and
the story having reached my ears, and my heart
also, I was on the tiptoe to render assistance.   I
remonstrated with the creditor, and obtained his
consent that the bed should be restored, which gave
me so much delight, that my feet were instantly
directed towards the farm-house where the bed was
deposited.   So great was my eagerness, that I quite
overlooked an engagement to meet the lady at noon,
and instead of spending two or three hours in an
unprofitable manner, I trudged away to be a mes-
senger of comfort.   The farmer had no servants at
home to convey the bed to the poor family; therefore, full of youthful ardor, I took it on my back,
and after toiling with great pleasure upwards of a
mile and a half, along a dirty road and under a
pleasant perspiration, I found the cottager's abode.
It was a miserable hovel indeed.   I did not stay to
knock, but opened the door without ceremony, and
found a poor sickly woman, with two small children,
sitting before a few embers, in a state of wretchedness.   The poor woman was speechless with surprise as I dragged the bed through the narrow door-
way; but a grateful smile illuminated her haggard
countenance when I told her that the creditor had
relented, and would not trouble her husband again.
Having endeavored to cheer her spirits, I threw five
shillings into the poor creature's lap and took my
leave, not a little pleased with my adventure.   I

now hastened to the waiting lady to account for my breach of promise. I was so well pleased with my own conduct that I thought every person would be the same, and particularly the lady in question; but to my great mortification, she did not approve of my having forfeited my word, even upon such an interesting occasion. From that moment I began to cool, and at length I received a point-blank discharge for neglect—a happy discharge for me. The new lover soon became cool also, and left the lady in the lurch; but she was afterwards married to a respectable surveyor in London. I now gave up all thoughts of physic, and returned once more to business.

My next attempt to quit the counter seemed to promise a greater prospect of success than any previous effort. I had imbibed a strong desire to become a clerk in the Bank of England. I waited on Mr. B——, a director, and was received with special kindness, but gladly returned to the work which I had so proudly sneered at, for I considered the salary of £50 to be very inadequate to the security required. This was £2,000; and though I had no relatives to help me, my character stood so high in the estimation of Mr. S—— of Maidstone, that he nobly came forward as my bondsman for the whole amount. I returned to my old quarters with a new resolution to be contented; and when my employer inquired if I was going to the Bank of England, I replied that "I had been to London to find out that I was better off in the country."

I went on in a most dangerous course for the

next seven years, not having the fear of God before
my eyes, and spending the Sunday with other riot-
ous young men who, like myself, with good charac-
ters for integrity, were in the constant practice of
immorality.   Frequently I did not enter a place of
worship for months.   Instead of looking into any
religious book on Sunday, I amused myself with
Paine's "Age of Reason," or Macleod's "Answer to
the Apology for the Bible."   I felt great pleasure
in these dreadful publications, therefore treated the
Bible as a "cunningly devised fable."   I not only
read these books myself, but preached them to
others.   Oh what an astonishing wonder that a holy
God did not consign me to perdition!

During all these seven years I was a member of
the Coxheath yeomanry cavalry, and was not a little proud of being a soldier.   I took great pains in
being well versed in the use of the sword; and having cherished Lord Chesterfield's maxim, that "if
it is worth while to do any thing, it is worth while
to do it as it should be," I was punctual in my
attention to duty and cleanliness, and was often
complimented on being one of the best soldiers in
the troop.

I was very regular at the business all the day,
so that my employer left it entirely to my care;
but my evenings were always spent in the company
of careless young men like myself.   If we sometimes went to church, it was more to see and be
seen than from any sense of religious duty.   I well
remember it once came into my head while at
church, that I would endeavor to suppose myself in

the immediate presence of God, and try to worship him for once in sincerity, just to see how I should feel. I shut my eyes and went through part of the Litany in this manner, fancying that God stood before my face. It was too much for me; I could not endure it. The thought of being holy and giving up my reigning lusts, or sink into hell, operated so powerfully upon my imagination, that I opened my eyes to get rid of the impression, and resolved never to try the same scheme again, but to go on as carelessly as before. Thus I completely turned my back on this ray of conviction.

I was blessed with a disposition to do good to any person in distress, and also to forgive any one who had offended me. Indeed I was all on fire to do anybody service, no matter who. I thought that thus I should rub out bad practices, and make a kind of balance between good and evil. I totally discarded the idea that a merciful God would ever punish the frailties of human nature. Oh the deceitfulness of the heart!

Thus I murdered away seven years of my time in all manner of sin, and yet preserved a fair character with the people of the world. Sitting one evening chatting with Mr. P——, a wine-merchant, he unexpectedly said to me, "I wish you would come and live with me as my clerk," and named his salary, which was more than I had ever received I now proposed to quit the scene of my boyish days, and although I had many times before endeavored to change my situation, yet now that I was on the point of doing so, my feelings were so much excited

that I was very unwell for several days. **But the**
pleasing hope of being enabled to render more
assistance to my impoverished mother operated as
a powerful stimulus; and following the impulse of
nature, aided by a sense of duty, I tore myself away
from the place in which I had remained from twelve
years of age until I had nearly completed my twenty-
seventh year.

Now commenced a course of life worse than ever.
Public-houses of all descriptions were to be visited
for my new employer at all hours, and where all
sorts of vile and low company resorted. I blushed
and shuddered at first; but the recollection that this
was now my path of duty soon reconciled me. And
yet I did not think so much of the evil connected
with my situation as I did of my wounded pride in
being obliged to enter the lowest kind of gin-shops
to ask for orders. To commit sin in a cleanly manner was not in the least unpleasant to my feelings;
but to be seen doing a dirty action was rather more
than my pride could endure. But Oh what filthi-
ness did I wallow in when the shades of night prevented the deeds of darkness being witnessed by my
fellow-sinners. Had not the Almighty God promised to turn the scarlet into snow and the crimson
into wool, the very remembrance of the depravity
in which I then encouraged myself would annihilate
every hope of mercy. But, blessed be His name,
with him there is plenteous redemption.

I was a deist in principle and in practice. Card-
playing and singing foolish songs were often my
Sunday amusement. I was so desperately hardened

that I could scarcely utter a sentence without making use of some blasphemous expression; but I was never known to tell a lie. This was a meanness which I abhorred, and therefore I was always honored with the title of an honest fellow, although at all times ready to join in revelry and dissipation. Little did I think that I should ever be brought to feel a burning and sincere affection towards that God whose written word I so lightly esteemed, and whose commands, except "Honor thy father and thy mother," my conduct openly defied. Yet I dare not say that conscience did not often accuse me, but my love of sin stopped my ears, so that I would not hear.

My daring and open avowal of infidelity reached the ears of the Rev. Mr. Cole, curate of Maidstone at that time, 1802, and he requested me to read Porteus' "Evidences of Christianity.' I was quite indifferent about the subject; but Mr. Cole entreated me with so much good-nature, that I determined to read the book merely from complaisance. Through the infinite mercy of God, my eyes began to see what they had never seen before. I found that I had been led away by sophistry. I commenced reading Porteus a second time, and became so fully convinced of the fallacy of Paine's "Age of Reason," that I took that infamous book from off the shelf and stamped upon it, denouncing the author as a liar. I then threw it into the fire, saying, "Go to the flames with you, Tom Paine; you've deceived me long enough; you shall do so no longer." One would naturally have thought that a

conviction so strong as this was would have produced some alteration in my conduct, but this was
reserved for a future day.

My situation as. a wine-merchant's clerk demanded that I should be continually in company
with persons who could drink and sing, and my
inclinations were in unison with these circumstances, although I never, at that time, indulged in private drinking; but the vivacity of my nature made
me the life and soul of a company. I went on in a
continual round of gayety till the latter end of the
year 1803, when a gracious God opened a way for
my escape.

On Saturday morning, September 24, 1803, I
was very much distressed on account of my dreadfully irregular and wicked conduct, and finding myself unfit for business, I determined to take a ride.
Without having any fixed course in view, I suffered
my horse to turn whichever way he pleased. He
took the road to Ashford, and as I rode along I was
led to reflect on the dreadful consequences which
would ensue if I should be cut off while pursuing
such a wicked course. The more I thought of this,
the more deeply was my mind impressed with the
danger which surrounded me; and yet it seemed
almost impossible to escape. As I passed up a
narrow lane between Harrietsham and Charing-
heath, my feelings so overpowered me that the tears
began to flow, and I cried out in an agony of distress, that if God would but open a door for my
escape, I would willingly give up my situation, however enviable it might appear to some, and would

be content to dig in a hop-garden, so that I might be rescued from such a dreadful state of wickedness. I believe I prayed with sincerity, and I well remember that I looked very sharp around me to see if any person had observed my conduct, for I felt half ashamed, although I was in hopes that I had not acted the hypocrite. When I reached the "Red Lion," the landlord said, "Mr. Hall, here is a newspaper, just brought by the postman, and perhaps you would like to read it while your breakfast is preparing." The very first thing that struck my attention was this advertisement: "An eligible opportunity offers, in one of the genteelest cities in England, for any industrious young man with a small capital, to take an old established business in the bookselling and stationery trade. For particulars, apply, etc."

I was struck with astonishment, because it appeared as if God had answered my prayer in the most extraordinary manner; for if I had not stopped at this very public-house, I should never have seen the newspaper, and if I had been a few minutes sooner or later, the paper would most likely not have arrived or have been sent out of the house. I felt an awful responsibility to answer the advertisement immediately. The situation was in the city of Worcester, to which place I repaired on the 5th December, 1803, and entered into such negotiations as led me to settle in that city on the 25th February, 1804.

From this important circumstance arose all the happiness which has since followed me, and which promises to end in my eternal felicity. Yet on the conclusion of this very journey, and after I had despatched this letter of inquiry, I became so intemperate that I rode my horse at full speed into Maidstone, and was thrown over his head upon the pavement, and picked up in a state of complete insensibility, but without any marks or outward appearance of bruises, although the horse was standing over me, with one of his feet close up to my stomach. Surely if God had not been slow to anger, he would have cut me down for this daring rebellion.

When I quitted Maidstone I felt like Jacob when he passed over Jordan with nothing more than his staff. I passed over the Medway with no more than five pounds in the world, except my clothes; and in addition to this I had my poor mother to support. I went to Worcester quite unconscious of any work of grace having been begun in my soul; but I was tired of what I now knew to be a sinful life, and therefore determined to reform and live a life of sound morality.

My character stood very fair, notwithstanding all my levity of conduct, and upon my character alone I borrowed £300. The house I had taken was well situated for trade, being in the High-street, but the business had been ruined by the idleness and extravagance of the two former tenants. I determined to be an example of industry, as well as to deserve the good opinion of those who had entrusted me with their property. I arose early and went to bed early, and constantly studied Franklin's "Way to Get Wealth." My conduct was soon noticed by the citizens, and new customers came daily to encourage my exertions. I broke off instantly from old habits of drinking wine, although my mother, who kept my house, frequently requested me to take a glass or two, as she was fearful that the sudden change might injure my health. Still I persevered in sobriety, and was blessed with abundance of health and strength.

On Sunday evening, 25th March, 1804, an evening never to be forgotten by me, I was strolling along the High-street, when a gentleman accosted me by saying, "What are you going to do this evening?" I replied that, being a total stranger in Worcester, I was merely sauntering about the city. "Come along with me," said he, "and I will take you to hear a funeral sermon." I accompanied him, and was so much pleased with the good language of the preacher, the Rev. George Osborn, that I made up my mind to attend regularly, and accordingly applied for a seat. My mother also attended with me. Being lame, she always walked to chapel leaning on my arm, and my heart was gladdened by the opportunity of becoming her stay and support.

The second Sunday of our attendance I was particularly struck with the serious deportment of a young lady who sat opposite to myself. When my eyes were not fixed on the preacher they came in contact with hers. I found that, similarly to myself, this young person was accompanied by an elderly lady, who appeared to be her mother; and the thought struck me that she might be a widow

blessed with a dutiful daughter. This thought was
too much in unison with the vivacity of my imagination to die away. I watched them out of the
chapel, the elderly lady leaning on the arm of the
younger; but as they were utter strangers, I had
to wait the tedious approach of another Sabbath,
when the same scene was renewed, and my hopes
and fears were again excited.

I now made up my mind that if this young lady
should prove to be a person of good character, I
would make an attempt to gain her affections, and
trust to Providence for the result. But I knew
neither her name nor residence. On Sunday, 20th
May, I watched her return from worship, and found
that she took the road which led across the bridge
into the village of St. John; and knowing that she
could not return to the afternoon service by any
other path, I posted myself on the bridge to await
the approach of my interesting unknown. She
came, and came alone. She passed me, and I spoke
with my eyes, but my tongue was mute. I followed
gently behind her till we approached the chapel.
From that time commenced an acquaintance which
has proved to be the happiest of my life.

The next morning a gentleman surprised me by
asking how long I had known Miss Teverill. "Miss
Teverill! Who is Miss Teverill?" replied I. He
answered, "The young lady with whom you were
walking yesterday afternoon." This was the very
thing I wanted to know; and the questions, "Who
is she? Where does she reside?" were asked all in a
breath. The reply was of such a nature that I said

mentally, "Then she is mine, if perseverance can gain her;" and I immediately commenced a regular siege. I soon obtained a very respectable introduction, and was admitted a visitor at the only house I thought of any consequence in the county of Worcester.

Every thing went on favorably. Mutual affection ripened apace; but an enemy was lurking unseen to poison all my hopes. Her father requested me to desist; but my affection was too deeply rooted to be extinguished, and the prospect of happiness too bright to be given up for trifles. My character was unimpeachable as to integrity and industry, and my natural ardor was not to be damped by a few heavy clouds. Her extreme youth was the next plea. I agreed to wait, but never to give up. I could not do it; it was against all reason, and against my nature, and therefore I stood as firm as Ajax. Opposition only strengthened our attachment.

Five days after this I was electrified by receiving consent to renew my visits. I supped with the family on the following Wednesday evening. On the Saturday following, only three days, a friend called on me, and made me understand that Miss Teverill had been hurried away from home to a friend's house about ten miles from Worcester. This was on a market day, when the city was full of people and my shop full of customers. But I was determined to follow her even to the world's end. It was towards evening, and my road lay near Pershore, to which town I directed my steps. Being

on foot, I availed myself of a butcher's cart returning from market. Night had now come on, and as
the country I had to travel was very intricate, I
passed the night at the Angel Inn, arose at three
o'clock the next morning, and set out for S——,
where, after innumerable inquiries, I arrived at six
o'clock. The family had not arisen, but a maid-
servant soon appeared, and I despatched her with
a note to Miss Teverill, to say that I had found her
retreat. I found she had been forced away at an
hour's warning. This only increased our attachment. We passed the day most happily together;
but this happiness was soon to be interrupted.

We were walking in the fields in the evening,
when suddenly a post-chaise appeared. We were
alarmed, and fearing the worst, renewed our vows
of constancy. The chaise slowly approached, con-
veying Mr. and Mrs. Teverill, and I desired my
Mary not to fear, but to take hold of my arm and
advance boldly. I civilly inquired after their welfare; and although I knew that a storm would soon
break forth, yet I could not help smiling at their
chagrin at finding that I had been too cunning for
them. This brought on a parley, and it was finally
agreed that she should remain at S—— in quiet, if
I would leave the house. I reasoned with Mrs.
Teverill on the impropriety of treating me with so
much kindness on the Wednesday, and then forcing
her daughter away from me in three days afterwards, without assigning any other reason than that
she had changed her mind. She was as hard as a
flint; and yet she afterwards became as fond of me

as if I had been her own son. During this discourse dear Mary had been ordered into another
apartment, and I was fearful that some scheme
might be planned to take her away without my
knowledge; therefore, to prevent a surprise of this
kind, I quitted the room a little abruptly, and found
out the post-chaise, from which, unperceived by any
one, I took away the pole, and deposited it in the
middle of a large field. Having thus prevented the
return of Mr. and Mrs. Teverill, I went again into
the room, and told Mrs. Teverill that I should not
quit the house until I had taken leave of her
daughter. I then restored the pole of the chaise,
and agreed not to write to Mary, provided her
friends allowed her to remain in quiet retirement
at S——.

I was miserably tormented by these circumstances, and my mother having left me, I had no one
to converse with after the business of the day, and
having lost all relish for reading, I began to spend
my evenings with the citizens at the Porter Rooms,
or "smoke shops," as they were called. This was
a bad resource, and bad it proved in the end.
Many and many a gloomy night, when the darkness
might almost be felt, I have stolen into the garden
around her father's house, and waited among the
shrubs to catch a glance only of her who had such
complete possession of my heart.*

* The autobiographer goes on to relate how the mental conflict
between love for her future husband, whom she could not resign,
and honor for her parents, whom she would not disobey, so seriously threatened Miss Teverill's health, that full consent to the
marriage was at length given.

The long-expected day at length arrived, and on Tuesday, the 26th of August, 1806, we were married at St. Clement's church, Worcester.

Having narrated the way in which it pleased God to bestow on me his greatest earthly blessing, I must enter my protest against the doctrine of chance. Chance did not lead me to my first situation. Chance did not preserve me there through all the attempts to quit it. Chance did not lead me to Worcester; neither did chance lead me to the chapel to behold for the first time her who was to become the happiness of my future life. Chance did not give me perseverance in pursuing that object; neither did chance bring it to a happy termination. Chance did not obtain for me my friends; neither did chance preserve to me that friendship when I deserved to lose it. Chance did not preserve my life under the various accidents which have befallen me; neither did chance raise me to be master in that house into which I first entered as a poor boy. Chance did not bring me acquainted with Dr. Day, who was the instrument in the hand of God to relieve me in a great measure from the influence of a dreadful malady; neither did chance restore my forfeited character. Lastly, chance does not give me a grateful heart to God for all his mercies; but it is God himself who has done all these things for me, to whom be all the glory.

CHAPTER II.

CONFLICT AND DEFEAT.

1810 TO 1813—AGE 36 39.

FEBRUARY 2, 1810. Almighty God, kindest Father of every thing, Oh look with pity, yet with just reproach upon the sad misdeeds of thy humble suppliant, and when he reads what may be penned in a moment of reflective intoxication—sad idea!— or in actual inebriety, may he be sensible of thy goodness in not snatching him to eternity in a moment so unprepared.

APRIL 16. My friend Mr. E—— kindly opened my eyes. No more smoke shops for me. John Vine Hall, be more careful how you walk. You have a wife and children. Do you love them? Then Oh forbear. Would you be a slave to the worst of tyrants? Rather prepare for a glorious struggle, and persevere till you conquer this hideous monster, then shall you be indeed a prince of conquerors. Come, John Vine Hall, listen to me, your true friend, Conscience; and if you have ever done any good actions, do not erase them by the indulgence of bad ones. I shall be sure to accuse you, and with great severity, if you shun my admonition; but if you will only obey my warning voice, I will surely promote your future happiness and draw a veil over the past. Rouse yourself then, and I will assist you in the battle. Think of the rich prize to be gained. Think of your affectionate wife, and let this day be the dawn of liberty and of glory.

JULY 24. Drunkenness—horrible depravity.*

JAN. 17, 1811. Never suffered so much from the bile in my life; will never have a repetition if I can help it. Must be careful, or die, and of all events that is what I am the least prepared for; but the time may come, and I trust it will. Once more returned to a sense of duty, and looking back with the deepest regret, I trust that these sentiments, and affection for my children and too good a wife, will unitedly prevail.

MARCH 12. Walked to H——, where I was most hospitably received. Mr. B—— and self drank out two bottles of wine, and from my being fatigued, it so overpowered me that, on going out of the house after dark, I lost my way. When I awoke next

---

* MAIDSTONE, Aug. 6, 1838. On looking over this journal, finding these blank leaves, I here record the astonishing mercy of God towards so dreadful a sinner as I have been.

At the time of the entries made on the preceding page, my business was gone, health destroyed, character ruined, a dear wife miserable. Oh what a change do I witness this morning! Business flourishing, health most perfect, my dear wife and children happy, my own character restored, and myself, through especial grace, a deacon of the Independent chapel. My house a house of prayer, my heart a heart of prayer; and twenty years have passed away, during the whole of which not a drop of spirituous liquor has ever passed the surface of my tongue. Oh what wonder has the Lord wrought!

MARCH 11, 1845. Again looking into this journal of my former depravity, I record the continuing mercy of my gracious God. Twenty-seven whole years without ever once having drunk a drop of spirituous liquor! Oh what mercy, that Jesus Christ ever lives in my heart a million, million times welcome guest, the joy of my soul, my only hope, my confidence and trust.

morning all was strange; yet, as I found myself alive and well, it so far satisfied me. On making inquiries, I found that I was in a public-house, to which I had been conducted by some man who had discovered me wandering in the dark, and who feared that I might fall into some one of the numerous coal-mines in that romantic country. I walked back to Mr. B——'s, and when I saw the path of my night wandering, I hugged myself to find what a lucky escape I had experienced from either being drowned in the canal or breaking my neck in a coal-pit. A strange frolic, but entirely owing to Mr. B——'s wine.

SUNDAY, FEB. 2, 1812. Attended Pump-street Chapel and took sittings. Mr. Byron preached two very searching sermons. No flattery; all plain truth, and home to the conscience.

MARCH 1-6. Drunkenness—six days drunk; awful ruin!

MARCH 14. My birthday; not only a birthday of nature, but, O God, a birthday unto repentance, and a forsaking of all sin according to thy most gracious call this very morning. Oh give me strength to make another effort to leave off every kind of sin. This morning, while busied in the shop, and being fretted, the effect of recent intemperance, I said with petulance, "Aye, aye, it's no use my endeavoring to become steady. My sins are too great to be forgiven." The fretful thought was stopped suddenly by a voice whispering in my ear, " If thou wilt forsake thy sins, they shall be forgiven thee." The emphasis upon *forsake* and

shall was so strong, that I could have fancied that
some person really stood behind me; but it was all
within, and I, who but the very instant before was
quite in a passion, was struck as with a flash of
lightning, and the tears ran down my checks, I
knew not why. The more I tried to suppress them,
the more they would flow. Finding it useless to go
on with business, I went up stairs; but there I got
worse, and I began to think, surely this is the voice
of mercy once more calling me to repentance. I
took up the Bible and hastily scanned my favorite
fifty-eighth chapter of Isaiah, and this affected me
so deeply, that I instantly fell on my knees and
poured out my soul to God, and confessing my sins,
implored most fervently, and with heartfelt sighs
and tears, that he would have mercy upon me. I
never knew—to my shame—what it was to pray
with the heart till now. I felt quite a new creature, and thus I trust that my birthday may become
a day of earthly and eternal joy.

SUNDAY, MARCH 15. Renewed my confessions of
sin, and prayed most fervently for mercy, and for
the first time—Oh shame!—since I have been in
Worcester, commenced family prayer. What a sad,
abominable life I have led, even while surrounded
by every blessing. Oh gracious Lord, make me
truly penitent, and preserve me to be a striking
monument of thy redeeming mercy. In the afternoon we had a church of our own at home. At
night we attended chapel again, and after supper
we had family prayer. Thank God for it.

MARCH 18. Farewell, a long farewell to thee, my

poor and long afflicted mother. Thou art gone to rejoice for ever in the presence of Jesus, whom thou hast long served with faith and patience under afflictions of the most excruciating nature for more than twenty years. Oh may thy God become my God, so that I may meet thee in those happy realms. My dear mother departed this life this evening, . under great bodily pain. She died praying two hours for me, her prodigal son. Her latest breath was for me, in earnest cry, "The Lord bless him— the Lord bless him—the Lord bless him;" and so she entered heaven. God of all mercies, I thank thee for thy goodness in raising me up to support, for so many years, a virtuous and afflicted parent, and didst make it my happiness to contribute to all her earthly wants.* I deeply lament my total unworthiness of thy favor; but Oh, have mercy upon me, and turn my heart from all evil.

MARCH 24. Mr. C—— took me to a Methodist class-meeting.

MARCH 28. Rather low in spirits, thinking I could not consistently receive the sacrament to-morrow. I prayed fervently several times in the day, and kept a strict watch over every thought, determined to resist every temptation to evil.

EASTER-DAY. The feast of the Lamb of God. Oh what a feast! Chapel at seven o'clock; again at half-past ten. In the afternoon upwards of four hundred sinners knelt before the Lord at his table. Realized the presence of Jesus Christ granting a free pardon and an assurance of protection if we

* His mother used to call him her "Joseph in Egypt."

persevere in forsaking our evil ways. My heart
beat high in rapture when I took the seal of the
covenant; and as a sick man takes from the hand
of his physician the long wished for medicine that
shall cure the raging disorder in his body, so did I,
with grateful tears, drink of that blessed cup which
was, through faith, to heal the disorder of a long
distempered soul.

MARCH 31. I went to the class this evening.
Such meetings are of great advantage to those who
are seeking the Lord Jesus. Private prayer is a
blessing indeed. Even my dreams are dreams of
prayer and happiness in religion. I this morning
made my first essay to pray with the family without a book.

SUNDAY MORNING, APRIL 5. Again I put up our
petitions from my heart without the aid of a book.
Oh may God make me as bold as St. Paul in the
gospel. What an honor it would be if I should ever
be allowed to become a champion in the cause of
Christianity, and to be the instrument of bringing
souls to God. Oh that He would give me a bold-
ness of speech to declare to many thousands that
"his mercy endureth for ever." Indeed his mercy
does endure for ever, or my soul would have been
cut off and destroyed many, many years ago.

APRIL 17. Mr. B—— induced me to become a
trustee to the new chapel, and I also entered my
name to lend £50 towards the building.

APRIL 24. I, even myself, made another effort in
public to show forth the goodness of God. I believe that my prayer aroused the gratitude of many

a heart in supplications for a continuance of mercy to me. Wonderful indeed that my sentiments should have been so completely changed as to enable me in six weeks to come boldly forward and declare in public prayer before the people the great and mighty things which God, through my firm faith in Jesus Christ, had done for me. O God of all mercy, continue thy work, and make a repentant prodigal useful to all people by declaring thy goodness in his life and conversation. Oh may he ever be upon the watch to resist temptation.

APRIL 30. P—— and T—— drank tea with us. We boldly declared ourselves Methodists. Yes, poor despised Methodists. I felt glad to show forth to my gay companions the change which religion had effected. This day I received a ticket of admission into the Society of Methodists. A great honor.

MAY 6. Mr. C—— and Mr. R——, old companions from Maidstone, called on me. I stopped Mr. R—— in his swearing, and rather surprised them both by a serious conversation. This evening, being at the prayer-meeting, I gave the people an exhortation to watch and pray.

MAY 18. I am suddenly fixed into four offices for the church of God: trustee, treasurer, committee-man, and prayer-man. See what the Almighty can perform in a short time. A sinner snatched from the very centre of hell, and made an instrument of public service in the house of God in a very few days. What a miracle, even in this our day.

MAY 19. I was so happy in prayer this morning that I could hardly contain myself.

MAY 21. At our class I expounded, and was blessed with a lively affection towards my hearers, and with gratitude for such a precious privilege. Oh my Saviour, though my sins have exceeded every thought, yet thy mercy is greater still. I am indeed a brand plucked from the burning, and Oh may I ever live to praise and glorify thy holy name.

MAY 28. Class-meeting. Oh what delight to have a spiritual appetite! Our gracious Lord furnishes the table with a delicious repast, "without money and without price." Now this is very contrary to the way of the devil, for his dishes are charged at a very high price indeed, and they turn sour into the bargain; but he is too cunning to suffer his guests to see what kind of food he has been cramming down their throats; he cruelly gives fresh poison to his already infatuated victims, and then lulls them to sleep in his infernal embrace.

MAY 30. Eleven weeks I have been preserved in the battle, and I trust in the assistance of my new Master for strength sufficient to drive that old dragon completely off the field. I know that he will keep continually skulking and prowling about the camp, but I hope to be guarded at every avenue, but not in my own strength.

JUNE 10. I was in such a state of serenity that I could not even fancy a doubt or a fear. As if a person approached me on my left hand with a demand for a debt, while in my right hand I held the means of paying it, and therefore no trouble could

arise on that account. So I trusted would be the case in any new trial. Yet boast not thyself, O young man, but rejoice with trembling and be humble before thy God. Some of my old gay companions would think me a madman, but God knows my heart and kills the fatted calf for his prodigal son, now brought back from feeding swine and wallowing in filth and mire.

JUNE 16. We had a prayer-meeting, and were all on fire; perhaps enthusiasts, says the world. No matter. Godly enthusiasts are preferable to devilish wise men.

JUNE 30. Half mad at having been quite off my guard, and by this means falling from a tremendous height into a most dreadful ambush of the enemy. Oh, how mournful for the saints and those who love God. Soaring too high without the wings of humility, I fell into the horrible pit of intemperance, while Satan hugged me again with his infernal arms. Horrible indeed! I could have shed rivers of tears. God have mercy upon me. There is not a greater sinner in existence.

JULY 6. Quarterly meeting. The brethren were all glad to see me among them again, although so unworthy. How brotherly is this regard for the welfare of each other's souls. I do not believe there is such another society in the world as the Methodists for the exercise of brotherly sympathy. Oh that I had not grieved them! Oh what sorrow does sin introduce; and when Satan gets his victims down, how cruelly he presses upon them. But the blood of Christ can overcome a thousand Satans.

The time will come—but stay in quiet, and trust in the mercies of the everlasting God.

JULY 29-31. Fighting most desperately night and day, by prayer, repentance, and abstinence—not having had any sleep for three nights—and have entreated with bitter tears that the Almighty would restore me. Oh what a hell does the soul feel that has once enjoyed the love of God and has lost it again by giving way to temptation. What punishment so great as an accusing conscience for having offended the best of Fathers. But the mercy of God is, like himself, infinite.

AUG. 1. Still in misery. Under a dreadful cloud. Satan, Satan, loose my bonds. Constant prayer and the firmest reliance on the blood of Jesus will surely prevail; yet how long must I wait for the sweet return of grace?

AUG. 13. Only eight persons at class. It is the race-week, but I hope that none of our people were present at the race-course.

RACE-WEEK. Dissipation. A drawing back from God.

SEPT. 9. Worcester music-meeting. Bustle, dress, singing, and dancing, and some pleased, and some otherwise. Poor Christian! Vanity fair after all.

SEPT. 13. A blessed relief from all the noise and confusion of the week. Find myself, by the sole support of my Saviour, quietly rising out of the slough of sin; but I am almost afraid to open my lips to any one, and I go about the house as quiet as a mouse.

SEPT. 21. Persons newly awakened are too apt to talk at a great rate, and then stumble. I hope my experience of the hellish anguish which accompanies drawing back from God will ever keep me humble.

OCT. 5. Worcester election. I intend quietly to perform my promise, and then stay within doors.

OCT. 17. Every thing out of sorts all the week, and a dreadful state of unsteadiness. Endeavoring to repent and pray. It is hard work, yet I am determined not to yield. What, shall I, who have experienced much of the love of God, yield to the devil? No. God and Christ forbid. Try again, try again.

OCT. 22. The bile. Never had it so bad in my life. What a mercy! I hope it will stimulate me to repentance. My poor Mary is incessantly kind, though she is very unwell through my misconduct. What a contrast, and how despicable does it make me appear; but I do hope that even yet I shall not only return unto the blessed Jesus, but unto my Mary also. Oh that my Saviour would draw me so close to him that I could never depart again.

OCT. 23. Very bad still with the bile, and worse with the deepest compunction.

OCT. 28. Oh how hard is the struggle, and what constant watchfulness and prayer does it require to enable a sinner to stand his ground even for a moment. I thank God that I do depend upon him, through Jesus Christ, with lively faith.

SUNDAY, NOV. 1. Oh that I could repent deeper and deeper and incessantly for all my past dreadful sins. The Lord's supper was administered this evening, but I retired; not that I doubted the mercy and pardon of God, but I had not been able to forgive myself, and therefore came home, and in private prayer implored the mercy and support of the blessed Saviour.

DEC. 13. Oh that Christ would warm my heart. I want more power to resist temptation, but thanks be to God that I am what I am.

DEC. 30. The bile and hell. Oh that God would blot out the last week from the sad catalogue of my sins, and give me grace that I may never sin again. What a horrible thing is sin, and the more so as God is so good. I quite abhor myself as being the most deservedly detestable monster in existence; and yet the mercy of God and the intercessions of the blessed Jesus unite to give me repentance. Oh come, repentance, come in thy humblest, fullest form.

EASTER-DAY, 1813. An encouraging discourse on repentance. It just suited my desperate case, and brought me from the verge of despair to cry out once more to God. Oh how true it is that there is no peace to the wicked. What a sea of misery has broken over me for the last fortnight, and how very, very dreadfully deep have I again fallen into that horrible pit, from which nothing but the arm of God can rescue me. Oh when will it end?

EASTER MONDAY. Full of anguish. Pleading with God for the gift of repentance. The heavens appear almost shut against my cry, yet I feel determined to pray unceasingly. Went to the prayer-meeting, and struggled against a hard heart, a flinty heart. Oh sin, sin, what a delusive tyrant thou art, and how galling are thine accursed bonds. I groaned and sighed, and pleaded the blood of Christ; but all was dark and dreary.

EASTER TUESDAY. After a restless night, spent partly in terrific dreams and partly in prayer, I threw myself on my knees and entreated for mercy. Horror and dismay now opened a battery against my soul. The Bible and hymn-book lay open before me, and I attempted to read; but it was all to no purpose, and the gate of mercy seemed closing, hell yawning wide to swallow up its victim, and devils anticipating their infernal joy. But stop; a gleam of light twinkling through the dark discovers the gracious invitation, "Knock, and it shall be opened." Yet even this promise seemed not to extend to me. But to stay on Satan's ground was certain death; therefore I prostrated myself before the throne in an agony of distress. Oh, it seemed to be a last effort, and I never in all my life prayed in such a manner before. God Almighty heard me, and by the blessed Jesus sent me an answer of peace and consolation. I arose in a flood of tears. My pain was gone, and my gratitude seemed as if it would drive me into a delirium of joy. Now this may be considered to arise merely from a strong irritation of the nervous system. Well, let all this be called by whatever name it may by others, I would humbly attribute it to the forgiving mercy of God. Could mere imagination change the soul of a man from grief to joy, make that a delight which was before a dreadful torment, and induce a man to endeavor to cut off a right arm and pluck out a right eye in the hope of becoming acceptable to God by the blood of the blessed Redeemer? I think not.

APRIL 12. Have made it a determination, by divine help, to pray unto God several times every day, that I may be kept in a spirit of watchfulness and gratitude, and be preserved from any kind of sin. O God of mercy, help me, for the sake of Christ, for I am weak and a profligate wretch indeed. But thou canst blot out all my offences, and blessed be thy name for giving me to believe that to forgive is one of thy chiefest delights, and that thou hadst rather pardon than destroy.

APRIL 25. By the blessing and power of God I have been preserved to this day in a spirit of watchfulness and prayer; but I want to feel a continual sense of my own depravity and ingratitude, that I may the more deeply repent before God Almighty, and be reconciled unto him once again, through and by the merits and sacrifice of Jesus.

MAY 2, 1813. Another week has been granted me of peace and comfort. Blessed be God.

CHAPTER III.

CONFLICT AND VICTORY.

1814 TO 1819—AGE 40-45.

On the 30th of January, 1814, I received a letter from my truly valuable friend, Alderman Christopher Smith, M. P. for St. Albans, and since Lord Mayor of London, acquainting me that my old master, Mr. B——, was dead, and that the disposal of his business had devolved upon himself; therefore he wished me to come to London immediately, in order to consult with our kind friend Mr. Pickard, as to his willingness to unite with Mr. Smith in raising a sufficient sum of money to enable me to take the whole of the business. This letter astonished me exceedingly, because I had no reason to hope for such a change of fortune; and even at the very time of receiving this intelligence I was suffering from a dreadful bilious attack, brought on by intemperance. But Oh the mercy and long suffering of God, who, while I was " dead in trespasses and sins," even then was at work for my good, and was opening a door for my future prosperity in temporals, and also preparing a way for my escape from my dreadfully besetting sin. In conformity with this letter, I set out on the 2d of February for London. I had but one companion in the coach, a student, a pious young man, and we did nothing but talk of the mercies and dealings of a gracious Saviour. At Oxford, I walked into a byplace at midnight, while the outside passengers were at supper, and kneeling down upon the stones, poured out my soul to God for his pardoning mercy and protecting care.

The weather at this season was excessively severe, the snow covering the ground everywhere, and the frost so intense that the river Thames was frozen completely over, and the ice so thick that booths were erected and skittle-alleys formed, and large fires kept up upon the ice from London Bridge to Westminster Bridge, and all sorts of pastime instituted. I went over the Thames upon the ice, which presented a dangerous appearance on account of the many chasms, and yet was crowded with thousands of men, women, and children. I was tempted to take a glass of wine, that I might say in aftertimes that I had not only visited the booths on the ice, but that I had actually myself taken refreshment there; but my mountain then stood strong, and temptation had no avail. I was mercifully preserved in this manner during the whole twelve days that I was kept in a state of idleness and suspense in London. There were many applicants for the concern, but my friend was so determined to put me into possession of what he considered an excellent opportunity of gaining a good maintenance, that he told me that he would sooner lose five hundred pounds than I should be disappointed. Mr. Pickard tendered his services by the loan of one thousand pounds towards the sum necessary. Oh the mercy of God in creating such a disposition in those whose hearts had been so severely grieved by my misconduct.

SUNDAY, FEB. 6. At Mr. Wesley s chapel, in the City Road, I heard a sermon by Dr. Adam Clarke. His sermon, which I took down from his lips, was on the thirtieth Psalm, which he divided into three parts : namely, Exultation, Distress, and Recovery. "This psalm," Dr. Clarke observed, "presents three different states of experience. The first state is of a soul when first brought to God; then the case which this state brings; then the presumption arising from this case, and the fall in consequence of this presumption, and the recovery by prayer." Oh how my ears were all awake at this beginning, because it seemed as if it was the very subject suited to my own individual case. In speaking upon the eighth verse, "I cried unto God," Dr. Clarke observed, "We are apt to think that if God were but to pardon, it would be well : no, not half well; we must be healed." In explaining the ninth verse, he observed that David might say, "If I am cut off in my backsliding, and yet am desirous to return to God, who will believe the promises, 'Return, thou backsliding Israel, and I will heal your backslidings; though your sins be as scarlet, they shall be as white as snow?'" "Therefore," said Dr. Clarke, "let no backslider ever despair." Oh how deeply did this sink into my poor wounded heart. I was all attention, all hope; and it seemed as if this sermon was preached for me alone. And it appeared the more so when the preacher went on to say that "some people will ask, How can a man who has

repeatedly trifled with mercy," exactly my unhappy
case, "expect that God will hear him again? Why,"
said Dr. Clarke, "if the man had no sorrow, we
should fear his state; but if the man desires to be
saved, we know that such desire comes from God,
and therefore he cannot be lost. And if this argument would but be taken hold of by poor backslid-
ers, they would not be unwilling to apply again
unto God, who is ever ready to hear their cry."
Oh, thought I, this is the very cordial for my
wounded soul, and heaven itself can bear witness
how earnestly I desire grace to live to the glory of
God, but am prevented by the strength of sin. "Is
it not the breath of God in your own souls?" said
Dr. Clarke. "As to your convictions of your own
unworthiness, that falls to nothing before the blood
of Christ; your sins can never be too great to be
forgiven. Take Christ in the front of your petitions,
and God will turn your mourning into dancing. If
you have lost your God, do not rest till you find him
again. Of what avail is it to the devil that he was
once in heaven; and what avail will it be to the
sinner that he once possessed the favor of God, if
he does not continue to possess that favor? But a
soul that is penitent can never be lost, for a single
spark of grace can never go to hell; and God stands
ready to receive the penitent, let him come whenever he will, or however deep his guilt." Well,
thought I, this is all for me; and as the Lord's supper is to be administered here this morning, I will
assuredly partake of it; and so I did, and my soul
rejoiced.

On Tuesday, 15th of February, I awoke very early, and prayed earnestly to God to blot out my sins and disperse every unholy thought, and I was for once so completely engaged in imploring salvation from sin into perfect obedience to the will of God, that I quite forgot to pray for my dear wife and children; but he who searches all hearts, knows mine also. I continued in a most anxious state of uncertainty about the business until Tuesday, the 5th of April, 1814, when a letter arrived saying that the difficulties were now removed. Accordingly, on Monday, the 11th of April, I arrived in Maidstone, and took possession of the whole concern.

Now then began a new career of life, and I found myself unexpectedly placed as the master over that very house which I entered as errand-boy on the 24th day of January, 1786, and remained till the 12th day of January, 1801. Oh how was my poor heart agitated with hopes and fears, and strong determinations never again to offend that God who had done such mighty deeds for one who had so awfully rebelled against him. But how weak are our best resolutions when made in our own strength; and so I soon found it to my cost and sorrow, for it was only on the Saturday fortnight, April 30, that some of my old companions came to congratulate me upon my arrival at Maidstone, and insisted on taking wine by way of wishing me success. Well, I thought a glass or two could not do me any harm, particularly as I had worked hard all the week, and had now obtained fortitude and resolution to stop at three or four glasses at the very outside. But how treacherous is the human heart! I went on, glass for glass, with my companions, till reason began to totter, and at this very moment, which I shall never forget, the door opened, and who should stand before my face to witness my folly and confusion, but Mr. Pickard? Yes; even my best friend, who had come down from London for the sole purpose of giving me comfort and advice in this trying moment. Oh how my heart recoiled at my own deep ingratitude towards such a benevolent friend, and I stood speechless. But he did not upbraid me, for his heart was too full of compassion to augment the anguish which he knew would take possession of my soul when reason resumed her seat. He gently retreated, and looking me full and expressively in the face, said, "I will see you in the morning." I dismissed my companions with reproaches and retired to bed, when I passed a restless night. As soon as I had breakfasted I waited on Mr. Pickard. When he saw me, he took my hand, and with a silent squeeze looked forgiveness. He soon proposed a walk, and we had scarcely got into the street when he turned upon me, and with a voice of sympathy said, "I do not condemn you, for I deeply pity you." This kindness entered my very soul, and I could only say, "God bless you, sir." Here again I have reason to bless that merciful Being who did not utterly take his loving kindness from me, neither suffer my friends to forsake me.

After this time I began to apply myself more earnestly to business than ever; but still my prevailing propensity kept fast hold, and although I was very circumspect at times for three or four weeks together, yet at other intervals I went off into the most dreadful indulgences, to the disgrace of myself and to the astonishment and grief of those who were truly desirous for my happiness. Among these was Mr. M——, who had known me from a child, and who combated the remarks of my enemies till at last he was almost in despair; and added to all this, and as the height of my depravity, I had been blessed with the best of wives, one who feared God, and whose life seemed to be bound up in myself, and whose tenderness towards me, even in the midst of my cruelty, was beyond all expression or description ; and although I was fully sensible of all this, as well as of the wonderful mercy of God in not cutting me down, still I had no power to resist my heart-rending propensity, although the happiness of my family and friends was all involved in my conduct. Added to all this was my own immediate danger of eternal misery, as also my frequently being rendered completely insane for several days after I had desisted from the use of wine or liquors. All these things only increased my weakness and my misery, for I often saw such dreadful sights and heard such dreadful sounds, when recovered from intoxication, that I was frequently led to exclaim, in all the horror of despair, that I was certain that my thoughts of religion were all delusion, and that I was doomed by heaven itself to eternal destruction. Indeed one day as I was shaving myself, after I had been in a dreadful state for several days together, the devil suggested

3*

to me that I had better cut my throat at once, for
I had outlived my former respectability, and was
become such a disgrace to my poor wife and children, that the sooner I was out of the way the better.   But again the same invisible hand preserved
me, and I kept on sinning and repenting at various
times during the remainder of the years 1814 and
1815; sometimes walking uprightly to the appearance of men for many weeks together, and continuing incessant in prayer to God for deliverance, still
hoping even against hope.   At length the time drew
nigh for my escape from Doubting Castle and from
the chains of Giant Despair.   I had been most
alarmingly ill of a bilious fever, brought on by intemperance, and was so near death that I began to
think I must now die, and go to receive the reward
of my sins; and yet hope was not entirely taken
from me, for when I was in the greatest bodily agony I remembered the words of David, and cried to
the Lord, and said, "What profit is there in my
blood; shall the dead praise thee?   O Lord, let
me live for Christ's sake, and let it be seen that
thine arm is not shortened that it cannot save.   Oh
save me, vile as I have been, that even yet I may
live to thy glory as a monument of thy mercy."
My tears and my poor heart went together, and a
voice seemed to say, "Thou shalt recover;" and
blessed be God, I did recover, with a broken and a
contrite heart.

I became much humbled, and thought if my
friends would place me in a private mad-house, or
some confinement, I should be content to live on

bread and water all the days of my life, if I could
be preserved from sinning against God. While I
was ruminating in this manner, and making fresh
determinations to set out again for the kingdom of
heaven, my dear wife and my friend Mr. M——
had been consulting whether there was any possibility of my being benefited by medical advice, and
had actually applied to Dr. Day, who gave great
hopes that if I could be brought to take such medicines as he should prescribe, a cure might be expected; but that the first great difficulty would be
to make me acquainted with their deliberations,
and to obtain my consent to conform to their plans.
At the very same time my gracious God was himself working in me a strong desire to make use of
every means that could be suggested. This was on
the ever-to-be-remembered first day of March, 1816.
Mr. M—— kindly came to visit me, though I was
then unworthy of his notice, and as I was deeply
deploring my sad, sinful, and ungrateful conduct
towards God and all my friends, I said, "I wonder
whether Dr. Day could possibly point out any plan
for my relief," as I was willing to undertake any
thing in the world to prove how desirous I was to
be freed from this dreadful wickedness. Mr. M——
and my dear wife looked at each other with astonishment, and she exclaimed, "The hand of God is
certainly in this thing." They then informed me
of what they had been doing, and how troubled
they were to know in what manner they should
make me acquainted with their plans, fearing that
I should be offended.

Here, my dear children, if ever you should read
this book, here was a ray of light bursting upon
your poor father's head, which led him from the pit
of despair to the gates of heaven. Here his hopes
were again revived; here your poor mother felt the
mercy of God pouring consolation into her almost
broken heart; and here a new song of praise arose
to that God whose mercy is everlasting. Dr. Day
was immediately requested to visit me, and after
putting various questions, he agreed to take me
under his care, and even went so far as to say that
he would never leave me until he had, through the
blessing of God, effected a cure. Oh what a day
was this; what hopes and fears alternately played
in all our minds! The very thought of being
healed of such a malady, and of being restored to
society and respectability, was too delicious to be
endured without showers of tears. I began to take
the remedies prescribed that very night, and was
enabled to trust in God for his assistance to enable
me to persevere. But it was not merely the medicines, but a great solace was given to my mind by
Dr. Day's kind commiseration of my situation,
which he declared demanded the full exercise of
pity, instead of that heavy censure which had been
cast upon me. The voice of pity! Oh how sweet
it is to the deeply burdened heart, overpowered by
a sense of its own depravity! In consulting with
my physician, I told him how deeply my mind was
impressed with a sense of the heinousness of my
sin against God, whom I desired to love, and yet
had no power to resist the dreadful evil which came

upon me periodically about once a month. His answer was, that he could not view my case in the same depraved light, for he was confident, from what he had discovered respecting my nervous system, that I could no more prevent the mischief when the fit came upon me, than any person subject to the gout could prevent a return of the same disorder. Oh what a valve of hope was now opened to my ardent imagination, to think even for a moment that there were persons who thought me less guilty than I had condemned myself to be. Yet still I considered this by far too favorable an opinion, for I had no desire to forgive myself, even though all my friends and even my Creator should do so. I desired to consider myself quite as vile as my outward conduct appeared to be, even though I had no desire to lose my hope in God; for all things were possible to him. The medicines were draughts composed principally of steel, mixed in about two ounces of peppermint water, to be taken twice a day; and with these he allowed me to take two or three glasses of port-wine after dinner, but to refrain entirely from the use of spirits in any way whatever; and to make use of toast and water at my meals, with a very moderate use of small beer or a little porter, but no ale.

I desired to feel exceedingly grateful that I was allowed so bountiful a supply, and the more particularly when so great a good was connected with it; for I had determined in my own poor strength that I would cheerfully drink nothing but water during the whole of my life, if such an expedient could at

all be the means of my escaping the dreadful evil
which had entwined itself around me for so many
years. I went on in a tolerably steady manner for
several weeks, strictly attending to my medicines
and watching against temptation, taking also especial care to read the Bible for nearly an hour every
morning before breakfast, with prayer and supplication for divine help, and as long as I continued
in this regular course I received daily blessings.
My health and strength were indeed renewed as
the eagle's, and I began to think that my mountain
would now stand against every attack of my secret
foe. Thus I became lifted up with pride, which led
me to be less attentive to prayer and reading the
Bible; and in consequence, at an unguarded hour
I was again the captive of my enemy.

Dr. Day again watched over me with the greatest tenderness, and desired me not to be discouraged, as he had not expected that I should overcome in a few weeks an evil which had been growing upon me for several years. I took fresh courage,
and set out again with a strong determination to be
so very watchful that nothing should surprise me
for the future. But how vain are the strongest
human efforts when unassisted by divine grace, and
how prone is human nature to refuse that powerful
aid which is so freely offered by the Creator of the
universe, "who giveth liberally, and upbraideth not."
This was not a battle between myself and another
of my fellow-creatures, in which superior strength,
or skill, or accident, might gain the victory; this
was a contest with inbred corruption and habits of

long standing and increasing growth, and which, if
not subdued, would inevitably sink the soul as well
as the body into endless ruin. However, I set out
again in the same manner as before, adhering to
my medicines and my Bible, and I thought myself
upon surer ground than ever, and particularly as I
had been recovered from my last fall in five days
instead of fifteen or twenty as was formerly the
case; and this circumstance gave my physician as
well as myself considerable reason to hope that we
had at least made some impression upon the force
and power of my strong propensity.

Still these hopes were delusive, for in nine days
afterwards I fell into the very same situation again,
and brought deep distress into my own soul as well
as poignant anguish into the heart of a beloved wife
and all my friends. I might be asked, How can
you have a sincere affection for your wife if you
indulge in these disgraceful extremes? All I could
answer would be that, from the bottom of my soul,
I detest and abhor my own conduct, and yet have
not the power to resist that which I hate. But to
proceed. Dr. Day himself was much chagrined as
well as myself, but he was not at all out of heart;
and when in the anguish of my mind I entreated
him not to leave me through disgust at my conduct,
he kindly reassured me that he would never leave
me till he had brought me through every difficulty.
And he the more insisted upon it that his hope was
considerably increased, because in these two last
times of falling into this distress I had been recovered each time in five days. Yet it would appear

very naturally to some minds that the blessings of the Almighty only served to render my heart more hardened instead of reducing it to obedience, for he had graciously given me another son, Newman, between these two last falls, the first of which terminated on the 18th of May, and the last of which commenced on the 27th of the same month; and in this interval I was so far recovered and so redetermined to persevere, that on the day my dear wife was safely delivered, which was on Wednesday, the 22d of May, 1816, I voluntarily drew up of my own mind, and wrote with my own hand, a complete grant of power to Dr. Day to make use of whatever means he should deem most expedient to effect my recovery, even to the confinement of my person; and this document I signed in the presence of Dr. Day and my friend Mr. M——, into whose hands I gave this writing, to be by him securely kept and brought forward in vindication of Dr. Day's conduct, if ever my situation should become so unfortunate as to oblige him to have recourse to severe measures.   Dr. Day and Mr. M—— were both of them deeply affected by this instance of my ardent desire to overcome this evil, and they felt constrained to acknowledge that I had by this act evinced all the sincerity that it was possible for a man to display; and they went away more strengthened than ever in their opinion that all would yet end well. Indeed I myself had stronger hopes than ever, because I felt an inward desire to live to the glory of God, even though my present conduct seemed to be directly opposite to every thing like

such a desire, and gave more encouragement than
ever to my enemies to hope for my speedy destruction. But He who had determined my deliverance,
had also determined that I should pass through
more trials, but at the same time he mercifully gave
me an increase of resolution to persevere.

Yet my mind underwent many painful struggles
through fear that, even after all that had been said
and done, it was still possible that I had been deceived in my hopes of recovery from so dreadful a
malady, and particularly as it had been a strongly
received opinion that persons addicted to drunkenness were very seldom recovered. However, I took
fresh courage, and felt my fears considerably abat-
ed when I read the lives of Bunyan, Perkins, Gardi-
ner, and Newton, all of whom had been notorious
sinners, and yet had all been rescued from destruction by the same almighty hand; and why should not
that same hand save even me, notwithstanding I had
outsinned them all? My faith in God revived, and I
commenced taking my medicines again on the first
day of June, and accompanied them with fervent
prayer and a strict attention to reading the Bible
every morning for one hour before breakfast. In
this manner I went steadily forward till the 23d of
July, when, to my dreadful grief and the grief of all
my friends, I yielded again to temptation, and fell
into the same dreadful state of intemperance and
distress as before. I remained under the effects of
this fall for six days, when it pleased God to spare
my life once more, and to renew my determination
to rise again and enter upon a new combat with my

mortal foe. But no language can depict the anguish
of my mind to find how dreadfully I had rebelled
against my Creator; and it seemed to be the most
incomprehensible thing in the world how I could be
so drawn aside, after having tasted and relished the
goodness of God and delighted in his ways; and
indeed it was such an astonishment to my own
mind, that I was frequently constrained to look
upon myself as the greatest hypocrite under the
sun, and yet I could not give up my hope that my
prayers, which I thought were at least sometimes
sincere, if not always so, would eventually be answered.

Under these circumstances I set out once more,
looking entirely to heaven for help, and continued
my medicines and reading the Bible with great
regularity every day. Thus I was helped forward
again, and my kind friends Dr. Day and Mr. M——
were every day anxiously overlooking all my steps,
and watching for the completion of their fervent
wishes. Hopes and fears now alternately rose in
my mind. The prize to be obtained was of immense
value, therefore the fears of losing it were great
indeed; and under these impressions I pressed forward with great circumspection, until I had become
so far established as to discontinue my medicines
entirely. But most unfortunately my dear wife
was absent at this time at Worcester, and having
no person to converse with in the evening after the
close of business, I frequently went into company,
when I should otherwise have been happy at my
own fireside. Still, however, through the mercy of

God, I maintained my ground, but not with so much firmness as I should have done if I had been favored with a companion to engage my vacant hours. Yet, notwithstanding all these dangers, I began to think myself fully established in such strength of resolution as to resist any temptation, and the more particularly as I had quite declined the use of medicine. But this was false security, for being invited to dine with Mr. A—— on the 10th day of September, 1816, in company with my kind and watchful friend Mr. M——, and several other good friends, I passed a very happy day; and although I did not drink more than a pint of wine, yet it was so much more than I had lately been accustomed to take, that it produced a stimulus in my system, which induced a desire for more when I got home, and I insensibly gave way to the desire, and thus staggered again out of the right path. But when I returned to my senses, and found what I had been guilty of in thus abusing the mercy of God, my distress was more poignant if possible than ever. I had seemed to be so near the attainment of all my best wishes, and of the hopes which my friends had so long entertained, that I had only to stretch forth my hand and seize the crown; yet it again vanished from my embrace, and the disappointment almost broke my heart. I wept rivers of tears, and prostrated myself before the mercy-seat of God, and implored his assistance even once more, that mine enemy might not have to boast that his power was stronger than the grace of the Most High. My prayers were heard, and I was restored from this fall in four days, and I immediately recommenced taking my medicines, being strengthened with a determination never to give up the contest.

During all these contests I had been allowed to take two or three glasses of wine a day, or a small quantity of spirits and water, according to circumstances; but then I had not prudence or resolution enough always to stop at the right point, and this often led to bad consequences. At length Dr. Day reasoned with me as to the necessity of confining myself wholly to water, small-beer, or porter, as the uttermost degree of strong drink that I might venture to take. My desire to conquer every enemy being now more deeply rooted than ever, I entered into my physician's views of the subject, and prayed for grace to help me in this my time of need. My dear wife was now also returned from Worcester, which made my home more comfortable, and gave new life to new resolutions. Accordingly I began on Sunday, the 22d of September, 1816, to relinquish the use of wine of every description, and also all kinds of spirituous liquors and ale, having also pledged myself that if porter or table-beer were too strong for my constitution, I would cheerfully confine myself to water rather than offend a merciful Creator. I continued taking my medicines with the greatest regularity till about the 10th of October, when my health becoming more and more established, I found them unnecessary, and after having taken three hundred and seventy-six bottles of the chalybeate draughts, I relinquished them entirely; and through the mercy of God have never had any occasion to recur to the use of these medicines from the 10th of October, 1816, even to the present moment of writing this passage, which is written on this 29th day of November, 1817.

During the whole of this period, that great Being who was accomplishing so wonderful a work, was also giving me an increasing desire to study his holy word; and through his constraining influence I have never passed a single day without reading the Bible for one hour, or nearly so, every morning before breakfast, besides at several other times in the day, and praying most earnestly to have my understanding illuminated, that the precepts and doctrines of the Scriptures might be deeply fixed in my heart, and form the constant rule of my life before God and man. By these means I have been kept in a state of continual happiness, my health has been uninterruptedly good, and all my comforts have abounded, and I trust that I am daily living to the praise of the glory of God, as a wonderful monument of his free grace and great salvation.

I would not have any one suppose that the great good here recorded was obtained without many struggles. It is no easy thing to overcome long-established habits, particularly when the natural inclinations are ever ready to contribute to their strength. And this was my case, inasmuch as I was of a lively, cheerful disposition, and fond of company; and because I could sing a good song or tell a good tale, I was continually invited into parties of drinking and pleasure. All this was to be overcome, and pursuits of an opposite tendency were to be encouraged with the utmost energy and perseverance. Now nothing short of divine help could possibly accomplish so desirable an end; but this help was to be had simply by asking it, with a sincere and contrite mind, of Him who has graciously declared that all who seek shall find. I am sure that I am a living witness of the faithfulness of God to all his promises. But did the seeking the kingdom of heaven make me less cheerful or less lively? Far from it; all this natural vivacity continued to flow, but it was turned into another channel. My business was pursued with as much avidity as ever; but the perplexities which used to occasion peevishness were now all softened by a serenity that made crooked things straight and rough places plain, thus exemplifying the words of Scripture, that the ways of religion "are ways of pleasantness, and all her paths are peace." Yet my feelings were often deeply oppressed when I beheld any poor creature tottering in the streets under the influence of intoxication, and the recollection of my own former distressing state impelled a fervent ejaculation that God would mercifully become the friend of these poor creatures, who had lost all friendship for themselves and were totally insensible of their danger. Indeed I never see persons in liquor but my heart groans for their relief, as I well know that nothing short of Omnipotence can stay the raging of such an unmerciful enemy. Those persons who had laid many bitter things to my charge all became quiet when it was known that I not only abhorred this conduct myself, but that I had also placed myself under the entire direction of a physician of long tried abilities, in order that I might be relieved from this formidable malady, which he most unequivocally denominated disease and not inclination; and that it was a disease induced by a strong affection of the whole nervous system, which rendered it almost impossible to escape the effects produced. This testimony softened the malice of my foes into pity; and when they were credibly informed that I was continually striving against it, they almost universally wished me success. My friends all gathered around me with the kindest expressions of encouragement, and this gave me a zest to persevere; and when I also beheld my dear children and a beloved wife all deeply involved in my fate, my heart was elevated to heaven at the very thought of being restored to them in health and happiness.

It was a Christmas day, 1816, when we were all sitting round the fire, my wife on one side and myself on the other, with our four healthy boys, Edward, Vine, Stephen, and Newman, playing between us, and ourselves enjoying a serenity of happiness springing from the mercy of our God, that the prospect of future bliss and the high enjoyment of present comfort quite overpowered our feelings, and with hearts lifted up in fervent gratitude to the Author of our blessings, we sang, "Praise God, from whom all blessings flow," and we sang it with the heart full in tune, while tears of unspeakable delight rolled down in sympathy with our exalted affections. It was a day of pure delight, such as

we had never witnessed before, because our affections were never before so sincerely fixed on our
great Redeemer. And besides all this, I had been
preserved ninety-four days without tasting even a
drop of any strong liquor, and this had never before
occurred since I was seventeen years of age. All
this increased our joy and gave additional vigor to
hopes of the future, and the more particularly as
God Almighty had himself given me strength to
pluck out a right eye and cut off a right hand in
order that I might enter the kingdom of heaven.
I now close this narrative with the strongest and
most powerful exhortation to my dear children, that
if ever they felt any affection for their father, or
would desire to reap advantage by his painful as
well as happy experience, they would closely study
and highly value that blessed book the Bible,
which is able, under the influence of the Holy Spirit, to make them wise unto salvation; and not only
happy with respect to eternity, but its precepts, if
followed, will soften all the cares of this life, and
enable them to pass through the world with honor
to themselves and with glory to that God whose
mercy is everlasting, and whose wondrous power
has changed the heart of their father from the very
spirit of infidelity to a decided belief and immov-
able confidence in the all-sufficiency of the atoning
blood of the Lord Jesus Christ, upon whom his soul
now securely rests for eternal felicity.

MAIDSTONE, MONDAY, SEPT. 22, 1817. What an
anniversary is this to my poor soul, and what pro-
digious blessings has the Lord bestowed upon me

during the whole of the last year; for it was this day twelve months ago that God himself enabled me to set out afresh for the kingdom of heaven, being released by his almighty arm from the dominion of my easily besetting sin. This dreadful sin was a constant desire to drink to excess, by which all my faculties were paralyzed, and my soul was sinking fast into despair; but at length the power of Jesus snatched my soul from that horrible pit over which it had long been suspended, and from which it seemed impossible to escape. But the mercy of God is from everlasting to everlasting upon those who fear him, and his grace alone has enabled me during the whole of the last year to resist every temptation to drink even a single glass of wine of any description, or to taste any kind of spirituous liquors or strong drink. Is it possible! Yes; and also God has given me the constant desire to study that best of books the Bible, which I have studied every day for one hour before breakfast to the edification and delight of my heart. He also has made it the delight of my soul to hold converse with him all the day long, whether engaged in walking or reading, or in the perplexities of business. But if any one should ever get hold of this book and read what I have already penned, I would not have him suppose that even this happy year was passed through without conflict. Far otherwise; it was a very severe struggle between life and death; and nothing short of the whole armor of God could have enabled me to withstand in the evil day. But by **the** grace of God I am what I am; and though I have been thus far preserved, still I daily tremble for fear that I may do something to dishonor the name of my God. When I reflect upon the strange events of my life contrasted with the lives of Newton, of Bunyan, and other dreadful sinners, and lastly, of St. Paul, who styled himself the chief of sinners, I am often led to exclaim, that they scarcely knew what sin was, when put into the scale against the depravities which have marked my progress, for I verily believe that I have outsinned them all together. I mention this to show forth the long-suffering of God, who has raised such a creature from the very centre of hell to sing his praises and to live to his glory, and to be a witness in these latter times that he is as willing as ever to receive all who call upon him in sincerity and truth.

THURSDAY, JAN. 1, 1818. Ah, my poor dear children, your happy father scarcely knows how to begin his record of another year. The mercies of the year that is past are so great, that your poor father hardly knows where to begin the praises of that God who has saved his life from destruction, and who has crowned him with loving-kindness and tender mercies. But, my dear sons, as I have already brought down my narrative to the 29th of November last, I will shortly state to you the simple occurrence of Christmas day. In the morning of that blessed anniversary, you, my dear children, together with your mother and your father, were all assembled round the fire before breakfast, wishing each other a happy Christmas, and being full of joy, we all joined in singing, "Praise God, from

whom all blessings flow." Your mother and myself, looking at each other and then on you our dear children, and feeling in our hearts the love of that beneficent Being who has been so merciful towards us, were constrained to lift up our hearts with gratitude, while our eyes did indeed overflow with joy. Even you, my dear children, young as you were, appeared to enter into these feelings, for you united in singing, "Grace, 't is a charming sound," and you sung it with all your might; after which we had family prayer, and at the proper time we attended the morning service at chapel. We spent the happiest Christmas day that we had ever known in our whole life before; yet neither your mother nor your father tasted even a drop of any kind of wine or liquor. As not even the cheerfulness of Christmas could move your father from his purpose, so your kind mother also was determined that she would not take any wine on this day. Have we not boundless cause to rely with implicit confidence on that benevolent Being who has already done such great things for us, and who has brought your poor father out of a horrible pit and placed his feet on a rock, and put a new song into his mouth, even the praise of God. Now, my dear children, this is the entire work of that gracious God, who has brought your father through fire and through water to feel unfeigned delight in studying his holy word every day for the last fifteen months; and the Bible has indeed been "a lamp to his feet and a light to his path," to guard him from evil and to guide him, under the influence of the

Holy Spirit, into the way of life everlasting. Oh
then listen to the admonition of your anxious parent, who is himself a striking monument of the
mercy of that God, who will surely answer your
prayers if you call upon him in sincerity and truth,
through the medium of his beloved Son, who not
only made atonement for your sins, but shed his
precious blood for the sins of the whole world.
Therefore I beseech you, by the mercies of God,
never to listen to the insinuations of Satan, that
your sins are too great to be pardoned, for that
can never be the case while Jesus Christ continues
to be our Advocate and Intercessor at the throne of
mercy; and there he stands for ever employed in
that glorious work till the final consummation of all
things. Therefore do not suffer any circumstances,
however desperate they may appear, to drive you
to despair, but consider what severe trials, temptations, and miserable falls David encountered, and
consider his repentance and restoration; and last
of all, consider the painful trials of your own once
miserable, but now happy father, who has been rescued from the very depths of hell by sovereign grace
alone, to enjoy daily and hourly communion with
God, under the liveliest hope of eternal felicity.

MONDAY, MARCH 2, 1818. Yesterday my dear wife
and myself joined with the church, at the Independent meeting in Week-street, in celebrating the
Lord's supper. I was admitted a member on Wednesday last, the 25th of February; and here surely
I may praise that merciful God who has brought
me into his banqueting house, and placed me under

his banner of love. O that I might "dwell in the house of the Lord for ever!"

I had brought down my narrative to the 1st of January last, but had omitted to mention that the Rev. Edmund Jenkins, pastor of the Independent meeting in Week-street, was an inmate in our family for nearly four months, until Wednesday, the 14th of February last, on which day he quitted us, and was married the next morning. During Mr. Jenkins' residing with us we experienced many blessings of a spiritual nature, particularly in having family prayer, which had long been abandoned before he came; but on the day of his departure it pleased God to give me grace and strength to go forward with this important duty, which we have regularly continued with great delight and inward satisfaction.

MONDAY, SEPT. 21, 1818. This auspicious day completes a period of two whole years, during which, by the grace of God alone, I have been most miraculously preserved from drinking any kind of wine or spirits, but have confined myself to porter or water. Yet I was seduced by a depraved nature to drink more porter than was right, by which I was brought into a distressing situation; but I have abundant reason to be deeply thankful to a merciful God, that when the enemy came in like a flood, his almighty arm was lifted up in my defence, and I was recovered from the snare in less time than ever before, being only one day under the power of my adversary. The last time was on Wednesday, the 15th of July, when, the weather being sultry in

the extreme, I drank porter till I became ashamed
of myself; yet the hand of God never forsook me,
neither was I suffered to taste even so much as a
drop of any kind of wine or spirits, although there
was a quantity of each within my reach, and no
human being present to prevent my taking it if I
had been so inclined. But my great Deliverer had
issued his sovereign mandate, "Hitherto shalt thou
come, but no further." I felt very deep anguish
for my transgression, and I entreated grace to give
up every idol. Porter had indeed been my idol,
and was to my taste the greatest luxury; but this
must also be given up. I pondered these things in
my mind without coming to a decision, till our faithful minister, in one of his pastoral visits, put the
following question to me in the most impressive
manner, "Do you love porter better than Christ?"
The appeal went home to my soul, and I instantly
resolved, by divine help, that I would not only give
up my long favorite beverage, but every thing else
that should retard my journey to heaven. Accordingly I ceased immediately from the use of porter,
and from the 19th of July to the present day, September 21, I have never tasted any other beverage
than my own table-beer and water. Here then I
have more abundant reason than ever to praise that
merciful Being who has thus subdued three of my
great enemies, and placed them under my feet.
Shall I ever again distrust the continuance of that
mercy which has been so greatly manifested in my
deliverance from so dreadful a bondage? Oh be
such a thought far from me, and let me ever rest

secure that He who hath begun the good work will indeed carry it out to full perfection. But let me take heed.

NEW-YEAR'S DAY, 1819. What an eventful year has the last been to me, and what astonishing mercies have been poured out upon my unworthy head. Who could have thought it possible, after what I have already recorded, that I should ever again fall into the net of my deadly enemy? Yet so unwatchful have I been, and so lifted up by pride, that I considered myself now completely secure against my former propensity, and that it was totally impossible ever to be overcome by table-beer. But one unhappy day I was thus again brought into disgraceful distress. Yet there was still abundant reason for thankfulness, as God restrained me from either spirits, porter, wine, or ale. But this table-beer was a little leaven which would soon have leavened the whole lump. Although God had enabled me to cut off the right hand almost, yet the retaining the use of beer was something like retaining one little finger of that hand. I was not suffered to remain long in this painful state, which commenced on Monday afternoon, the 16th of November, for on the Wednesday following I was seized with a most dreadful fit of the bile, and then began to recover. I felt myself to be an ungrateful, sinful creature, and desired to fall before a throne of grace, that I might obtain mercy and strength to set out again in the right path. I now found, by bitter experience, that it was absolutely necessary to give up every thing that could bring my soul

into similar distress from a similar cause, and that
if I had a spark of sincere love towards God, I must
from this hour give up the use of all kinds of liquid
containing any spirit. Accordingly, having received
from God himself a holy desire to live to his glory,
I called upon him to give me strength, and set forward again on Thursday evening, the 19th of November, with the determination never to allow any
thing stronger than tea or coffee to enter my lips
again. In this blessed resolution I have been enabled, through divine assistance, to continue to the
present moment, and have uniformly substituted
water for malt liquor with my meals, and instead of
a glass of beer after my meals, I have experienced
unspeakable comfort in taking nothing but milk
and water. Oh, the greatness of the power of the
grace of God! It is indeed unconquerable, and I
am a living witness of its miraculous influence.
May my benevolent Creator grant, for Jesus Christ's
sake, that I may remain a faithful witness to all
eternity.

OCTOBER, 1820. How many humiliating circumstances do I find when looking over my ledgers. Entries scarcely legible, yet piercingly plain as to the
miserable state I was reduced to through the abuse
of wine when such entries were made. I view them
with agony and grief. I then turn with grateful
astonishment to the present circumstances of my
spared life, and ardently desire to be filled with
deep repentance before a gracious and patient God.

I rejoice on account of my beloved wife and dear
friends, who are no longer fearful of evil tidings as

heretofore when my name is mentioned, and who are no longer ashamed of their relationship to a person who had caused them so much grief. What a contrast to those dreadful times when such fearful sights appeared before my eyes, that if I were not at this present time in the full possession of my senses, the very mention of such scenes would create a suspicion of insanity. At one time, being in bed and fully awake, with my dear wife sitting beside me, I saw the figures of two frightful looking men extending their bodies apparently over the top of the bed, with long whips in their hands, with which they were flogging me, amid dreadful imprecations, on account of my evil conduct. I caught fast hold of my wife, and screamed out in an agony of fright, which so alarmed her that she endeavored to escape from me; but so great was my terror that I held her fast in my arms, fearing that these demons should carry me away if she quitted the room. She alarmed the house, which brought her sister and two maid-servants into the chamber; but I would not allow her to leave me during the night. This was after a fit of intoxication had subsided, but which had so deranged my nerves as to produce temporary insanity; yet I recollect the circumstances as plainly as if they were in action at the present moment.

At many other times strange figures appeared before me, accusing me of all my former sinful practices, which were as plainly brought before my recollection as if they had but recently taken place. Sometimes flashes of lightning appeared to pass be-

fore me, and when I inquired of these figures what
such appearances signified, they would seem to answer that they came from hell, and that they were
commissioned to drag me there. All these things
appeared real to my poor agitated mind, and almost drove me distracted. One Sunday morning,
while the people were passing to church, I jumped
out of bed to follow a spirit with which I had
been conversing; the supposed phantom leading
me down stairs to the door, which I opened to ad-
mit of its departure. At this time I was perfectly
free from intoxication, but my nerves were all deranged in consequence of a very late fit of intemperance.

Appearances of the strangest kind were continually presented not only to my mind, but to my
eyesight, and from this circumstance I can account
for the tales of apparitions which have seemed to
appear to persons laboring under nervous irritation. But still these things appeared to be real,
and were frightfully distressing. At other times I
have been tempted to destroy myself, that the world
might be rid of such a monster; but now here I am,
with my life redeemed from destruction, my health
renewed like the eagle's, my soul and body devoted
to God, to the honor and praise of his almighty
power; and for this reason, because "his mercy
endureth for ever."

Often have I taken the dreadful glass into my
hand, and looked at the wine with a sort of sensible horror, yet had no power to resist the strong
impulse to let it pass my throat. Many and many

a time has conscience plainly told me that this conduct would assuredly bring me to ruin, my children to beggary, and my wife to an untimely grave; yet, with all these reflections, the dreadful habit was so strong, that I gave way to its force. Many a time also I have looked with strong emotion upon poor ragged children playing in the streets, and when my sympathies have been excited even to tears, the same faithful monitor has whispered to my mind, "Such will be the fate of your own children, unless you break off this destructive habit." But all these things were unavailing; affliction, tenderness, conscience, had no power, and nothing short of Omnipotence could perform the mighty act.

My happiness is now unspeakably great, arising from constant temperance and sobriety, and from being also at all times ready to meet the business and difficulties of the day, thus living in some very small degree to the glory of God. Even in the midst of all these blessings, how much anguish does it occasion my soul to catch myself sometimes musing over scenes of past sensual indulgence, till former sins appear to be almost recommitted. What but the precious blood of Christ could atone for such deeply-rooted pollution? I have been often pained by the most abominable thoughts crowding upon my mind, even in the midst of secret prayer as well as in the house of God, and have therefore been led to suspect whether I was truly sincere in the profession which I had made. These things are very painful, and yet I not only delight, yes, greatly delight in the ordinances of God, both public and

private, but feel great pleasure also in the society
of those who love his blessed name, and who by his
grace are enabled to praise him in their lives and
conversation. I do indeed feel great delight, unspeakably so, in the company of a sincere Christian, and I hate every evil way and every thing
within myself as well as others that would dishonor
the Son of God. It now affords me great, unspeakable pleasure to point out to poor perishing sinners
the willingness of God to forgive all who repent and
turn from their sins, and also to stand forth as a
witness to his faithfulness and power to subdue the
most inveterate habits. I, who was a most dreadful drinker, even I am become one of the most sober
men in England, through the power of God alone.

CHAPTER IV.

EMANCIPATION.

1819 TO 1821—AGE 45-47.

FEB. 18, 1819. Blessed be God that thirteen weeks have now passed in which I have enjoyed the uninterrupted gratification of never tasting any other liquids than coffee, tea, or milk and water. Oh what mercy! And so much have I enjoyed this latter beverage, that it becomes sweeter and sweeter to my taste every day, and my health and spirits are kept in a finer tone than ever, through the rich mercy of that Redeemer whose power and goodness have been so resplendently displayed in healing all my diseases and redeeming my life from destruction. The peaceful state of my mind, and my prospects of futurity, are beyond description; and I now look forward with ineffable delight, accompanied with a brilliant hope that I shall be enabled to spend the remainder of my days on earth to the honor and glory of God, and to be with him for ever in heaven.

MARCH 14. The rich mercy of God has permitted me to see another birthday, after struggling for seven years against a most fatal evil; and although his goodness has prevented my being cut down as a cumberer of the ground, yet how many have entered the gates of death by the very same path from which, by the most astonishing mercy, He has rescued my soul. I deeply lament that my gratitude bears so little proportion to his goodness; and the more particularly when the contrast is so very and so awfully striking between my present condition and the fate of my old companions. My early friends snatched away, and gone — where? J. S——, my bosom-friend, died at thirty-six—gone; J. T—— died suddenly, in a shocking state of disease, at forty—victims of intemperance. My old companion Lieut. R——, wild and intemperate, cut off at thirty-one. J. S—— at thirty went the same dreadful path to death. T. K——, paralytic, beginning in intemperance, died at thirty-nine. W. C—— at twenty-eight, the same. J. P——, a man whom one would call excellent at times, died raving mad from intemperance, at forty-two. Why was it not my fate? T. E——, whom I often envied for his sobriety, became so much the victim of intemperance as to be removed to a mad-house, where he now lies, insane. And yet I, the most unworthy of all, I am preserved to tell the dismal tale. And not only these my companions have fallen, but others also, with whom I joined in the midnight revel, are reduced to beggary, and are now wandering about in misery and contempt. I feel deeply on their account,

> "And fain my pity would reclaim,
> And snatch the firebrand from the flame;
> But feeble my compassion proves."

None but God!

JULY 19. Blessed be God that a whole year has now passed away since I tasted any thing stronger

than table-beer. And yet I desire to look back with
humble sorrow that even table-beer was too strong
for me in November last. But again I desire to
rejoice in the strength of that grace which has enabled me to give up what I was so exceedingly fond
of. I cannot, I will not restrain the rejoicing of my
heart and soul in consequence of the goodness of
my redeeming God in removing one propensity
after another, to make way for my more complete
enjoyment of his blessed self. Had I all the powers of all the finest orators upon the earth, I could
not describe the inward joy that I feel in being
brought to love my God. When my feet were first
turned from the ways of sin, I was exceedingly anxious to know what the world thought of me, but
now I seem only concerned to live in close union
with Christ my Lord, through the sanctifying influences of his Holy Spirit. I am indeed a brand
plucked from the burning of hell, and now my soul
burns towards the living God. The being saved
from the power of my former habits causes this
great exultation; and now that, by the grace of
God, I am enabled to live to his praise in the bosom of my family and before the world, I find my
heart filled with ineffable delight in being myself
brought out to speak to his faithfulness, who has
declared that he willeth not the death of a sinner.
My appetite for holy things increases. I love the
people of God, and it is my delight to open my
house and heart to receive his ministers. Daily do
I delight to study the Scriptures, and I feel an increasing desire to obtain a knowledge of the whole

counsel of God, that I may, in my poor way, be at all times ready to give an answer to myself and to others. I have also abundant reason to rejoice in the goodness of God in making all my enemies to be at peace with me, and in continuing to me the friendship of good men. He also condescends to make me useful to others, and to dispose my heart to support his cause to some considerable extent, although it is grief to me that I have not a pocket equal to my desires. These things, my dear children, I write for your example, entreating you always to be liberal towards God, and never withdraw your hand from doing good. God will assuredly bless you most abundantly; I am his witness. You will have many difficulties, but the greatest of all will be the opposition of your own heart to the ways of God; yet all these things, which are the lions, the grace of God can surmount. Remember your poor father. Remember how he used to kneel with you, morning and evening, in prayer to God, and how he used to join with you in repeating hymns, and in singing, "Praise God, from whom all blessings flow." Remember these things, and do not forget that your father was once averse to all such engagements, till the grace of God enabled him to fight every battle, and to conquer—for his glory, the glory of the Lord.

JULY 28. The Rev. J. Liefchild and the Rev. J. Slatterie supped and slept at my house.

SEPT. 23. Had the pleasure of entertaining six ministers this evening : namely, G. Burder, J. Slatterie, J. Roffe, J. Chapman, G. Bentliff, and E. Jen-

kins, and I felt it a delightful honor to entertain
so many servants of my Lord. What a wonderful
change has the Almighty made in my heart and
mind, that it should be my greatest delight to min·
gle with those persons whom I formerly despised,
at least despised their holy conversation.

I often look back with astonishment at my presumption in engaging in public prayer at Worcester, and I now tremble at every temptation of my
own mind even to think of engaging in such a manner again. My place is to be still, and see and
hear.

JAN. 14, 1820. Temptation—a flattering one.
This day J. B—— gave a dinner to a select party
of eight gentlemen, and invited me to be one of the
number. The invitation was highly flattering to
me. There were also some peculiar circumstances
respecting this dinner, in which I was principally
concerned, by having been the instrument of effect-
ing a reconciliation between two of the persons invited; but I declined, stating that I never drank
wine, and therefore could not sit at table with any
comfort where the party were to meet for the express purpose of enjoying a glass of wine together.
Mr. B—— urged his request by saying that if I
would only favor him with my presence, I should
be allowed to drink nothing but milk and water;
and this he urged with so much good-nature, that
it seemed hard to refuse, and I told him I would
consider the matter and send him an answer. I
instantly repaired to my closet, and kneeling before
a throne of mercy, entreated power from God to

withstand this temptation, half inclined to yield
Satan had finely gilded this invitation by the insin-
uation that my company was so much esteemed,
that if I would but join the party, they would excuse
my drinking wine. The snare did not take. The
Lord was my defence, strength was given me to
stand fast for the honor of Christ, and I wrote Mr.
B—— a polite note, stating that I could not overcome the obstacle to my accepting his polite invitation. Blessed be God, who giveth power to the
faint.

I was tempted in the same kind of way about
four months ago to dine with the grand-jury, when
I was one of that body, and the temptation was
strong from within as well as outwardly, and I began to reason with myself, but started as from a
dream, and mentally exclaimed, "No, Lord, no; and
for thine own honor I pray thee give me strength
to resist every solicitation." I quitted the party
and sat down to dinner with my own family; but I
had not been seated five minutes when the foreman
called for me to accompany him to the dinner. He
was astonished at my refusal, and went away declaring that he would levy a fine for my non-attend-
ance, which was accordingly done, and I escaped
as a bird from the snare of the fowler. Blessed be
God!

MARCH 14. The eighth return of that memorable
day in which God was pleased to commence his
work in my soul. He has mercifully kept alive his
love in my heart, and my bodily health and temporal comforts have been uninterrupted since my last

birthday. I have also experienced much delight in
the daily study of the Bible, committing to memory
twenty-five hymns, with seven of the prose psalms--
27, 34, 51, 103, 116, 121, 139—and these were quite
a treasure to me, either in walking or in retirement,
so that my religious stock is much enriched with
knowledge truly precious. My desire after heavenly things has likewise considerably increased, and
instead of God being never in my thoughts, as in
former times, he is now always in my affections,
whether at my desk or at any other employment.
Indeed his mercy is so great in giving me power to
resist temptation, that I conceive it to be impossible for human language to express my love towards
him, or my fervent desire to be holy; and yet, with
all these gifts, I tremble more than ever I have
done before through fear that I may do or speak,
or even think, any thing that should bring dishonor
upon his blessed name, a name more dear to my
soul than ever. Many talk of the great merit due
to myself for giving up every kind of liquor and
abstaining from company, but this is a sort of blasphemy to my ears, and I never allow any person to
leave my presence without warmly declaring that
the whole work is the work of God alone, by whose
strength and grace, shed abroad in my heart, all
these blessings are maintained. "I will praise thee,
O Lord; for thou hast delivered my soul from the
lowest hell." I may indeed say from the lowest hell
when I consider my former miserable state. So
dreadful was the effect of intoxication upon my
body, that my face and eyes after a fit remained so

swollen and disfigured as to be truly frightful even
to myself. My hands and fingers were also hard
and stiff, my beard grown long and hard, and more
like the hair of a horse than a human creature.
My mind full of horror and the most dismal apprehensions, temper irritable and irritated at the least
noise or movement; body full of agony and entirely
sleepless for several days and nights together, wandering from room to room with feelings of anguish
and despair, attended with dreadful temptations to
commit suicide, that the world might be ridden of
such a monster. A man was kept in the house for
three months to watch me at every step and to supply my wants. All my former sins harrowed up my
soul, accompanied with temptations to doubt the
power and willingness of God to forgive so great a
rebel. This is but a faint picture of the fulness of
trouble brought upon one who seemed lost beyond
hope. The exceeding riches of the mercy of God
shone forth and rescued me from the iron hand of
Satan, and brought me out with a victorious arm as
a monument of the power of divine grace. "Oh to
grace how great a debtor!"

My dear wife was now made completely happy.
She had faithfully and tenderly watched over me,
and instead of uttering reproaches, only reproached
me by her tears, and still encouraged me not to despair, as she considered that I was sincerely desirous to conquer my besetting sin. She was incessant
likewise in her applications at the throne of mercy,
praying even against hope. The Lord heard her
cries and mine also,* and with a hand all divine

snatched me from the arms of Satan to erect a family altar to his praise and glory. I was formerly termed a good singer and a jovial fellow, which frequently led me into dissipation. But now, blessed be God, I sing the songs of Zion, and have strength given me to reject every invitation to join the social board, and am more respected than ever, even by the persons with whom I refuse to associate. My bodily health is also superlatively good, being free from every kind of pain or disease, having at all times an excellent appetite, and confining myself to plain food, and never drinking any other liquors than tea, coffee, milk and water, or toast and water. Thus has a merciful God completely changed my appetite as well as my inordinate desires, and he has made me to be the happiest man in the world. Blessed be his name.

SEPT. 30. I have made it a constant rule, for the last eighteen months, never to quit the shop, when it has been closed at night, without kneeling and expressing hearty thanks to God for his gracious care over me; and I never quit my room, when I go at eleven o'clock to dress and shave, without kneeling before the throne to return thanks for preservation to such part of the day, and to implore a continuance of divine aid for the remainder; for I feel myself so very weak and so liable to sin, that I dare not trust myself even for a moment.

OCT. 6. I have been thinking, should I die this day, what are my prospects of futurity, and should I live many years, what do I expect to obtain from a life of holiness as a merit. If I could attain to the holiness of an archangel, still the blood of the Son of God must be my only plea, my only trust; therefore, if I am not safe in Jesus now, even at this moment, I cannot expect that any advance in holiness will entitle me to a place in heaven as a reward. All, all must be of the free mercy of God, in and through and for the sake of his beloved Son, who shed his blood for me individually as well as for the whole world. These are my present prospects, and Christ is all my trust. But shall I not fall again into my besetting sin? No. Although I feel my weakness, yet the promise of God is my support. He will not forsake the work of his own hand. The honor of Christ is also on my side, a strong defence, and my hearty love to Christ and to his cause is also another defence. Christ is also my Shepherd, to protect me against the assaults of my foe; and yet with all this I feel it every moment necessary to cherish the apostle's admonition, "Let him that thinketh he standeth, take heed lest he fall."

CHRISTMAS DAY. How many mercies have we to thank thee for, O Lord. This day our aged mother passed the day with us in happiness and comfort, surrounded by our children. After dinner we sang, "Praise God, from whom all blessings flow," and then we repeated hymns in rotation, beginning with myself, my dear wife, down to the youngest that could speak, even our Eleanor, who, though only two years and a half old, could repeat three or four hymns in a very pretty manner. Oh, it was delightful to hear a whole family engaged in praising our glorious God for his infinite mercy in preserving our feet in the path to heaven. May we all press forward to the end.

SUNDAY, JAN. 14, 1821. Why am I permitted to hail with joy the opening of this day, and to feel an ardent desire to go to the house of my God that I may worship him with a grateful and contrite spirit? Why am I not now lying on yonder couch, as aforetime, in a state of intoxication and madness, disgraceful and disgusting? Why is all this change, all this reverse? It is because the compassions of my God fail not. Why is it delightful thus alone to meditate on the blessed expectation which my God hath given me of a happy immortality, mixed with a fervent desire to honor him in all my ways? It is because he hath blotted out my sins, for his own name's sake, that in me, as well as in Paul, yes, even in me, He might show forth all long-suffering, and exhibit his sovereign power over the heart of the stoutest rebel that ever was turned from the path of sin to delight in the Lord his God. Dear Jesus, it is to thy sacrifice that I am indebted for all the happiness that surrounds me, and for that lively hope which ever lives within me. Oh help me to live to thy glory.

JAN. 17. Went to see poor Mr. B——. Found him lying in bed in a most dreadful state from recent intoxication, a living picture of what I once was. Poured out my heart in thankfulness to God for his unspeakable mercy and forbearance towards myself in having raised me up from the depths of hell and granting deliverance from my dreadful foe.

Entreated the Lord to have mercy on poor B——,
and raise him up to become a monument of sparing
mercy. Warned, exhorted, and encouraged him still
to trust in God. Told him that millions of sinners
who were once in as bad a state had been recovered. Desired him to look at myself, who had
been worse than he had ever been, though now a
wondrous monument of the power of the grace of
God. Bade him look up with lively hope.

JAN. 20. Mr. B—— called on me this morning
in a state of deep penitence, and quite recovered.
He was full of sorrow, and expressed determination
to set out again in the ways of God. Said he was
sorely tempted at J. M——'s, but resisted every
solicitation.

MARCH 14. Birthday. This day commences my
forty-eighth year, under brighter and happier prospects than any former year of my life. May I not
then call upon my soul to bless God's holy name?
This morning I renew my covenant with my God,
and call upon him to take me under the shadow of
his wings, and grant me strength to walk before his
face in happy obedience and cheerful confidence,
trusting solely in the sacrifice of my Lord and Saviour Jesus Christ.

APRIL 24. This being a remarkably fine morning, my dear Mary, self, and children, went down
the river in a boat, and we sang "Praise God" over
the very spot where I once fell into the water, twenty
feet deep, and escaped with my life.

MAY 22. As soon as I alighted from the coach
in London, I stepped aside and mentally thanked a

gracious God for his protection, and entreated he would keep me from all kind of sin. When I arrived at home, I stepped into the churchyard before going to my own house, and then poured out my heart to God in thankfulness for having protected me throughout the day, and for having enabled me, by his powerful grace, to go to London and back again without tasting any kind of refreshment on the road, and drinking only a glass of water, except breakfast, all the time I was in London.

Mrs. S—— of Strood is a remarkable instance of the goodness of God towards me in favoring my exertions to render service to others. About twenty years ago she lived in Maidstone as under-servant, and having been ill-treated, she made her complaint to me, which prompted me instantly to insert an advertisement in the paper for a housekeeper's situation. In consequence of this she was engaged as housekeeper to the late T. S——, Esq. Her conduct was so exemplary that within two years he made her an offer of marriage, which she accepted, and became the wife of a man possessed of two thousand a year in landed property. Mr. S—— died about four years ago, and bequeathed to his widow five hundred pounds per year during her life. Mrs. S—— very lately acknowledged her obligations to my instrumentality. I thank God for this great instance of his goodness, and desire to say, from the bottom of my heart, "Not unto me, O Lord, but unto thyself be all the praise."

PROVIDENCE. I had been walking by the side of the river, and having arrived at the place where a poor widow resided who had received me into **her** house in July, 1818, at the time that I was close to the water, and insensible from drinking, I was induced to call and see the person who had kindly sheltered me. She was at the washing-tub hard at work, but exceedingly dejected, and shed tears as I approached her. I found that she had been hard pressed for repayment of two pounds which she had borrowed and was not able to pay, and being threatened by the lender, she was greatly distressed. I told her that I saw the hand of God most clearly in directing me to her house at such a crisis. The poor creature's countenance soon became brighter, and I thanked God for having enabled me to repay the kindness I had experienced from this poor woman.

CHAPTER V.

"THE SINNER'S FRIEND."

"THE SINNER'S FRIEND." MARCH 1, 1821. Reflecting upon the astonishing goodness of God towards such a great sinner as myself, and considering
how much benefit and encouragement I had received
from the perusal of "Bogatzky's Golden Treasury,"
I felt deeply concerned that books of this nature
were not more easily attainable by the poor. It
was suggested to my mind that a small selection
might be made from this valuable little work, and
distributed at a low price, or gratis, throughout the
town of Maidstone, whereby it might please the
Lord to awaken or encourage the downcast to seek
for mercy. I determined to set about the work, but
was immediately deterred by the fear of having
been led to think of this plan more for my own
honor than for the glory of my God. This harassed
me considerably, and the more I felt desirous of
prosecuting my plan, the more I became fearful of
indulging self-complacency. I hesitated several
days, and finding that I could not overcome the
first suggestion, I made it a matter of fervent prayer
to be directed how to act. After struggling three
weeks, I was brought to a resolution to make a
small selection of the most encouraging portions
from Bogatzky and print them as a tract. I thought

half a sheet, containing sixteen portions, would be
sufficient, and for this purpose I selected about fifty
of the choicest, from which I intended to cull out
sixteen; but when I had proceeded thus far, I found
that so many good portions still remained behind,
that I could not bring myself to give them up;
therefore I extended my views from half a sheet to
a whole sheet. Again and again I prayed the Lord
to take the whole matter into his own hand, and
root out of my heart every disposition contrary to
his honor and glory.

Having fixed upon thirty portions from Bogatzky, I wrote two portions myself by way of introduction, being the first and second, and put the whole
to press.* At first I thought of printing only five
hundred copies; but considering that if I should
find this number insufficient, I should have much to
regret after the press should have been broken up,
I resolved upon printing a thousand, which were
completed on the 29th of May, when my little book
appeared, in a neat, blue cover, bearing the title of
"THE SINNER'S FRIEND." I was now puzzled to
know in what manner to get them into circulation,
as I wished to do it as secretly as possible, having
never mentioned the circumstance to any person.

MAY 29. This morning, with an anxious heart,
and having first entreated of the Lord wisdom and
discretion, I set out to distribute my little book. I

---

* From time to time the compiler of "The Sinner's Friend"
wrote a page and substituted it for one of those originally extract
ed from Bogatzky, until at length it was almost entirely his own
work.

put three dozen into my pocket, and proceeded over the bridge towards the houses of the poor in West Borough, and the first person I met was Mr. F——, who had been an old associate at cards and dissipation, to whom I presented the first copy. I then walked up to the houses, but had not courage to open a single door; and while I stood pondering what to do, a poor woman approached, leading a little child. I plucked up courage and requested her to accept a little book, which she received with an expression of countenance that led me to think she knew the truth, and she kindly undertook to deliver ten copies to her neighbors. I was pleased with this beginning, and thanked God for it. I then went under the cliff and left four copies at three poor houses, and from thence I went to the top of Stone-street, and gave twenty-four copies at different houses, including four to strangers whom I met on the road. I prayed the Lord to bless them to poor sinners. I returned home and replenished myself, and left six copies at each of eight little shops, to be disposed of at threepence each; and to encourage the people to put them into their windows, I gave them the books to sell for their own benefit.

I had not returned home more than half an hour, when a stranger came with one of the books in his hand, which he had purchased at one of the places where I had left them for sale, and requested to have a dozen, which I gave him, but refused to take any thing for them, stating that I was authorized to distribute them gratis.

JUNE 2. This evening being Saturday, I walked to and fro upon the Barming road, and distributed twenty-two copies among the poor people returning from market. I have thus disposed of two hundred and thirty-nine copies in various ways. Some I threw into the houses where I found the door or windows open, and left them to the mercy of God to bless them to the inmates.

JUNE 5. This morning a poor old woman inquired for the gentleman who had given away "The Sinner's Friend" at the different houses. She said that a neighbor had lent her one of them, which she had read, and she should be thankful to procure one for herself. She said it was a sweet book. I asked her how she came to think so. She replied, "Because she was a sinner, and it just suited her." Miss E—— picked up one of the books in the passage leading into her uncle's house, and was surprised at finding it there. Supposed some travelling bookseller must have left it, but she could not imagine how the man should know that she was a sinner; said the book just suited her case, and she would not part with it for any money.

JUNE 9. I disposed of thirty-five at the poor houses behind Week-street. In one of these saw three hearty children sleeping on the hearthstone before the fireplace, huddled together with their arms around each other's necks. The father and mother were out at work, and had left the two youngest, three and four years old, under the care of the eldest, about eight years old. It was now afternoon, and they had not had any food since the morning, and did not expect to have any till their father and mother came home at night. While the eldest was telling me this tale, the youngest cried out to me, "More dinney." Poor little creatures! The eldest boy said that his father worked on Penenden heath from morning till night, and his mother at the paper-mill; that himself and brothers were left at home all day, and had only a bit of bread in the morning and the same at night. Gave the eldest sufficient to purchase a loaf of bread and cheese, and away they all scampered to the chandler's shop.

JUNE 14. Gave eight to Mr. P——, who said that a person who had seen one of them, had been led to make inquiry for the way of salvation in consequence of being alarmed at what he read in "The Sinner's Friend." As my little book was now inquired for, and as many persons expressed their comfort from having perused it, I found it necessary to pray for a humble, watchful spirit, that I might not be led away by any notions that I had done any thing of myself, and I told all the people to give their thanks to God, and not to me.

JUNE 16. Saw Mary S——, who said she had received a book called "The Sinner's Friend," sealed up and directed. She said that when she read the words, "Sinner, this little book is for you," she felt hurt, and thought it was an insult; but when she read the contents, she was convinced that the book was sent to her from the best of motives, and that she intended coming to chapel to hear Mr. Jenkins preach. I now began to be very thankful that I had not been so narrow-minded as to print only five hundred copies.

JULY 20. Having now disposed of all my copies of "The Sinner's Friend," I desire most humbly and most heartily to bless my God for all his mercy towards me, and to entreat a constant supply of grace to keep me ever watchful against pride, self-sufficiency, and complacency, on account of having been employed in his blessed service.

Nov. 13. The second edition, two thousand copies, of "The Sinner's Friend," was published this day.

Four copies of "The Sinner's Friend" dropped in the street, and saw them picked up by laboring men going home from market. Twelve to Mr. M——, a most notorious blasphemer about two years ago, but he has become a wonderful instance of the transforming power of divine grace. He told me that he had given one to a swearing man at Stilebridge at the very moment he was pouring forth the most horrid imprecations. The man took the book in his hand, looked earnestly at the title, paused, heaved a deep sigh, and instead of letting loose a volley of oaths, he tremblingly said, "I am sure there is something good in this book, and I shall keep it for your sake;" and then with great emotion he added, "I shall never forget you."

Six to my friend N—— on a visit at my house which gave me an opportunity of entreating her to seek the Lord with the fullest purpose of heart.

Four to a poor woman who had repeatedly obtained them to distribute among her poor acquaintances. Three to H——, and conversed with him on the necessity of seeking the Lord.

NEW EDITION OF "THE SINNER'S FRIEND." Through the mercy of God, I have been allowed to publish a new edition—three thousand copies—of "The Sinner s Friend," and having already had the pleasure of distributing upwards of three thousand copies gratuitously, I propose to sell the present edition at or about prime cost.

Three days' journey to France. Distributed "The Sinner's Friend" to sailors belonging to the pier at Dover; to a lady and gentleman at the inn, and spoke to them on the mercy of God; to a gentleman on board the packet-boat; thrown into the cabin; to a lady at Calais; to the minister at Calais, etc.

John Akhent called to remind me that four years ago I had given him six copies, one of which was made useful to his poor mother, who was then in great grief on account of her eldest son having been killed by an accident. At this time she read the portion on the eighth page, "Despair not," etc., and the Lord was pleased to bless it to her soul.

Thirteen to a wagoner's mate, James Crouch of Staplehurst. This lad, seventeen years old, came to purchase a copy of "The Sinner's Friend," which gave me an opportunity of speaking to him on the way of salvation, and I was delighted to find this humble peasant in his round frock rejoicing in the Lord. Fifty to Mrs. W——, the woman who keeps the entrance to the castle at Hastings, to dispose of to visitors who go to inspect the ruins. She wrote

5*

me requesting a few more copies, as she had disposed of those left her by my dear wife a few weeks ago. How merciful is the Lord to open this new way of placing "The Sinner's Friend" in the hands of persons visiting the castle.

Six to a poor lame man, and preached the Lord Jesus to him with energy and fire. The poor man was exceedingly thankful. Four to a poor dumb woman. There was something exceedingly interesting in this case. This poor creature, a stranger, came into the shop and spread open a sampler on which was worked a verse indicative of the joys of heaven. She motioned me to read it, and then pointed to some blue-covered memorandum-books, and holding threepence in her hand, gave me to understand that she wanted one. I laid them before her, but she did not want a blank-book, and she pointed to the letters on the sampler to make me comprehend that she wanted a printed book. I put several before her; still she was uneasy, and again pointed to the verse on the sampler to make me understand that she wanted a book about salvation. I was still at a loss, but as she still presented the threepence, I was induced to lay "The Sinner's Friend" before her; but as it was in a brown cover, she was still dissatisfied, till I opened the title-page, and then her eyes sparkled with joy, and she again offered me the money, which was refused. I gave her four copies, when she instantly put out her hand and shook mine, then put her hand on her bosom and looked upwards, pointing with her finger, and with a grateful smile indicated

that she had got what she wanted, and she immediately went away. It occurred to me afterwards
that she must have seen one of the former editions
of "The Sinner's Friend" in a blue cover, and this
led her to point to the blue-covered books when she
first came into the shop.

Three to Dick S——, a notorious drunkard.
Saw him this evening in a sober condition, and
spoke to him of sin, and of Christ to pardon. The
poor fellow listened with great attention. On my
knees implored the Lord to have mercy on this
poor man, and save him from drunkenness as he
had done me.

The chaplain to the county prison called and
acquainted me that he had distributed these little
books to some of the poor wretches in prison. He
said he had no book so calculated to do good to
the prisoners. Blessed be God for his mercy in
thus favoring my little book, and may the Lord
have all the praise.

Twelve copies to the Rev. Rowland Hill personally at my house.

Three to a poor sailor who knew James Covey,
the poor seaman who lost both his legs in Lord
Duncan's victory, and of whom a tract is circulated.
Spoke to him of Christ. He said that James Covey
used to give him good advice, and tell him to seek
the Lord. The poor man shook hands with me to
express his feelings of gratitude. God be thanked
for granting me this mercy.

APRIL 26, 1830. Six to Rev. Rowland Hill's
coachman, D——. He said "The Sinner's Friend"

had been made useful. Thanks, ten thousand thousand thanks to my gracious God for having spared my life to the present hour, and granted me the opportunity of distributing 9,000 copies of the little work gratuitously, besides the sale of 5,835 copies, making 14,835 since it was first published in 1821. Surely the Lord's blessing and mercy is indeed in this thing, and to his name I desire to render grateful praise.

Twelve to T. C——, a staff-sergeant at the battle of Waterloo. Had been in twenty-two engagements and escaped unwounded. After Waterloo he became converted to the Captain of salvation, and was employed by the Naval and Military Bible Association to distribute the word of God. He had been lately out of employ, and leaving his wife destitute in London, he went all the way to Brighton to present a memorial to the king, to which no reply was given. Last week he walked from Brighton to Maidstone to wait upon General B——, but without success. In this extremity he addressed a letter to Lord R——, and yesterday took the letter himself, and had an interview with his lordship, who dismissed him unrelieved. The poor humble follower of Christ had prayed earnestly to the Lord of glory to appear for him in his utter destitution, and the Lord heard his cry and answered it in the following remarkable manner.

In the evening, after returning from Lord R——'s, the poor man received a letter from his lordship to wait on him the next day. The poor man was naturally surprised, and while he sat mus-

ing in a small apartment occupied by one Epps, a
tanner, who should open the door but Lord R——
himself! Something which the poor soldier had
either said or written had made such an impression
on Lord R——'s mind, under the influence of the
Spirit of God, that he could not rest till he saw this
poor man again, and instead of waiting till three
o'clock in the afternoon, according to his own appointment, he was with him so early as noon, and
sat nearly an hour patiently listening to a poor soldier detailing the wonderful ways of the Lord; and
then Lord R—— presented the poor penniless servant of God with no less a sum than one hundred
and twenty-five pounds sterling, and quitted the
house. "Oh that men would praise the Lord for
his goodness, and for his wonderful works to the
children of men!" Had I not taken the notes into
my own hands, I should scarcely have believed it,
but I found them to be genuine and good. It is
impossible to account for Lord R——'s conduct in
any other way than by ascribing it to the immediate influence of God in making his lordship the
instrument of his mercy towards his poor servant
in the distressing hour, because Lord R—— is not
a man likely to be led away by any enthusiastic
feeling, nor by want of judgment or sound discretion; therefore it is the Lord's doing from beginning to end. I received the above astonishing narrative from T. C—— himself, who had come to
purchase a small pocket-book in which to secure
his treasure. He returned to London this afternoon by the three o'clock coach, furnished with the

means of liquidating his debts and softening the
anguish of his poor wife, who had been turned out
of her lodgings since he quitted her a few days since,
and their bed and furniture had been taken away.

JUNE 11, 1831. It has pleased a merciful God to
spare my life to publish a new edition of this little
work, which he has so greatly honored with his
especial blessing as to bring it into increasing demand. This morning the eighth edition was published. I laid the first copy before the Lord, pouring out my heart before him in thankfulness for
past mercies, and entreated him to keep me exceedingly watchful and humble, that I might not be
lifted up with pride and self-complacency, and thus
forfeit his future protection of my little book, which
I had dedicated anew to his tender care. Oh may
his Holy Spirit ever preserve me in a humble, watchful, penitent, and believing frame of mind, that I
may live unceasingly to his glory.

Six to B——, a pious bricklayer, who told me
that he had lately heard of two instances in which
"The Sinner's Friend" had been made a blessing.

I visited Mr. S——; he said, "Words cannot
express my thankfulness for 'The Sinner's Friend,'
and for your kindness in coming to see me." On
asking him what portion of "The Sinner's Friend"
had been useful to him, he said, "Pardon for the
worst of sinners," page 10. My heart was instantly
overpowered with thankfulness to the Lord for his
great mercy in thus honoring this portion, which
I had written expressly for the purpose of meeting
the case of the most abandoned. Mr. S—— said

that when he read that murderers were pardoned,
he was immediately filled with hope, and from that
hour the Lord began the work of conversion in his
soul.

Nov. 24. One personally to W. Wilberforce, Esq.,
the champion for liberating the slaves in the West
Indies. Mr. Wilberforce is residing with his son
the Rev. R. Wilberforce, the rector of East Far-
leigh. I walked over to see Mr. Wilberforce, who
received me with Christian courtesy, and chatted
for some time, and shook me kindly by the hand as
a brother in Christ. Mr. Wilberforce is extremely
feeble, almost worn out with old age, yet lively and
cheerful.

Thirteen to a poor man, James Perry, from
Chatham, to sell for his own benefit. This poor
but very decent man had walked from Chatham
this morning to sell matches. There was something so exceedingly prepossessing in his appearance, that I was constrained to speak to him of
Christ, and to my great delight I found him to be
one born of the Holy Spirit. He had seen better
days. Gave him money and food. He had prayed
the Lord to direct his course to some Christian
friend who might relieve his wants.

My dear friend Mr. Slatterie told me that a
young man at Chatham, nephew to Mr. Foster,
dated his first impressions of serious things of eternity from reading "The Sinner's Friend." This
young man joined the church of Christ.

March 14, 1833. This morning, on which I entered my sixtieth year, I am permitted the great

privilege and happiness to bring forth the tenth
edition of "The Sinner's Friend," which I humbly
dedicate to the Lord, with earnest prayer that he
would be pleased to bless these as he has done
those gone before.

Twelve to Lady Le D——, on her calling purposely for conversation.

Ten on going to Gravesend. Six at six cottages
on Boxley Hill. Had some interesting conversation with a respectable female in the van. Gave
her a "Sinner's Friend," which she received with
great emotion, saying, "This is the book which was
made the means of conversion to a young relative
of mine, who has since joined Mr. Slatterie's church."
Blessed be the Lord.

FEB. 11, 1834. This day I had the happiness of
publishing the eleventh edition—seven thousand
copies—of "The Sinner's Friend." With heartfelt
gratitude I took twelve copies in my hand, and
kneeling before the Lord, humbly dedicated them
to him, with thankfulness for past blessings on this
little work, and earnest entreaty for his favor on
every copy of the new edition, for Christ's sake.

A young man, J. T——, now residing at Green-
street, near Sittingbourne, received his first impressions of religion from reading "The Sinner's Friend,"
and he is now become a preacher of the gospel
which he once despised.

A poor woman at Shaftesbury informed me—
"You sent several copies of 'The Sinner's Friend.'
I heard that the wife of H——, who lately ran away,
was in great affliction of body and mind. I sent

her a copy of 'The Sinner's Friend,' and from the time she first received this little book till the hour of her death, it was scarcely ever out of her eager grasp. She said that it had made her very, very happy. She slept with it upon her pillow, and died literally clasping it to her bosom." Blessed, for ever blessed be the Lord for so many and such repeated proofs of his wondrous goodness in overshadowing this little work with his especial favor, to the conversion and salvation of souls. I was so overpowered by this renewed token of mercy, that tears of gratitude rushed forth to the Lord. Oh may I be more humble and watchful than ever.

FIFTEENTH EDITION, 7,000 COPIES. MAY 25. Blessed be the Lord God Almighty for his great mercy in making it needful to print a new edition of "The Sinner's Friend," which he has so largely favored by the conversion of sinners. Oh may my heart be more than ever humble, that I lose not his precious favor by the allowance of pride or self-complacency or any kind of sin. Twelve to Mrs. B——, the first copies of the new edition. Laid these twelve copies before the Lord, imploring his blessing upon them and upon every copy of the new edition. When shall my wondering soul begin to praise him for so much mercy to so great a sinner as I am?

On board the steam-packet from Gravesend to London. One to a lady who sat on the deck reading a book. Four to a gentleman who sat reading. I addressed him by saying, "I am an agriculturist sowing seed for the kingdom of heaven; permit me,

sir, to present you with some of the seed." I spoke
also to two other gentlemen on the way of salvation.

Thirteen to various persons on my journey to
and from Westerham, with earnest prayer that the
Lord would bless every copy to the glory of his
own most holy name and for the honor of his blessed Son. No tongue can tell, no mind can conceive
of the ecstacy of my soul when exercised in pro-
moting the glory of God. The name of Christ, or
rather, the love of Christ, puts me into a perfect
blaze, a very fire of ecstacy and delight. Oh may
the Lord preserve me from extinguishing this fire,
and may his grace uphold and keep me from the
indulgence of any kind of sin.

By the infinite mercy of the Lord, I am spared
to see the twentieth edition of "The Sinner's
Friend." What can I possibly render unto the
Lord for all his benefits towards me? I took
twelve copies of this new edition in my hand, and
kneeling before the Lord, implored his blessing
upon the work of his own hands.

I had purposely dropped a copy of "The Sinner's Friend" in the pathway, and a gentleman
picked it up and came to me with the book in his
hand, saying, "Sir, this book just suits me, for I
am a sinner." He then said, "My name is Bar-
nett, the 'Le Fevre of No Fiction'" He afterwards accompanied Arthur and myself in our chaise
nearly four miles, entertaining us with his strange
adventures.

TWENTY-FIRST EDITION—IN WELSH. Six thousand
two hundred copies now printing in London

Fifty to Captain P——, bound to Quebec with emigrants. I had intended these for A. T——, to take with her to Demarara, but not being able to find the ship, I hailed the *Martha*, and requested to speak with the captain, to whom I expressed my wishes, and to my great delight, he most readily complied, and said that he would take care to put them into circulation, which he did instantly, in my presence, to the officers and men who were on deck; and I saw the sails hoisted, and the ship get under weigh for America. Oh, how did my heart praise the Lord for this most unexpected opportunity of sending the gospel invitation abroad, by a person whom I had never seen before, but who I hope is a willing disciple of the Lord.

I had the high gratification this day of learning that it had pleased the Lord to put it into the heart of some kind lady to translate "The Sinner's Friend" into the Irish language.

While at Tunbridge Wells, I received a letter from dear Mr. Knill, thanking me for "The Sinner's Friend," and stating that his brother Williams, a missionary from Tahiti, considered "The Sinner's Friend" to be the very thing for the people of the South Sea Islands, and that he would translate it into Tahitian if I would find paper and printing. I laid the matter before the Lord, and he gave me a determination to run all risks and have it printed instantly, and then beg for the means of payment. The first person to whom I named my determination was Mr. C——, who gave me thirty shillings; Lady B——, one pound; and the third person, Lord

B——, gave me ten pounds. Praised be the Lord,
who instantly answered my prayer. Received from
the Bishop of Chester a sovereign towards the translation of "The Sinners Friend" into the Tahitian
language.

·Nov. 17, 1836. The total number of copies of
"The Sinner's Friend" sent out of our house this
year, from January 1 to the present day, November
17, is 75,878, in 322 days; 235 per day average, and
208 over. Oh the goodness of the Lord! Blessed
be the Lord for opening fresh streams everywhere
for extending the circulation of "The Sinner's
Friend" in so many parts of the world, and accom-
panying it with his especial blessing.

FEB. 21, 1837. This morning I had the inex-
pressible pleasure of receiving a letter from Mr.
Hallock, the Corresponding Secretary of the American Tract Society, announcing the delightful fact
that the Society had adopted "The Sinner's Friend,"
a copy of which was enclosed, with a kind hope
expressed that they might circulate tens of thousands of this little work. A tract, "The Wonderful
Escape," was also enclosed, containing my speech
at the Temperance Society at Exeter Hall, in May,
1836.* This tract is adopted and published by the

---

* "In the town where I reside," he said, "were twelve young
men who were accustomed early in life to meet together for
indulgence in drinking and all manner of excess. Eight of them
died under the age of forty, without a hope beyond the grave, victims of intemperance. Three others are still living in the most
abject poverty.

"One more, the last of the twelve, the worst of all, remains to
be accounted for. He was a sort of ringleader; and being in the
wine and spirit trade, his business was to take the head of the

American Tract Society, (No. 358.) O may the Lord mercifully bless every copy of each of these messengers of mercy, to the conversion of sinners and the glory and honor of the Lord Jesus Christ; and may I myself be preserved from pride and self-complacency, and never forget the immensity of my own obligations to the Lord for his delivering grace and tender mercies.*

table at convivial parties, and set up whole nights drinking and inducing others to do the same, never going to bed sober. He was an infidel, a blasphemer, a disciple of Tom Paine, both in principle and practice.

"One dark night, being in the neighborhood of Stourbridge, he had been drinking to excess, wandered out of the house, and staggered among the coalpits, exposed to fall into them and be lost. He proceeded on till he fell, and rolled down the bank of the canal; but God, who is rich in mercy, had caused a stone to lie directly in his path, and the poor drunkard was stopped from rolling over into the water, where, by one turn more, he would have sunk into eternal ruin. His senses returned for a moment; he saw that if he attempted to stand, he would fall headlong into the canal, and crawled back again into the road. But this miraculous preservation had no effect upon him; he merely called it a lucky escape."

* The English edition here contains an interesting chapter of Mr. J. V. Hall's persevering and evidently successful "Labors for Prisoners," especially George Dunk the forger, and Hartley the murderer.

CHAPTER VI.

"WISDOM'S PATHS PEACE."

1822 TO 1824—AGE 48-50.

MARCH 14, 1822. I am forty-eight years old this day. Ten years ago, on this blessed day, my gracious God sent his arrows of conviction through my rebellious heart, and brought me to a sense of my dreadful situation as a lost sinner. Ten years has the Lord assisted me in the great conflict which I have had to sustain daily and almost hourly with myself and Satan; and this morning my soul is overwhelmed with grateful feelings for the mercy which has been so largely bestowed upon me. Mingled tears of bitter sorrow and unspeakable delight rolled down my face while before the Lord this morning in private; and while the ingratitude of my former days stood in view before my awakened imagination, my heart seemed overpowered with the weight of mercy which a gracious God had poured out upon my unworthy and polluted soul. I hope that I do indeed bless the Lord with all my ransomed powers, and that I feel more happy in his love than ever, and more truly desirous that I may constantly, under all circumstances, live to his glory. My fervent desire is that the Lord Jesus may ever have full possession of my heart, and there reign without a rival and with uncontrolled sway.

What great reason have I also, in a temporal

point of view, to bless and serve the Lord. Ten
years ago my character was ruined, my trade fast
declining, misery in my family, and misery in myself. But now, my character reëstablished, my
trade overflowing, and instead of misery in my family, we are all happy in the favor of the Lord our
God. Oh how can I ever sufficiently praise and
honor the Lord, who hath done such great things
for me! He hath indeed delivered my soul from
the lowest hell, and established my goings, with a
song of thanksgiving continually in my mouth.
Blessed be his name for ever and ever. Amen and
amen. Watch—watch—watch.

MARCH 21. Notwithstanding my ardent desire to
live to the glory of God, yet I seem to be more harassed than ever with evil thoughts. My soul is
grieved beyond measure at the depravity of my
own heart; and I constantly pray God to fill me
with his Holy Spirit, that every evil imagination
may be destroyed, and that my every breath may
be holy.

MAY 1. Experienced more than usual delight at
a throne of grace this morning. I had dreamed of
having taken the forbidden draught, and I remember that, even in my dream, I felt ashamed of myself; but, blessed be God, I awoke in safety, and
had only seen in vision what had once been my
unhappy state. I thanked my God for having heard
my former petitions in regard to the study of the
Bible, and for having made it my delight during
the last six years, and I entreat grace to make it
my daily study to the end of my life, and not to

read it that I might merely say I had read so much,
but that I might study it effectually, in order to live
to his glory; and that henceforth the Bible might
ever be the food of my soul, the delight of my life,
and the light of my path; that its precepts might
be bound around my heart and fixed in the centre,
and that the influences of the Holy Spirit might
enable me to live according to the rule of the word
of God in all things.

AUG. 14. I desire to bless God that for several
months past a secret impulse has often led me into
the summer-house, there to bend my knee before
God. This delightful exercise grows upon me, and
becomes a kind of second nature ; but I have prayed
the Lord that it may never rest in mere habit, but
that it may be the earnest desire of my soul to lie
prostrate before him at all times in humility and
deep repentance. I have found prayer to be very
strengthening to my soul, and a powerful support
in my daily walk, amid ten thousand temptations
from without, and a far greater number from within.

OCT. 24. HIS BIBLE. For the benefit of my dear
children, my sons and daughters. I have now
searched this blessed book to the end of the second
chapter of the first of Peter for the third time, and
my soul is filled with unutterable delight arising
from desire and anticipation of beginning the Old
Testament again, to search and enjoy more than
ever the heavenly food so profusely prepared for
those who love God, and who are by his especial
mercy brought to live upon his holy word. This
increasing desire to study the Bible in preference

to every other book, is the gift of God in answer to earnest prayer, and it has preserved me from thousands of evils. I therefore affectionately entreat you, my dear children, to seek earnestly and constantly for this grace. My daily prayer has long been that the word of God may ever be the food of my soul, the increasing delight of my life, and the light of my path, that its precepts may be bound around my heart and fixed in the centre, and that the influences of the Holy Spirit may enable me to live according to the word of God in all things, that thus living I may live to his glory and to the honor of his beloved Son. I write these remarks with fervent prayer that they may be made a blessing to my dear children when I, who was once the greatest sinner upon earth, am singing before the throne of God as one of those who have been redeemed by the precious blood of Christ. J. V. HALL. I have found the pearl of great price, blessed be God.

CHRISTMAS DAY. This day my dear wife and self, with our seven living children and our aged mother, all united in singing, "Praise God, from whom all blessings flow." My poor heart danced for joy, while tears of gratitude started forth in honor of my God, and for his mercy in preserving me from the dissipation of Christmas festivity which reigns around, and in which I was once most deeply engaged, sitting up whole nights in revelry and iniquity. But the grace of God alone preserves me, and the sense of this mercy overwhelms me with unspeakable gratitude. I daily read accounts of the dreadful effects of sin—men dying in a state of

intoxication. I cannot express the thousandth **part**
of my feelings on account of the love and mercy of
God towards me.   His service is indeed my greatest delight and the joy of my heart. When I look
around and perceive that all my old associates still
remain in the bonds of iniquity, while I am emanci-
pated, is it any wonder that I should express myself
so warmly? The very stones would cry out were I
not to declare the goodness of the Lord.

MARCH 14, 1823. Awoke this morning about three
o'clock, with a heart full of gratitude to my gracious
God for having permitted me to live so long as to
see the commencement of my fiftieth year. When
I arose, I went to the Lord and renewed my covenant with him to be his devoted servant. I seem
to fear nothing so much as offending my God; yet,
notwithstanding this fear, I continually sin against
him. Without the blood of Christ, I feel assured I
can never be saved. What is all the boast of reformation to do for a poor sinner? Nothing! Nothing but the efficacious sacrifice made on Calvary
can satisfy my soul; and that does satisfy it. Blessed be God for this living faith, which banishes every
fear. Still I say, "Watch and pray."

APRIL 24. When I feel how deeply I have sinned
against the Lord, I feel astonished that I have any
hope of salvation; yet I have not only a hope, but
a very lively one; and I do trust that, through the
alone righteousness of Christ, I shall one day stand
before the throne of God with a golden harp in my
hand, singing with a loud voice, "Glory, glory to
God in the highest!" I cannot look upon my sins

and not feel horror, deep horror and shame, at their enormity and magnitude; neither can I look upon the blood of Christ without feeling a thrill of delight run through my whole soul, as it does at this moment while I am penning these words. Yes, the eternal Son of God is all my hope, trust, and desire. I desire to have him always in my heart, as my King to rule over me, that every act of my life, every wish of my soul, and every breath I draw, may all tend to his glory. This blessed theme may possibly form part of our rejoicing with our friends in heaven, where, I have no doubt, we shall know each other. My opinion of the tender mercy of the Lord is, that whatever may increase our felicity in heaven will form a part of the inheritance; and we must think that it will afford amazing pleasure to tread the golden streets with those who accompanied us on earth in our walk to the celestial city.

Isms. I desire to bless the Lord that I embrace no isms. Show me the man who loves the Lord and hates sin, and who desires to honor God in every thought, word, and deed, depending on the influences of the Holy Spirit to enable him to do so, that man is my brother, whatever be his color, nation, or sect. My daily prayer is that the Lord may be pleased to prosper every society, of whatever denomination, which has for its object the glory of God and the honor of his beloved Son. My dear children, you who will read this book when I am gone to my rest, to you I bequeath this principle as the best gift of an affectionate father, although you can only possess it through the mercy of a gra-

cious God and under the influences of his **Holy**
Spirit. Pray for it, and it is yours; but remember
to pray for it as for a gift that will free you from
bondage.

JUNE 21. I can truly say that Scott's Bible has
been an unspeakable blessing to myself during the
last seven years, in the course of which time I have
studied it daily, and have read the whole of the Old
Testament twice, the New Testament three times,
and have just finished reading the gospels for the
fourth time, with increased delight and thankfulness to God for his mercy in having preserved to
me a spiritual appetite. My daily prayer has long
been that the word of God may ever be the food of
my soul, the increasing delight of my life, and the
light of my path; that its precepts may be bound
around my heart, and that the influences of the
Holy Spirit may enable me to live according to the
rule of the word of God in all things; that thus living, I may live to his glory and to the honor of his
beloved Son. This prayer the Lord has answered,
and does continually answer, to the joy of my heart.
Who on earth has so great reason as I have to bless
and praise the name of the Lord?

JUNE 26. Spent half an hour at the bedside of a
dying saint, who said he was happier than a king.
To behold a dying saint beckoning death to approach, and looking upon his dart with unutterable
delight, what a pleasure. No murmurs, though
nothing but bare walls and parish allowance. One
cannot call this dying. *Happier than a king!* I
think I shall never forget these words, nor the ani-

mation with which they were uttered. This is the
grandest sight I ever beheld—better than a corona-
tion. I repeated to him the whole of the twenty-
fifth Psalm, with which he appeared pleased. I
desire to praise the Lord for having caused so many
portions of Scripture to be delightful to my own
soul, and also for having given me grace to commit
many of them to memory, that they may be useful
to others as well as to myself. I have now upon
my heart and mind the following Psalms: 25th,
27th, 30th, 34th, 51st, 91st, 103d, 116th, 121st, 130th,
139th, and 145th; also twenty-four choice hymns.
These form the principal part of my living stock,
being always fresh upon my memory, and ready for
use on all suitable occasions.

Among the hymns are those commencing, "Come,
my soul, thy suit prepare;" "God moves in a mys-
terious way;" "Guide me, O thou great Jehovah;"
"Oh for a thousand tongues to sing;" "Jesus, and
shall it ever be;" "Oh for a heart to praise my
God;" "Oh for a closer walk with God;" "When
all thy mercies, O my God;" "Grace, 'tis a charming sound;" "When with my mind devoutly pressed;"
"How sweet the name of Jesus sounds;" and "The
star, the star of Bethlehem."

How infinitely superior are these "Songs of
Zion" to my old, foolish, worldly vanities! Blessed
be God. With what delight do I take up the language of the ninety-first Psalm; for the Lord hath
indeed made me to "tread upon the lion and the
adder"—wine and spirituous liquors; and he hath
truly "delivered me and honored me" in a most

peculiar manner. The Lord has honored me with the friendship of his chosen people; and some of the ministers of the everlasting gospel are now among my dearest friends. The Lord has also honored me by making me useful among the poor, and also in distributing religious books, particularly "The Sinner's Friend." Nothing on earth is so truly delightful to my soul as to speak boldly for the honor of the Son of God whenever I have an opportunity. Great thanks to the Lord for this gift.

JULY·9. Rev. H. Townley took up his abode at my house. He had recently returned from Calcutta, where he has been laboring during the last five years as a missionary. About thirteen years ago, he followed the profession of the law in Doctors' Commons, and lived in a style of luxury and dissipation, frequenting operas and masquerades. He was also a sceptic in religion, delighting in the works of Voltaire, Hume, and other infidel writers. On looking over a newspaper, he saw an advertisement of a new edition of Paley's "Evidences of the Christian Religion," and never having heard of the work, he sent one of his clerks to purchase a copy, which he perused with the greatest eagerness; and so wonderfully was conviction fastened on his mind, that on the very next Sabbath-day he became a preacher in his own family, by reading the word of God, and commencing family prayer. While Mr. Townley was relating this circumstance my heart bounded for joy, and I told him how the Lord had dealt with myself, by turning me from deism. On

the Sabbath morning, after family prayer, he addressed my four sons : "Here are your father and I,
we have known other gods, but we found that they
could not save us. We now know the true Lord,
and him we desire to serve." Ah, how great is the
mercy of the Lord to have called me by his grace,
and to have delivered me from my abominations
before my children had arrived at an age to have
witnessed such heartrending depravity. I may well
say, "I love the Lord, because he hath heard my
voice and my supplications, and hath delivered my
soul from death, mine eyes from tears, and my feet
from falling." Blessed be his holy name! Even
the very smell of wine is become disgusting, and I
rejoice in the thought that my mouth will never
again be polluted by strong drink of any description. The Lord feeds me, as he did Daniel; and I
have more strength of body and health of countenance than ever I had when I drank my pint or
bottle of wine each day.

JULY 20. My four dear boys assembled with me
this morning, and we sang a hymn and then read
the fourteenth and fifteenth chapters of St. John,
verse by verse alternately, and then sang another
hymn. I then exhorted them to seek the Lord
with full purpose of heart, that when I should be
removed, they might have God for their Father
and their Friend.

One day, on leaving Dr. D——'s house, I spoke
to his footman on the necessity of seeking the Lord.
Gave him "Scripture Help," "Bickersteth on Prayer," and "The Sinner's Friend." He was exceed-

ingly thankful for my advice. This man called on me six months afterwards, and with tears of gratitude said, "I thank God, sir, that you spoke to me in the manner that you did one night when you were leaving my master's house, as till then I was going on in a wild path; but now I am seeking the Lord, and feel happy in his service."

JULY 27. Saw Dr. D—— this morning at his own house. Found him in a low, desponding state. Endeavored to encourage and comfort him. I told him if he had, in his own person, committed all the sins that ever were committed by the whole world, from Cain to the present hour, still the blood of Christ was more than sufficient to blot them all out.

AUG. 16. My case is somewhat like a poor man placed on the top of a very high house surrounded on all sides by fire; the spectators below unable to afford relief, while the poor man keeps running from side to side to escape the rising flames; but suddenly, and just at the moment when every hope is given up, a hand is seen issuing from the clouds, snatching the half-distracted man from his perilous situation and placing him securely on the ground. Would the man thus rescued from destruction ever forget his benefactor? And when speaking of his marvellous escape, would not his heart be full? Just so I have been snatched from the fire of hell by the hand of the Lord; therefore I can never speak but with enthusiasm when opening my lips to the praise of God.

FEB. 28. A stranger came to purchase Dr. Malau's Tracts, and said they were delightful tracts, but that Malan was now dreadfully persecuted at Lausanne, and was silenced, being forbidden to preach the gospel. I replied that there was no occasion to go to Lausanne to find persecution. "No," said the stranger, "for as soon as we express love for the Lord Jesus Christ, the enmity immediately appears. Many persons will speak of the mercy of God, but if the Lord Jesus Christ be named, and the necessity of being found in him, then they are deemed enthusiasts and madmen." The stranger then went on in an animated manner to speak of the love of God in Jesus Christ, and of the necessity of the influences of the Holy Spirit, and also that we should never be ashamed of the cross. He drew from his pocket a Bible, and turning to the fifth chapter of the first epistle of St. John, read in an energetic manner the tenth to the fifteenth verse. I looked at him with great delight, wondering who he could be, and my curiosity was upon the full stretch. I said to him, "Sir, I know not *who* you are, but I know *what* you are, and I desire to bless God that he has shown you the way of salvation, and granted you his Holy Spirit. I rejoice also to see that book in your hand, because it speaks for itself."*

MARCH 10. I find a great portion of vanity and self-complacency mixed with all my actions; but if we abstain from exertion till vanity be eradicated,

* This proved to be the Earl of ——, between whom and the author a very cordial correspondence on religious subjects was maintained for many years.

we shall become totally useless; therefore we must
not allow ourselves to be cheated of opportunities
to do good, but pray to God to keep us ever humble, watchful, prayerful, penitent, and obedient.

MARCH 14, 1824. Jubilee. Fifty years! I feel
such an overwhelming sense of the mercy and goodness of God towards me, that I scarcely know where
to begin to praise him :

> "When all thy mercies, Oh my God,
>   My rising soul surveys,
> Transported with the view, I'm lost
>   In wonder, love, and praise."

I have not only been preserved, but have been
indulged with many privileges for which I can never
be sufficiently thankful. It has been my great happiness to attend the dying beds of several individuals who are now singing before the throne of God;
and I have also been favored with the unspeakable
pleasure of repeated conversations with rich and
poor on the love and mercy of the Redeemer. I
have also had the pleasure to distribute 2,787 copies of "The Sinner's Friend," in various directions,
among high and low, rich and poor. And above
all, I have been brought to feel more than ever my
own innate depravity and the absolute need of a
Saviour, as well as the continual influences of the
Holy Spirit to sanctify and keep me in the path of
holiness. I long to be holy, and because I am not
so I feel increasing grief. I am also still pursuing
the daily study of Scott's Bible, which has been the
increasing delight of my life during the last eight
years. This is a great mercy. I have also had the

enjoyment of entertaining the ministers of the Lord, and have been profited by their prayers and pious conversation. I love the messengers of Zion, whatever may be their talents, and I bless the Lord for this great and happy change in my affections, seeing there was a time when I would sooner have shut my doors against a minister of the gospel than have admitted him under my roof.

"Oh to grace how great a debtor!"

What great things the Lord hath done for me! Blessed be his holy name.

When I approach the footstool of the Lord in the first of the morning, I feel constrained to say, "O Lord, to thee alone am I indebted for these comforts, and it is from thy mercy alone that I am not stretched on this floor in drunkenness, or in a workhouse, or in a madhouse, or lifting up my eyes in endless torment. Having done such marvellous things for me, O Lord, mercifully prevent my doing the slightest thing to dishonor thee, or bring disrepute on the name of thy beloved Son." This is my daily, hourly prayer; and I pray also that the least motion of inward sinfulness may give me exquisite pain, that I may fly instantly to the Lord for shelter and support. I seem to think that no one can possibly have so great cause to love the Lord as I have, because no one can have sinned so much against him, and yet have received so many favors and such signal displays of his almighty power. He has not only removed from me every disposition or inclination for strong drink, but has mercifully

implanted so opposite a feeling, that the very smell
of wine or strong drink in any person creates a
shuddering and horror beyond description, and I
ejaculate, "Is it possible that my mouth was ever
polluted with such filth?"

AUG. 13. I had the pleasure of sending my old
friend Mr. S—— an acknowledgment of his great
kindness to me many years ago, when he was in
prosperity; but he is now in adversity, having run
through a fortune of thirty thousand pounds, and
remaining totally ignorant of Christ. Who has
made me to differ in opinion as well as in circumstances? Oh that all my old friends had found the
Lord. I pray for them daily, beseeching the Lord
to bless them with a knowledge of himself.

AUG. 26. Wedding-day. Blessed be the Lord
that I have been spared to witness and rejoice in
the eighteenth anniversary of this auspicious day,
which finds my beloved wife and self in excellent
health, and more dear to each other by far than
when we were first united. Our blessings are of
the most exalted kind, the love of God filling our
hearts, giving us unspeakable delight. "What
shall we render to the Lord?" May we ever remember and honor the Lord our God with the first
fruits of all our increase, and give ourselves unreservedly to him who hath done all these things for
us.

SEPT. 10. I went with my dear wife to visit a
poor despairing widow. The Bible lay before her.
She was in the most disconsolate state, because she
could not believe in Jesus Christ. A professed

deist had ruined her peace of mind. With uplifted hands and in mental agony she exclaimed, "Oh, what will that man have to answer for, who has thus deceived me and ruined the soul of my poor departed husband!" I never saw so pitiable an object in my life. I tried to encourage her. How can I ever be sufficiently thankful to the Lord for his wondrous mercy in rescuing me from this delusion of the devil and Tom Paine.

SEPT. 11. Poor widow B——. I had been solicited to visit this poor aged widow, seventy-nine years of age. I found her in great distress of mind, with the Testament open before her. I spoke to her at considerable length on the mercy and goodness of God in Christ, and took her hand in mine with as much tenderness as I could express. She then said, "I am so glad you are come, sir; it is so comfortable to hear you talk so. I knew you, sir, thirty years ago, when you were a very gay young man and knew nothing of this language. But what a change!" I replied that my old companions considered me mad; that I had expressed my wishes to them that the Lord would make them equally mad.

When I entered my own house I found a gentleman waiting to see me. He was well dressed, in black, and had twelve copies of "The Sinner's Friend," which he had purchased. He surprised me by saying, "You do not recollect me now, sir, but you gave me one of these little books when you came to the prison where I was confined, and spoke upon the mercy of God to poor prisoners. It cheered my heart and did me good." The Lord was pleased to visit him in prison, and to humble his heart; and he himself now proclaims the news of salvation to poor sinners in the neighboring villages of Gravesend, where he holds a respectable situation, and is a teacher in one of the schools.

SEPT. 15. I find when my mind has been considerably disturbed, if I can but sit down to my Bible, for even a few minutes only, there comes a season of refreshing which quiets the agitated feelings and enables me to take a fresh start. Blessed be the Lord for that mercy which has placed me in a situation where not a day passes without my having the supreme happiness of speaking to one or more persons, high or low, on the way of salvation : yesterday to Lady ——, the day before to the Hon. Mr. N——. I have also poor brethren and sisters in the Lord, who come to my door with matches; so that my cup does indeed abound, and "the lines are fallen to me in pleasant places."

Nov. 19. I frequently entreat the Lord to put his restraining bridle upon me, and keep it tight in his own almighty hand. My soul is daily grieved at the prevalence of sin, and when I see a drunken man staggering along the streets I shudder involuntarily and call upon the Lord to have mercy upon the poor lost, fallen creature. When expressions of blasphemy are uttered, I feel as though some sharp instrument had been pressed against me, while the prayer of pity arises in my heart, and I remember with grief and shame that such was I before the Lord embraced me with his saving love. Let any

person whose mind soars above the very folly he
commits, yet feels an overpowering propensity to
indulge in strong drink which he would forsake but
cannot, think of my case, and be comforted with the
assurance that if he will but go to the Lord and
penitently entreat his aid he shall surely become a
conqueror. There are doubtless a vast number of
persons who have been seduced, step by step, into
intemperance, but would give the universe to be
enabled to retreat from their accursed bane; yet
from the almost insurmountable difficulty of the way,
they remain engulfed till death overtakes them with
all the horrors of a guilty conscience. I have been
upon the very verge of this destruction, but the
Lord stretched forth his mighty arm and snatched
me from the yawning gulf. I knew personally a
fine young man in Worcestershire, the eldest son of
a wealthy baronet, who accompanied one of his college friends into Scotland during a vacation, and
while there imbibed such a habit of drinking whiskey, that when he returned to his father's house he
found the dreadful poison to be irresistible; but,
being a young man of superior attainments, the
degradation of his mind became insupportable, and
in an agony of despair he committed suicide to avoid
the shame of being a drunkard. I have been tempted to do the same, but God preserved me.

Dec. 10. STUDY OF THE SCRIPTURES. Although I
have now studied the blessed Scriptures many years,
yet I find new beauties every day, and I have a
clearer perception of passages which had not shone
in my view before, or had been but little regarded.

This is to me a decisive proof of the influences of
the Holy Spirit in enlightening by degrees the mind
which could not at first have encountered all the
effulgence of divine truth. I rejoice in this gradual
unfolding of the precious truth, because the soul is
thus continually receiving new enjoyment, as well as
renewed impulse to search after hidden treasure.

DEC. 21. My dear boys were now returned from
school; we were all seated round the table. My
heart was surcharged with gratitude to God for his
goodness in having preserved us. I could not refrain from tears. I addressed my dear children on
the mercy of God, and told them how great would
be our happiness in heaven when we should all sur-
round the throne of glory. Requested them to unite
in singing, "Praise God, from whom all blessings
flow." I was so deeply affected that I found it difficult to set the tune. Afterwards we joined my
dear Mary and her infant A——, and now there
were nine of us, all united in love. Praised be the
Lord.

DEC. 22. DEATH OF MRS. TEVERILL. Our joy of
yesterday was interrupted this morning by the almost sudden death of our dear mother. It so happened in the providence of God that the dear and
respected old lady, who once endeavored to prevent
my becoming the husband of her daughter, had long
found a comfortable retreat in my house, and she
had also become sincerely attached to me.

CHAPTER VII.

"WHO MAKETH THEE TO DIFFER?"

1825 TO 1838—AGE 51-64.

JANUARY 1, 1825. SICKNESS. A woman had been hired to nurse my dear wife. She had just come from nursing a man who had died of typhus fever, but having fumigated her rooms she was not supposed to be liable to convey the contagion. About Christmas day, 1824, I began to droop. My surgeon entreated me to take wine to strengthen me. I positively refused. My two daughters now appeared to be declining very rapidly. Mary the worst. At this juncture the nursemaid was attacked and soon lost her senses, while I was in great danger, and my dear wife expected to be bereft of child and husband. Dear Mr. Slatterie came over twice from Chatham on purpose to see me. He knelt at my bedside and earnestly entreated the Lord's compassion. During the fortnight of my extreme illness the Lord nursed me in the hollow of his hand, and prevented any wicked thoughts coming near me. I lay in his hand like a little child, and my heart was incessantly overflowing with the most intense gratitude. It was not affliction, but a continued outpouring of mercy.

When I partially recovered, Dr. S—— prescribed wine or porter. I replied that I neither could nor

would take either, but that I could and would trust
in the Lord to give me strength without wine or
porter. I knew that he had raised up Daniel upon
pulse and water, and he could, and I doubted not
would, in tender mercy do as much for me; especially as it was my heart's desire to honor the Lord,
whom I took at his word: "Because he hath set his
love upon me, therefore will I deliver him; I will
be with him in trouble, I will deliver him, and honor
him." All this did the Lord accomplish in my case,
and caused my strength to return without the aid of
strong drink. My heart did indeed rejoice in this
faithfulness of the Lord to a poor creature who had
put his whole trust in him, in opposition to the advice
kindly tendered by the physician. There was a still
greater mercy developed by this trial, inasmuch as
the Lord proved that he had removed every disposition towards drinking wine; for had this propensity only lain dormant, how gladly would sinful nature
have embraced the opportunity. But no, the Lord
had completed the work of his own hands, and to
his name be all the praise.*

MAY 3. A trip to France. My health had con-

---

* Some may regard the autobiographer's refusal to take wine
medicinally, and his confidence that God would restore him without
it, as the error of enthusiasm. But it must be borne in mind that
in certain cases the smallest indulgence in alcoholic drinks arouses
the old passion, to subdue which total abstinence as a means is
absolutely essential. Many reclaimed drunkards have gone back
to their former habits of excess through taking wine medicinally.
There may be cases where it is far better to run the physical risk
than the moral. The present instance was one of these. At the
same time it must be borne in mind that what is now known as
"teetotalism," renounces wine as a *beverage* only.

tinued gradually to amend, but my friends insisted
on my absenting myself entirely from business, that
I might enjoy the benefit of a few days at the sea-
side; therefore on Tuesday, the 3d of May, I set out
for Dover. The next morning I arose in excellent
health, knelt before the Lord, read the fourteenth
chapter of John, and at seven walked round Dover
harbor down to the sea, and put up prayer and
praise to the Lord while the foaming waves were
rolling at my feet. I gave a "Sinner's Friend" to
each of three sailors who were watching the ships,
and then returned to my inn to breakfast. At Calais
I was struck with the surprising difference between
the manners and customs of people who resided at
so short a distance from each other. It appeared
as though one had got into another world. In the
evening I strolled through the streets much pleased
with the happiness which seemed to pervade all
ranks. Not a sad countenance to be seen. I sat
down on a bench and watched the old men smoking
their pipes at their doors chatting with their wives,
while the children were playing around them—all
happy. I thought of my own dear wife and children, praying the Lord to bless them. At Boulogne,
having paraded the streets, I turned my horse towards Bonaparte's pillar. The sun was shining in
splendor, the larks were singing melodiously over
my head, and the whole scenery was so enlivening
that as I rode along I put up a fervent prayer of
praise and thanksgiving to my gracious God, entreating him to keep me holy and fill my heart with
heavenly love for Christ's sake. As the vessel enter-

ed Dover harbor, I poured out my heart in praise for God's mercy in having preserved my going out and my coming in. Blessed be his name. I had thought much of the Lord during my journey, and my heart was continually lifted up to him to preserve me from every evil thought and way. He did preserve me. Arrived in safety at my own house, I returned thanks to a gracious God for finding my health and strength greatly increased by this excursion, though it had been for only four days and a half.

TUESDAY, JAN. 24, 1826. Forty years! On Tuesday, Jan. 24, 1786—forty years ago, the same day of the week and the same day of the month—I left my father's house on Snow Hill, London, and came to the house I now occupy, a little errand-boy not twelve years old. Then I was the youngest in the house; now the oldest, and raised up to be master over all. I know not how to express my gratitude when reflecting on the goodness of God during so many years. Rebellion and ingratitude not only marked my younger days, but have reached even to my grey hairs, and yet I live, and am not cut down as a cumberer of the ground. Yes, I live; but it is in, through, and by my blessed Jesus that I live, resting on him who has borne with my manners in the wilderness for forty years, and by whose mercy I have been raised from the depths of hell to delight in the way of the Lord my God.

> "Jesus sought me when a stranger,
>   Wandering from the fold of God,
> He, to rescue me from danger,
>   Interposed his precious blood."

Precious to me indeed; and Oh may I never lose the influence of that blessed Holy Spirit, by which my heart is quickened, cheered, and warmed into a flame of heavenly love. To the Lord be all the praise. "O Lord, truly I am thy servant; for thou hast loosed my bonds, and brought up my soul from the grave, and kept me alive, that I should not go down to the pit."

My former companions in iniquity, where are they? Tremendous thought! Almost all cut down in their sins in early life, while I remain to tell the wondrous tale of redeeming love. Of eleven young men who, with myself, at the age of twenty, rioted in all manner of sin, often sitting together around the same table, drinking and singing and swearing, of these eleven not one is left; the whole of them have passed into eternity without a shadow of hope or the least desire to know the Lord. How marvellous then are my mercies, and how great my responsibility. I have been spared to study the word of God with great delight and with constant prayer, searching every word of the sacred pages with an increasing appetite, earnestly desiring to have the precepts of the Lord bound around my heart as the rule of my life in all things, that I may live to his glory and to the honor of his beloved Son. But I must refrain. There is no end to this blessed theme.

AWFUL CHANGE! Why not John Vine Hall? Only the mercy of God. Mr. G——, a student at R—— college, preached the gospel; but afterwards turned wine-merchant, became a drunkard, and a cruel husband. Died in a hospital, aged thirty-three. Was once a good-natured man, but became cruel through strong drink. Why was it not I? Oh how great are my obligations to the mercy and grace of God!

SEPT. 1. To the Hon. S—— T——: "Perhaps I cannot do better than open my heart before you and detail my own once miserable case, and thus convince you how truly desirous I am to assist you out of the snare of the devil. Sometimes I sank into the dreadful practice of drinking two bottles of wine per day, for ten or twelve days in succession, rendering myself unfit for business or society, as well as exciting such a nervous irritability of temper, that I was waspish and cruel even to those whom at other times I most tenderly loved. After so terrible an indulgence and abuse of the mercies of God, I frequently, when quite alone, saw the most extraordinary phantoms dancing before my eyes, eluding my grasp, while strange noises and voices assailed my ears, drawing me into conversation, so that I became nearly like a person in a state of insanity; and when I recovered from these fits of intemperance, I was so enraged with myself that I could not endure the sight or conversation of my dearest friends. I have envied the very dogs in the streets. I appeared to be lost even beyond the reach of hope. At last the late excellent Dr. Day was consulted as to the possibility of affording relief to overcome so dreadful a propensity by the use of medicine. The doctor gave a favorable answer, and the Lord made me willing to submit to any trial, and I placed myself entirely under the care of this dear physician, whose prescription, under the immediate blessing of God, accompanied with fervent prayer, enabled me in the course of six months to discontinue the use of wine or spirituous liquors. My life has been ten years redeemed from destruction, as well as crowned with loving-kind-ness and tender mercy, and I am now the living monument of the power and mercy of that gracious God who is become my light and my salvation, and who will become yours also, my dear sir, if you will only put your trust in him and submit to be guided by his counsel. He will do so for the sake of his beloved Son. Arouse yourself then. Think what you are and are likely to be in society; but Oh, think also what you must become if you live and die in sin.

"I took between three hundred and four hundred bottles of steel-draughts in six months, and had I taken five thousand, the result would have been a rich reward. I have now dealt with you as though you were my own son. Think, Oh think of your poor soul. You may die to-morrow, or this day. Oh then set out instantly for the kingdom of heaven, and may the blessing of God attend you. You may be made whole if you are but willing. The way is now clearly pointed out to you by one who has proved the efficacy of that way, and who has been in a thousand times worse condition than yourself, but has been long restored to be a comfort and

* Sulphate of iron, 5 grains ; magnesia, 10 gr. ; peppermint-water, 11 drachms; spirit of nutmeg, 1 drachm. This forms one draught ; two draughts to be taken each day.

encouragement to others, and who prays the Lord
to bless you with a firm determination to forsake
every idol for the sake of Christ."

APRIL 22, 1828. We had the privilege of entertaining at our house the Rev. Rowland Hill, eighty-
three years of age.

FEB. 25, 1837. Poor Bob S——. This man had
been one of my old wicked companions in very early
days. He was now an inmate of the workhouse-
hospital, where I had attended during the last five
years on the Sabbath to read the Scriptures and
exhort the people to turn to the Lord. He was one
of my hearers during the last three years, and it
pleased God to touch his heart while he heard from
his old companion the joyful news of salvation.
Many a time have I seen tears of repentance roll
down his cheeks when speaking of the mercy of
God to his soul as the vilest and most undeserving.
He was taken ill, and confined to his bed when I
visited him. Two days before he died he said to
me with intense feeling, "Christ is the greatest
comfort I ever felt in my life." He then put up his
hands in fervent prayer, to which I added my heart's
Amen. He prayed like a man who felt the need of
a Saviour.

FEB. 28. This day I had the thrilling pleasure
of receiving intelligence from Mr. G—— of Glas-
gow, that he was about to publish "The Sinner's
Friend" in the Gaelic language, for the use of the
Highlanders. The above encouraging testimony
brought me on my knees before my gracious God
for this new testimony of his mercy and goodness.

MARCH 10. This day it has pleased the Lord to grant me the great privilege of witnessing an edition of "The Sinner's Friend" in the Irish language, translated under the direction of the daughter of the bishop of Meath. Oh may the divine blessing attend every copy in that benighted country. I humbly dedicate these to the Lord with earnest prayer and thanksgiving.

MAY 5. At the Tract Meeting in Exeter Hall, the Rev. J. Williams said that "he held in his hand a valuable tract, entitled 'The Sinner's Friend.' The editor had told him that if he would translate it into the Tahitian language, the means should be furnished of enabling him to print twenty thousand. He had accomplished the work, and the tract was published."

SEPT. 22. This day completes twenty-one years since even so much as a teaspoonful of wine of any description has ever passed the surface of my tongue. On the contrary, the very smell of strong drink is most abhorrent to my feelings. Oh the wondrous change which the grace of God can effect upon the renewed soul! I never drink any thing but tea, or coffee, or milk, and yet at sixty-three years of age I am stronger in body and mind than I was thirty years ago when indulging in all kinds of strong drink. But it is not my body only which has been strengthened, but my soul, blessed be God, has been growing in grace, producing the most exquisite enjoyments in this new life devoted to God. During all this time my aim has been to direct poor sinners to the "Lamb of God who taketh away the sin of the world," and the Lord has been pleased to bless my efforts in the most astonishing manner. To the Lord alone be all the praise, and to him I desire most humbly to devote every power of body, soul, and spirit. In Jesus, my salvation, my only hope and trust, I desire ever to be found, in full assurance of faith that he will never cast me away from his presence, nor suffer my soul to be lost. His word standeth sure, and I am safe in him—in his righteousness, not in my own, nor in any change of heart or life, but solely, wholly, and fully in the righteousness of the everlasting Son of God.

JAN. 14, 1838. Dear Mr. Williams, who translated "The Sinner's Friend" into Tahitian, dined with me this Sabbath, and I presented him with the stereotype plates, for which he was exceedingly thankful. He returns to the South Seas in a few weeks, taking with him 20,000 copies of "The Sinner's Friend" in the Tahitian language. May the Lord be pleased to bless every copy for Christ's sake.

FRAGMENTS OF TIME. How little do people in general think how much may be gained by gathering up the fragments of time. In my walk every morning from my cottage on Penenden Heath to Maidstone, I thought I might gain food for my soul by reading the New Testament for ten minutes. Being quite alone, I enjoyed this refreshing repast almost every day, blessing and praising the Lord for giving me such an appetite for heavenly food, and it was with no small gratitude that I found this morning that I had thus completed reading the whole of the New Testament.

MAY 9. Deep conviction of sin. In consequence of my son's absence, I slept at the house in High-street. When I arose this morning surrounded by mercies, not the least of which I had deserved, I felt my heart overwhelmed within me, and poured out my soul before the Lord nearly as follows :

"Unto thee, O Lord, do I lift up my soul this morning, in the very place, in the very room where I have committed so much iniquity. On this very spot do I desire to sink into the earth with shame at the remembrance of my past sins, crying out, 'Unclean, unclean ; God be merciful to me a sinner !' And, O Lord, I pray thee to cleanse me from all my pollution, in the name of him who has given me hope by declaring that they who come unto thee by Him shall in no wise be cast out. Help me, O Lord, to rise above every fear, and do thou mercifully destroy within me all sinful inclinations, and let holiness to the Lord fill my heart and be exemplified by a happy obedience to thy commands. Oh keep me humble, watchful, penitent, prayerful, and believing, that I may live increasingly to thy glory. And Oh thou blessed Spirit, come and prepare my heart for the ever blessed Son of God. And Oh thou blessed Jesus, thou who art the Chief among ten thousand, the Altogether Lovely, Oh come and abide in me, and help me to abide in thee as a branch of the true vine, bringing forth much fruit to the praise and glory of God. Oh my God, preserve me in my eyes, thoughts, and desires, that

all my ways may please thee, and that I may bless
thee at all times and have thy praise continually in
my mouth."

I had arisen from my slumber in the very chamber where, in the days of my youth, nearly fifty
years ago, I had often deeply sinned against the
Lord; and finding myself now in the way to Zion,
I felt my past sins rush upon my mind in all the
horror of their depravity, and this recollection
brought me to cry out the more earnestly for the
blood of Christ to wash my filthy soul from its
abominable pollution. I do trust that the Lord
did indeed hear my prayer, the breathing of a contrite soul. My sin comes before me so powerfully
every morning of my life, that when I look upon it
I am astonished that I have not destroyed myself
by my own hand. No one can possibly conceive of
the bitter anguish of my mind. O God, remember
not my sins. Hide thy face from them. Blot them
out of the book of thy remembrance. Oh mercifully grant me the joy of thy salvation. Oh the
agony, the agony, the agony of an accusing conscience. O Lord my God, hold me fast for Christ's
sake. I cannot look back upon my past sins but
with an abhorrence which no language can reach,
no heart feel like my own. "God be merciful to
me a sinner," is ever uppermost and accompanies
me everywhere—never absent. Oh what should I
do without the appropriation of the precious blood
of Christ to my own individual case. I must perish. Were I given to intemperance, suicide would
immediately follow.

June 14. Blessed for ever be the Lord for his great goodness and patience in sparing my life to witness an edition of "The Sinner's Friend" in the Manx language, for the poor people in the Isle of Man. By the kindness of a few followers of the Son of God, I shall have the happy privilege of sending five thousand copies gratuitously.

July 19. Twentieth anniversary of the Lord's mercy. "He shall tread upon the lion and the adder, the young lion and the dragon," strong drink, "shall he trample under feet." "I will deliver him, and honor him. With long life will I satisfy him, and show him my salvation." Surely the Lord has mercifully and abundantly verified his own word in my own individual case, and this blessed day testifies that twenty whole years have passed away since I discontinued the use of porter, of which I was extremely fond; but not a drop has entered my lips since the 18th day of July, 1818. But this is only part of the Lord's mercies towards me. He has kept me in the hollow of his hand, filling my heart with increasing love to him, making it my supreme delight to make known his salvation. He has also preserved to me my dear, affectionate wife, that best of gifts, except his beloved Son, whose affectionate tenderness and patience were with me in all my wretchedness; and when sunk in transgression and shame, this dear wife never forsook me a single hour, but continued her kind attentions with earnest prayer that the Lord would be pleased to pity and have mercy upon me, and deliver me out of the hand of my strong enemy. The Lord has answered

these prayers to the rejoicing of her heart. But
when I recollect my former unkindness, the effect
of strong drink, against this dear wife, my heart is
agonized almost to distraction; grief is never absent from my mind, and I should certainly take
away my own life were I to fall into the sin of
drunkenness as heretofore. I mourn in secret. I
strive to keep it from everybody. I dare not, cannot disclose the whole of my agony. I mourn in
the midst of plenty, and groan in the midst of gospel privileges, even with my soul truly devoted to
God. Well may I cry out, "Why art thou cast
down, Oh my soul?" "My life is smitten down to
the ground." "But why should a man complain
for the punishment of his sins?" Still I would cry
out in the name of Christ, "God be merciful to me
a sinner." Notwithstanding all this painful experience, no one but the Lord can tell the yearning I
have increasingly after souls to bring them to
Christ.

The Rev. T. W. C——, dean of Trinity college, Cambridge, wrote me the particulars of the
conversion of a profligate young man, converted,
by especial mercy, by reading "The Sinner's
Friend," portion page 10, "Pardon for the worst
of sinners." Blessed, ever blessed be the name of
the Lord.

FRENCH AND GERMAN EDITIONS. The Lord in his
tender mercy has been pleased to put it into the
hearts of two pious ladies to send me an offer to
translate "The Sinner's Friend" gratuitously into
these languages, if I would undertake to publish

them, which I have gratefully assented to do. May God add his blessing for Christ's sake. Amen.

OCT. 14. America. Received a letter from New York, stating that the Tract Society at New York has printed in the whole 64,000 copies of "The Sinner's Friend," and 94,000 copies of my speech at the Temperance meeting at Exeter Hall.

CHAPTER VIII.

"BRINGING IN SHEAVES."

1839 TO 1841—AGE 65-67.

JANUARY 24, 1839. No tongue on earth can tell the rapture of my soul when speaking for the Lord Jesus Christ. Every power in me all on fire, in a perfect blaze, when telling of redeeming love. But when I look at myself, and see the blackness of my heart and remember my dreadful sins, my soul sinks within me, and had I not a clear view of the mighty, the almighty sacrifice for sin, I should sink into despair. But Christ says, "No, I have redeemed thee, poor sinner. Thou art mine, and none shall ever pluck thee out of my hands." Thanks be to God for his unspeakable gift. I, once a poor drunken blasphemer, have now been many years a deacon of the church of Christ. Oh marvellous mercy! Surely I may well say,

> "Who could believe such lips could praise,
> Or think my dark and winding ways
> Should ever lead to God?"

MARCH 14. This day commences my sixty-sixth year—a poor sinful creature, laden with iniquity, yet overwhelmed by the mercy and goodness of my gracious God, who has plucked me indeed as a brand from the burning. On Monday evening, March 11, I, in the absence of our beloved pastor, was presiding at the prayer-meeting, and while

standing at the desk reading the blessed word of
God, I was quite overcome with the recollection
that on the same evening, March 11, 1811, I was
wandering, a poor drunkard in a dark night, among
the coal-mines at Stourbridge, and having passed
and escaped these horrible pits, I rolled down the
bank of a canal, and in one moment more, had not
the Lord held me, should have rolled over into the
canal and should have been lost for ever. Is it any
wonder that I should have felt the vast difference?
Why, the very stones would cry out were I to hold
my tongue. How wonderful that such a wretch
should have been raised up from the very depths of
hell to send invitations to tens of thousands of sinners to seek the Lord; and more wonderful still,
that the Lord should have blessed those invitations
to the conversion of many souls. Paul says that he
was raised up as a pattern of long-suffering to those
who should hereafter believe. I am sure that I
have been raised up as a witness of the forbearance
and long-suffering of an offended God, that no sinner, however vile, may despair. I returned home
weeping with an agony of gratitude, talking with
the Lord, telling him of his marvellous loving-kindness, and praying him to keep and preserve me
from pride or any kind of sin. I felt like a poor
wicked child before a tender father—a prodigal
returned. God be praised. Oh the matchless,
boundless love of God!

I have always before me the remembrance of
sin, filling my heart with unutterable anguish. But
what astonishing things has the Lord been pleased

to effect by the instrumentality of my little book!
What numbers of poor sinners have been brought
to seek the Lord by this simple means! My Lord
has also given me a son to be an ambassador for
the Lord Jesus Christ. But the marvellous change
is all of God, to whom I burn with ardent desire
that every breath may be to his glory, through my
gracious Redeemer, now my chiefest delight, ever
in my heart, a million, million times welcome guest,
there to live and reign.

The Rev. J. Black, Dunkeld, June 13, 1839,
wrote me the blessed intelligence of a remarkable
conversion of a colonel by the reading of "The Sinner's Friend." I fell on my knees with tears, clasping my hands, crying, "Lord, accept my thanks,
accept my thanks, and keep me humble. Oh keep
me humble, but accept my thanks for Christ's blessed sake."

JUNE, 1839. That dear servant of God, the Rev.
H. P—— of the Established church, has been giving
a lecture every Wednesday evening from "The Sinner's Friend," and in a letter of the 5th of June, 1839,
writes me, "We shall take the last page of 'The
Sinner's Friend' on Wednesday evening, July 3.
And now what I desire is, that you write us a letter
which I may read to my congregation on conclud-
ing your little work. Rejoice with me, my friend,
that a young female, about eighteen years of age,
has been turned from the power of sin and Satan
unto God by my lecture on the thirteenth page of
'The Sinner's Friend.'"

JULY 15. French edition, 3,000. Blessed be God

for his great goodness that a French translation of "The Sinner's Friend" was published this day, and humbly dedicated to the living God. Oh may his rich mercy accompany this little work, now circulated in ten languages in various parts of the world, to the comfort and conversion of many sinners.

I stop and ask myself this question: Am I doing these things from sincere love to God and to his beloved Son; or am I led away by any desire to obtain the good opinion of my fellow-sinners? I am so jealous of myself, that I dare not answer the question, but cast myself at the feet of Jesus, and like poor Peter, say, "Lord, thou alone knowest whether I love thee or not." But I do pray most earnestly that my whole heart and the warmest affections of my soul may be entirely and unreservedly given up to thee.

JULY 30, 1839. To Col. H——. "Like you, I was the fiddle of every convivial party. I could take the head of the table, and sit all night, drinking, swearing, playing cards, and every abomination. At a ball I was always sure of a partner, because I could dance well and was never tired; therefore the cry was, 'Oh, we must have Mr. Hall, for he will keep us all alive.' But Oh, how does my heart now grieve to think of these things; and how astonished am I to think that God did not cut me down in my horrid blasphemies and daring rebellion against him; and then to think of the wondrous change! The blasphemer an ambassador for Christ! The drunkard a Rechabite! The prayerless rebel presiding at a prayer-meeting!

"'Wonders of grace to God belong,
Repeat his mercies in your song.'

The companion of the licentious the friend of the pious! The bawler of profane songs the author of 'The Sinner's Friend!' Oh, how does this exalt the glory of the grace of God, for nothing else could possibly effect such a change. How does it exalt his mercy—higher than the heavens. What reason have we then to fear, my dear friend, that God will ever leave unfinished that which he has so manifestly and so gloriously begun? Oh no, no, never. But then those evil thoughts; what are we to do with them? Why, my friend, you must do as I do with them; carry them to the foot of the cross, the only place to get rid of them. I was myself most distressingly plagued with fears on this account till I read 'Owen on Indwelling Sin,' and here I found that the people of God harassed themselves by the expectation that they were to get rid of indwelling sin before they get to heaven, which can never be the case; and it should be enough for them to know that, although sin dwells in them, yet, by the grace of God, it does not reign over them as it once did. This gave me quite a new light upon the subject, and made me content to be always fighting, trusting in the Lord. I remember also hearing a dear silver-haired preacher of the gospel comforting his hearers by saying, 'The devil will worry the saints all the way to the very gate of heaven; but, blessed be God, he can never get in after them.'"

Nov. 25. This morning I started from Maidstone at nine o'clock on a journey to Norwich, to a meeting of the Norwich Union Life Office. I supplied my bag with a goodly number of "The Sinner's Friend," praying for opportunities. There were three passengers and myself in the coach, and before we had got four miles I had the happiness of introducing the subject nearest my heart. They listened with earnest attention to what I had to say of redeeming love. Early next morning I left London by the Norwich coach. When daylight appeared I began to look round upon my fellow-travellers, but was no way encouraged. We went on silently for about five miles, when I took out a copy of "The Sinner's Friend," as though I were going to read it, when a lady passenger immediately said, "You have got a most interesting little book, sir." "How do you know it to be so, madam?" "Oh, sir," she replied, "I know it well, and that it has had a most astonishing circulation." The lady said she knew the author, naming a gentleman of Norwich. This brought on the desired conversation, and we kept on praising God to the very last minute, as the coach drove up the streets of Norwich, and then my fellow-passengers gave me a hearty shake of the hand, repeating their thanks.

Mr. T. G——took me to a large meeting of the teachers of the various Sunday-schools. How great was my surprise to hear my own name pronounced by the chairman as the author of "The Sinner's Friend," and that I would address a few words to the company. I arose and opened my mouth for the Lord, who mercifully, as he always does, gave me utterance, and I hope I did not bring any dis-

honor upon that blessed cause which I so dearly
love. Before the meeting broke up, I requested
Mr. G—— to procure three hundred copies of "The
Sinner's Friend" from the bookseller in Norwich,
and present a copy to each person in the room.

Mr. G—— took me with him the next morning
to a select prayer-meeting, consisting of six dear
devoted men who had met for prayer that the blessing of the Lord might attend the annual meeting of
the City Mission, at which it was planned that I
should speak. Mr. G—— then took me with him
to visit a poor dying woman anxious for her soul's
conversion. "The Sinner's Friend" was lying on
the chair by her bedside. She was very feeble,
but when Mr. G—— told her that I was the person
who wrote "The Sinner's Friend," her countenance
brightened up as she exclaimed, "Do I indeed behold the gentleman who wrote that book which has
afforded me so much comfort?" I reminded her
of the words of the Lord Jesus Christ, who had
most emphatically declared, "Him that cometh to
me I will in no wise cast out," and, "None shall
pluck you out of my hand." I then told her, if
Satan should suggest doubts and fears to her mind
as to her safety, to look immediately upon this note
of hand, signed, "Jesus Christ the Son of God,"
"None shall pluck you out of my hand."

At the meeting of the City Mission there were
upwards of one thousand persons. In the strength
of the Lord I boldly declared my obligations to
God's mercy, and then brought forth four instances
of the value of missionary efforts, either in speaking

to people living in sin, or going to their houses, or being faithful at their bedside, or in giving a tract. I then gave an account of the Lord's dealings with my own soul, and said that the way of my deliver-ance was so wonderful, that it would appear almost as a fable invented for effect; but the man of whom I had been speaking, as I had spoken in the third person, was now alive and in good health; then pausing a moment, I concluded by saying, "And it is from his lips you now hear of the goodness of that God whose mercy endureth for ever." There was a dead silence; the feelings of the people had been wrought up to a high pitch; not a sound was heard, but several dear people upon the platform came up to me and pressed my hand in the most expressive manner. They felt the goodness of the Lord; so did I. He was with me from the begin-ning to the end. Praised be his name. One gen-tleman came up, and with a half incredulous inquiry asked me if I was really the person who had lain at the edge of the canal.

FEB. 25, 1840. On looking into my journal this morning, I turned to the entry made on the 15th of March, 1812, when I was in great distress on ac-count of my sinful course; and on reading the peti-tion which the Lord at that time put into my heart, that I might become a signal monument of the power and goodness of God, I was overwhelmed with gratitude at his wondrous mercy in answering prayer in so remarkable a manner, that for upwards of twenty-three years not a drop of wine or spirit-uous liquor has ever passed my tongue, and that I

have been enabled to be an ambassador of Jesus
Christ. I fell on my knees and with tears of gratitude endeavored to thank the Lord for his wondrous
long-suffering. Oh what encouragement does my
case afford to the most abandoned sinner to cast
himself at the feet of Jesus, who has promised that
none shall be cast out who come to God by him.
No heart was ever so much at enmity against God
as mine; and yet how dearly do I love him now,
and have done for many years. This is all his own
work, not mine. Blessed be his name.

MARCH 14. This day commences my sixty-sev-
enth year. What shall I say of the goodness and
mercy of God to so vile a sinner? I stand astonished
at my new nature, scarcely believing my own senses:
that I, who hated holiness, should feel the most
exquisite as well as the most unutterable delight in
walking in the ways of God; that this blessed feeling
should also have occupied the chief place in my heart
for upwards of twenty years, without the smallest
diminution, daily, hourly, momentarily increasing,
till my whole soul glows with a constant blaze of
heavenly love. I cannot hear the blessed name of
the Saviour without feeling a fire within me stealing
into my eyes with streams of gratitude for what he
has done for my soul. I could praise him for ever.
And Oh, how many opportunities has he given me
for doing this within the last year, in journeys by
coaches or steam-boats, or otherwise; and how has
my heart been enraptured in such opportunities in
proclaiming to persons whom I had never seen before the amazing love of God in the person of his

beloved Son. Oh wondrous grace, matchless mercy! Yes, blessed be his name, I am his, and nothing shall ever separate me from his love.

JERUSALEM. It is impossible to express the exquisite pleasure which I experienced, May 29, by the receipt of a letter from the Rev. J. N——, dated Mount Zion. He proposes to translate "The Sinner's Friend" into the Hebrew and Arabic. I was overjoyed at the letter, which I laid before the Lord on my knees, with thanksgiving that "The Sinner's Friend" had been accepted in that very city where my gracious Redeemer shed his blood for the sins of the whole world, and for me. Blessed be his name.

Mr. A. W—— went to France on June 4, principally to circulate "The Sinner's Friend" in the French language. Mr. W—— took five hundred copies for that purpose. Oh may the Lord be mercifully pleased to bless every copy for Jesus' own sake. Mr. B—— has been circulating "The Sinner's Friend" in Spain, from whence he was driven. "The Christian Spectator" publishes a Papal edict against it.

JUNE 30. This day the seventy-first edition of "The Sinner's Friend" was published, with three entirely new portions which the Lord had mercifully put into my heart to write. I took one of these copies in my hand, and kneeling before the Lord, humbly dedicated them to him with earnest prayer for his blessing to attend every copy.

JULY 13. Wrote Dr. Pinkerton that I wished the Frankfort Tract Society to adopt "The Sinner's Friend;" that I would send them gratuitously one

thousand copies; and also would present them with
the stereotype plates. I laid my letter and the little
book before the Lord, and on my knees entreated
him to influence the Committee of the Frankfort
society to adopt "The Sinner's Friend."

AUG. 13. For a long time my heart has been
irresistibly drawn to the exercise of prayer about the
middle of the day. When the men have gone to
their dinner, I have retired to the printing-office for
a few minutes to kneel before the Lord with thankfulness and praise for the continuance of his great
and many mercies. I have felt it refreshing thus to
hold communion with God in the very midst of
business, to arm me against the many vexations
which momentarily assail me. I am sure it is good
often to run to the Lord, to take shelter under the
shadow of his almighty wings, that he may protect
us from ourselves as well as from the world and
Satan.

AUG. 16. This day I received from W——
R——, Esq., Russian merchant at St. Petersburg, a
letter saying his son-in-law "gave 'The Sinner's
Friend' to Baron H——, a colonel in the Grand
Duke's regiment. He is delighted with it, and calls
it the best epitome of the gospel that he ever saw.
His copy is lent out, and is going a round among
his friends; but he wants a French copy, to lend to
those who do not understand German. We shall
also lose no time in having it translated into Russ.
It will suit the Russians."

SEPT. 5. This day I had the exquisite pleasure of
sending off by Hamburg steam-packet, the stereo-

type plates of the German edition of "The Sinner's Friend," as a present to the Lower Saxony Tract Society, in the name of the Lord Jesus. O may his richest blessing accompany every copy.

OCTOBER 14, 1840. Wednesday morning, seven o'clock. Is Christ really precious to my soul; or is he not? Is Christ dear to my heart; or is he not? Is it my earnest desire to have him ever with me; or is it not? If called to die this very moment, is my confidence firm in Christ; or is it not? What answer does my soul give to these questions? Surely I can truly say that Christ is indeed the altogether lovely, precious to my soul, and my supreme desire; with the deepest sorrow for sin, yet with the most implicit confidence in that precious blood which cleanseth from all sin, even my sins. Then if called to die this day, or even before I finish this entry, I am now safe in Christ, and a thousand years of holy living would not make me more fit for heaven than at the present moment; for I can enter heaven only an unworthy sinner having no righteousness of my own, but all in Christ, for he is my sanctification, my peace, my way to God. Such are my thoughts at this moment with the word of God before me, and before I proceed to read its blessed contents. Blessed be God for this lively faith in his beloved Son.

J. V. H.

Nov. 7. O blessed be the Lord that I live to see the day up to which he has mercifully enabled me by his great bounty to give away upwards of forty thousand copies of "The Sinner's Friend." O what can I render to the Lord for all his goodness tow-

ards me, so great, so utterly undeserved? I desire
to give him my whole heart, and to devote all my
life to his blessed service for Christ's sake. O Lord,
accept my heart, and seal it thine.

Nov. 16. I wrote the Religious Tract Society an
offer of "The Sinner's Friend," to print it as a tract.
To this proposition they assented. May the Lord
add his blessing. Amen. [Up to midsummer, 1843,
the Tract Society published ninety thousand copies,
in fifteen editions.]

A note from the son of the Bishop of Calcutta
announces that "The Sinner's Friend" is already
translated into Bengalee, and widely circulated.
Praised, O praised be the Lord.

MARCH 14, 1841. This day completes my sixty-
seventh year. I can scarcely believe it possible
that I am so old. My health vigorous, and my soul
all on fire for the Lord Jesus. O what wondrous
things has the Lord done for me during the last
twenty-five years, making me not only a Rechabite,
but a follower of the Lord Jesus Christ.

MAY 12. A new portion for "The Sinner's Friend,"
"What must I do to be saved?" In reading in
my usual course the sixteenth chapter of Acts, I was
impressed with the importunity of the poor jailer to
know what he could do to be saved; and as many
persons are anxious to know this, I felt as it were a
sudden call to write a few thoughts on this passage,
and then transfer it to the pages of "The Sinner's
Friend." I immediately laid the matter before the
Lord, imploring his aid to warm my heart, and then
instruct me what to write in strict accordance with

his holy word. In answer to this petition, the Lord was mercifully pleased to direct my mind to write the new portion which will appear in the new edition, eighty-eight, on page 4, "Salvation through faith—not by works." May the Lord accompany it with his blessing, for Christ's sake. Amen.

The Rev. J. Angell James, Birmingham, writes, "I greatly rejoice with you in the usefulness to which God has called you by the publication of this little work. It will outlive its author, and be sending up converted and glorified saints to heaven to follow him to the realms of bliss. How sweet is the thought of doing something for Christ even after we are dead."

June 8. Awoke early this morning out of a heavenly dream, in which I had been engaged with several persons in a house of prayer. I was myself apparently engaged in the exercise of most earnest supplication, with an intensity of energy far more than when I am awake. This blessed vision was in answer to earnest prayer the last thing before I closed my eyes in sleep. It has long been my custom, when I get into bed, to pray the Lord that, if it be not too much to ask, he will be pleased to preserve me from sinful dreams, and that when my body is locked in sleep my soul may be engaged in his blessed service, either in praise or prayer; so that, whether sleeping or waking, I may always be engaged in his blessed service. I have reason to bless the Lord that he continually grants my requests to the rejoicing of my soul, so that with David I am

enabled to say, "When I awake I am still with thee."
Blessed be the Lord.

THE FAITHFULNESS OF GOD TO HIS PROMISES. What
a blessing is prayer; and Oh what mercy that God
should hear us! It has been a great comfort to me
in my pilgrimage to trust in the promise of our dear
Redeemer, "Whatsoever ye shall ask in my name,
that will I do." The Lord is ever faithful to his
word. I have proved it to be so in a most remarkable manner in the following instance. My love
and reverence for the Lord have led me to leave the
whole direction of my concerns in his hands; praying him to make me holy and acquiescent in his will,
rather than specify to the Lord any particular blessing. But a few years ago my beloved wife was laid
on a bed of sickness, and considered to be within a
few minutes of eternity, not the slightest hope; so
that the physician told me that her duration in life
would not exceed ten minutes. She had parted,
finally as we thought, with myself, and I had retired to another apartment, while she sent for my
eldest son to attend her bedside to receive her blessing. I stepped gently into her room again unob-
served by any one, to catch the last sound of her
dear voice, and while I was thus remaining in most
painful suspense, even then unwilling to dictate to
the Lord, but rather feeling, "Though he slay me,
yet will I trust in him," and love him too, a voice
from heaven whispered in my ear, "There is a promise laid up for you in the trying hour: I know your
faith, your love, and that you would rather not specify a blessing, but would humbly trust my mercy;

but now make use of this promise, 'Whatsoever ye
shall ask in my name, that will I do.'" With a half
suffocated voice I cried out in agony, "Lord, I beseech thee, for the honor of the word of thy dear
Son, do grant me the life of my wife." I sank back
in my chair, overwhelmed with the intensity of my
feelings, and could say no more, not a syllable. I
could only weep. But Oh the mercy and faithfulness
of God! The angel of death, his arrow poised, was
forbidden to strike; and from that very moment my
beloved wife began to recover, and she who was supposed to be within ten minutes of death has been
many years, and is now, the solace of my life, the
joy of my heart, uniting every energy of heart and
soul with myself in the work of the Lord, having
herself written one of the portions, "Word to the
Poor," in "The Sinner's Friend." Blessed be the
Lord.

SEPTEMBER 22, 1841. Twenty-five years of emancipation. I discontinued wine and spirituous liquors
Sunday, September 22, 1816. I am more full of life
and fire at nearly seventy years of age than I was
at thirty, when I drank freely of every thing. By
not taking malt liquor I never feel the pain of thirst,
therefore do not require liquid aliment in the same
degree as heretofore, tea and coffee being sufficient.
But besides this, it has pleased God to put "a new
song into my mouth;" and he has enabled me by
his almighty grace to live to his glory, a monument
of redeeming love.

"THE WONDERFUL ESCAPE." This tract, the sub-
stance of my speech at Exeter Hall, at the anniver-

sary of the Temperance Society, May, 1836, was adopted and 136,000 copies printed by the New York Tract Society entirely without my knowledge. Blessed be the Lord. Who would have thought, when I made this speech, that it would have been made a blessing in America?

DEC. 1. Mr. E. M—— died this day, aged sixty-three. He was one of my early companions in a society of twenty or more gay young men indulging in folly and sin : we two were the only persons left; all the others cut down in the prime of life. I had spoken and written to Mr. M——, and I gave him a copy of "The Sinner's Friend," with strong entreaty that he would read it with attention. His death is a warning. The whole society, of which I was a leader, is now broken up, all gone except myself. Shortly I too must die. I behold David and Saul and Peter, a murderer, a blasphemer, and a back-slider, yet all these three are in heaven, notwithstanding their misdeeds. How came these to find a place there? Because God is long-suffering, gracious, and merciful to all who seek him through Jesus Christ. Though all men may deem me beside myself, yet no philosophy nor argument can ever dissuade me of my firm belief that Jesus Christ lives and reigns even in my heart, which once dared to despise his rule, and which was determined to indulge in every kind of sin. David said he was "a wonder unto many;" so am I and have been among my former acquaintances, but I am the greatest wonder to myself. But "wonders of grace to God belong." It is all wonder from beginning to end.

Some of my friends seem to think that I have a peculiar warmth of manner in expressing my love to Christ. Ah, dear friends, ice itself would become fire with indignation, were I not to burn and blaze whenever my dear Redeemer's name is the theme. The wonder is that I am not in the hottest hell instead of singing the praises of God. If any inquire why it is that I love so much, I refer them to the Saviour's own words, "Because he hath much forgiven." Glory, glory, glory be to the Lord. Amen. Lord, keep me humble, keep me humble for Jesus' blessed sake.

CHAPTER IX.

CONTENT.

1842 TO 1852—AGE 68-78.

MARCH 14, 1842. This day ended my sixty-ninth year, and the thirtieth year of my new birth. The Lord has indeed fulfilled his word in my case: "With long life will I satisfy him, and show him my salvation," Psa. 91: with long life, inasmuch as I have now outlived all my friends, the associates of my youth. My own time must, however, shortly come. But I have not the slightest fear. Not because of my new nature, a total change of heart, but from the impossibility of God to be unfaithful to his word. And he has said by his beloved Son, that whosoever believeth on him shall have everlasting life. By the grace of God I do believe in Christ, although I was once an infidel, and he has become the very chiefest object of my affections, with a constant hatred of all manner of sin. In my old age, and with plenty of this world's goods, I am still a beggar, begging my way from earth to heaven every hour of my life. But I feel enriched by free, unmerited grace. It is my desire ever to lie at the foot of the cross with deep repentance and love towards that divine Redeemer who ever lives and reigns in my heart. This blessed feeling has been increasing daily in my soul more than twenty years. God be praised evermore. O may my beloved wife and all my dear children enjoy the same heavenly delights, that we may all meet round the throne in blissful union to sing for ever of redeeming love.

A letter from the Religious Tract Society informs me that "The Sinner's Friend" is to be printed at Athens in the Greek language. How wonderful, that where Paul made known the then unknown God, and possibly even on Mars hill, "The Sinner's Friend," by the blessing of God, may be the means of directing some poor sinner to the cross.

MAY 2. When the late martyr Williams was at my house, I wrote an affectionate letter to Makea, king of Rarotonga, which Mr. Williams engaged to deliver to him on his return to that island; but as Mr. Williams was murdered, I never expected to hear any thing about my letter. To my surprise, a letter was delivered to me this day from Makea David, son of the late king of Rarotonga, translated by Mr. Buzacott, resident missionary, saying, "I understand that Jesus the Messiah is your rejoicing, by what you have said in your writing to Makea. I also understand the little book, 'The Sinner's Friend;' a book very excellent, and enlightening to read."

APRIL 19. This morning dear Newman and self set off from Rotherham to Thorne, on our way to Hull. In the packet were several emigrants for America, to whom I spoke of the mercy of God. In the cabin I also found four dear Christians, to whom I opened my mouth for the Lord, encouraging them to put their trust in Him. At Hull we were most courteously welcomed by Sir William Lowthrop. In the evening to a prayer-meeting, which was being

held at Mr. Stratten's chapel to implore the divine
blessing upon the new chapel to be opened on the
morrow. Mr. Stratten astonished me by saying,
"A stranger, who is now here, unknown to us personally, but well known as the author of 'The Sinner's Friend,' will, I hope, engage in prayer when
the hymn has been sung. As soon as the service
was over, about a dozen ministers and others came
round me with kind shakes of the hand. O how
great is the goodness of the Lord towards me. On
our return we found the Rev. Dr. Raffles and Dr.
Harris, who had come to officiate at the opening of
Albion chapel on the morrow.

APRIL 20. OPENING OF ALBION CHAPEL, HULL. The
Rev. J. Stratten commenced the service by a dedi-
catory prayer. The Rev. Dr. Harris preached from
"Thy will be done." There was breathless attention for an hour and a half. In the evening the
Rev. Dr. Raffles threw open the gate of mercy wide
as infinity, from "The grace of God that bringeth
salvation hath appeared unto all men." Oh it was
enough to awaken the dead, and I trust that many
a soul was made glad indeed in the Lord. I had
some very pleasant private conversation with Lady
Lowthrop upon the mercy of God to sinners. Afterwards I spoke to the butler about the way of
salvation. He said he was not a converted man, but
he hoped to become so. He appeared truly thankful, and promised to attend to my admonition. I
spoke to him a second time, urging him to seek the
Lord without delay. I entreated him so warmly
that he appeared deeply affected.

APRIL 22. At Sheffield a respectable woman addressed me, "Sir, you gave a very instructing little book, 'The Sinner's Friend,' to a person here, the other day. Would you be so kind as to give one to me?" She asked with such a look of importunity that I said, "Oh yes, and I bless God that you have asked me." I then took hold of her hand in a kind manner and said, "Do you know Jesus?" The tears started in her eyes, and she looked that she knew him. Shaking her kindly by the hand, I commended her to the blessing of the Lord; and when I got into the street I could scarcely refrain from crying aloud, "Lord, thou art ever blessing me; and thou knowest that it is the joy of my heart ever to be praising thee. My heart, my heart praises thee, O God." I was quite in rapture at this very unexpected opportunity of speaking for the Lord.

APRIL 25. Mr. W——'s butler walked with me to the railway station, which gave me the opportunity of speaking to him on the great importance of being decidedly a Christian. At the station-house I conversed with a young female on the necessity of being found in the ways of God. Gave her a copy of "The Sinner's Friend," thankful to God for the opportunity of beginning the day in his service.

JULY 13. HULL. This day it pleased God to allow my dear wife and self the privilege of witnessing our dear son Newman's being ordained a minister of Jesus Christ. Newman had been unanimously invited by the deacons and church of Christ assembled in Albion chapel to take upon him this

important office, and this day about twelve ministers were assembled for the service. The Rev. T.
James proposed the usual questions to Newman,
whose straightforward account of the principles of
his faith and the motives which had led him to
desire the office of a Christian minister, awakened
the deepest sympathies, and drew tears from many.
I wept with gratitude to hear him declare that from
a child he had been taught the way of the Lord,
early instructed by his dear parents to walk in the
way of holiness and truth.   He spoke of his early
advantages, but acknowledged that his religion was
merely outward, until a circumstance aroused him
seriously to seek salvation in Christ Jesus. This
was simple, but made effectual by the Holy Spirit.
It was a letter from a younger sister.   Here again
I had abundant reason to praise the Lord that my
dear children had not been taught in vain to seek
Him.

SABBATH-DAY, JULY 17. Albion chapel, Hull.
Dear Newman commenced his arduous services as
pastor.   His first text was, "Brethren, pray for us;"
and in the evening, "I am determined to know
nothing among you, save Christ, and him crucified."
The Lord's supper was administered after the evening service to about eighty communicants.

JULY 19. I embarked on board the Vivid steam-
er; there were four Wesleyan ministers on board,
and when the company were assembled to tea, one
of them asked the divine blessing upon our refreshment. I could not refrain from expressing my pleasure, and at the same time saying that I should be

very glad to have a prayer-meeting in the saloon at half-past seven o'clock, when about twenty persons united in prayer and praise until half-past nine. The next morning at half-past ten we renewed this exercise for an hour.

Aug. 6. At Hull I had the opportunity of speaking to many persons, particularly to Sir W. L——'s butler, that he might overcome his besetting sin of intemperance and find a refuge in Jesus Christ. I took him by the hand and spoke to him tenderly, till his eyes told the feelings of his heart. My son Newman says in a letter from Hull, "On Thursday last H—— came to offer himself as a member for church-fellowship, and stated that it was my father who first led him to think seriously of his soul. How my heart rejoiced for one of the first batch of new members to be my father's spiritual son." When I read this I fell down on my knees in joy and gratitude, and could only articulate with convulsive accent, "O my Lord, mercifully accept my thanks, and bless that man with establishing grace for Christ's sake, and keep me humble." What delight have I experienced in speaking for Christ in steam-boats, coaches, railways, omnibuses, and anywhere when opportunity has occurred. It has been my highest delight to "bless the Lord at all times, and to have his praise continually in my mouth," and to say, "Come and hear, all ye that fear God, and I will declare what he hath done for my soul." This is the second instance of a gentleman's servant having been brought to think seriously of his soul in consequence of my admonition.

OCT. 20. A servant provoked me by obstinate argument when I endeavored to explain to him his error. I felt angry, and spoke hastily. I was sorry for it, and immediately fell on my knees beseeching the Lord to pardon my sin. "Set a watch before my mouth," etc. How needful this for every professor of religion.

JAN. 4, 1843. Newman writes that one of the members admitted to church-fellowship last week attributed to reading "The Sinner's Friend" her first religious impressions. Also that he had been sent for to see a sick man who had been without any religion or hope; but a copy of "The Sinner's Friend" had been lent him, and Newman found him sobbing with penitence and joy.

JOURNEY TO HULL. MARCH 12. In the afternoon of this Sabbath I had the pleasure of conducting the service at Wincobank chapel, near Sheffield. About three hundred present. I spoke for an hour, my soul all on fire. March 14. Hull. Arrived at Dr. Gordon's. At Dr. Gordon's met ministers of the Established, the Presbyterian, and Independent churches. We heartily agreed upon the essential points of the gospel—none but Christ. How delightful to meet with sincere Christians of every denomination. March 17. Accompanied Sir W. L—— to the prison, and addressed a few words to the debtors. Afterwards addressed the female prisoners, who were also assembled in a room, where Lady L—— was reading to them from the Bible. March 19. Bethel Floating chapel. Conducted the service on board the Floating chapel, and spoke for about an hour to six hundred persons, sailors and others. The ship was literally crammed. March 23. Mrs. H—— of Welton told me that a gentleman who was taken ill requested particularly that she should be sent for to speak to him about a Saviour. Mrs. H—— read several portions from "The Sinner's Friend," which so comforted his soul that he pressed the little book to his bosom with gratitude, and shortly afterwards died. March 26. Penitentiary. Sir W. L—— and Miss M—— took me to address the inmates, twenty-six young females. Spoke tenderly to these unfortunates, many of whom wept exceedingly. I felt that I myself was far worse than any of these poor females. The Lord has saved me; why not save them? March 29. Unceasingly alive to his mercy, I felt constrained, as I walked along the streets, to be continually praising the Lord. I hope it is indeed the true desire of my soul that my God may be glorified by me in every word and thought and deed, and that Christ may occupy every space of my heart, to the exclusion of every kind of sin. March 30. Enjoyed a walk of three hours with Lady L——, who kindly introduced me to many exceedingly poor Christians, living in such obscure places that I was surprised she had found them out; but she was in the habit of reading and praying with them. In these visits I heard of two persons who had been brought to the Lord through "The Sinner's Friend." April 8. Home. Dear Mary and self knelt together before the Lord to thank him for his great mercy during our absence, and for the kindnesses from the whole

8*

of our friends during our stay in Yorkshire. I had
never had so delightful a relaxation from business.
My dear Mary being my companion, made my joy
complete. Blessed be the Lord.

MARCH 14, 1844. Seventy years of age. Were it
not for a correct reckoning of the past years, I could
scarcely believe it possible. No lassitude, no disease whatever. I may well call upon my soul and
all that is within me to bless the Lord. I awoke
very early this morning, praising him for preserving my health and causing me to rejoice in Christ
as my all-sufficient Saviour. But in the midst of
mercies almost beyond compare, still my nature is
prone to sin. I lament it deeply, with earnest cry
for a truly penitent heart.

MARCH 26. This day we took possession of our
new residence, and my dear Mary and self knelt
together before the Lord to dedicate ourselves and
our new tenement to the Lord, beseeching his blessing to accompany us in this and in every circumstance of our future life. In the evening, at our
family altar, we again, with our children and servants, repeated the same heartfelt offering to him.

"The Sinner's Friend" is now adopted and published by the four largest Tract Societies in the
world; also in India by the Calcutta Translation
Society, under the superintendence of Bishop Wil-
son, in various dialects. Oh what do I not owe to
the Lord for his wonderful mercy in thus bestowing
such great honor on my little work!

MAY 8. It was again my privilege to speak to
the people in Week-street chapel, our dear pastor

being absent in London. My principal design was to urge the great importance of being one with Christ, and in every situation of life to have him always with us. The blessed reward of being one of his sheep—eternal life. The security—never perish; "No man able to pluck them out of my hand." Blessed security! Although I had no thought or desire to have been thus engaged, and would rather have relinquished it to any other person, yet when I was so engaged my heart was all on fire, overflowing with the most intense feeling to induce my fellow-sinners to seek a close union with our blessed Redeemer, and through him to be one with the Father.

SUNDAY, MARCH 2, 1845. The Lord's supper. It was on Sabbath, March 2, 1818, that I partook of the Lord's supper for the first time in Weak-street chapel, having been received on the previous Friday as a member of Christ; and this day I had the great privilege to officiate as a deacon, to which office I had been unanimously elected many years ago, and the Lord has mercifully preserved me until the present day. I felt overwhelmed with gratitude, and I requested our dear minister to return thanks to the Lord publicly on my behalf.

HULL. MARCH 24. Walked about the docks to circulate "The Sinner's Friend." This evening a district meeting of Christian friends was held in Sir W. L——'s drawing-room. To my unspeakable gratitude five or six persons referred to "The Sinner's Friend" as having been made a blessing to their souls, by directing them to the Saviour. Oh

how merciful is the Lord to me, the very chiefest of
the worst of sinners. Nobody knows how bad I
have been but myself. Yet the Lord knows it all;
but blessed be his name, the blood of his dear Son
cleanseth from all sin—from my sins.

JUNE 7. This morning Mr. O——, a perfect stranger, came to Maidstone for no other purpose than
to pay me a visit. He addressed me in the most
enthusiastic manner, saying that he had distributed
many thousand copies of "The Sinner's Friend,"
and knew of the good that had been effected by its
circulation, in cases almost exceeding credibility,
only he knew them to be true. The Rev. J——
from Tahiti came in the evening. So that the
Lord was this day pouring forth a river of delight
in bringing me into close communion with his dear
people. On this day we had the great pleasure of
entertaining the missionaries, etc., who had come
to attend the annual meeting. Our room was literally crammed. Twelve ministers among them. I
was truly thankful for a house and a heart to receive
the friends of my Lord.

AUG. 26. Anniversary of our wedding-day, com-
pleting thirty-nine years united to my beloved
Mary, more beloved than ever. But Oh, how my
heart aches at the remembrance of the pain I have
occasioned her to feel; and Oh, how my soul mourns
at the recollection of my sins against a holy God
The very mercies of God made me quite miserable,
because they were so greatly undeserved. I was
indeed and always am truly sorry for my sin, but
I have implicit confidence in the blood of Christ

to atone for all my guilt, although of the deepest dye.

SEPT. 23. Astonishing that such a wretch as I was should be permitted to speak for Christ. But the ways of God are not our ways, and he in infinite mercy first grants conversion to the most unlikely, like Saul of Tarsus, and then bestows upon them a commission, saying, "Feed my sheep." The change is truly as great as from darkness into light, hell into heaven. "But," says the sceptic, "where is the proof?" To such a one I would say, "Look at yonder wretched object, prostrate on the ground, covered with filth, frightful to behold, his eyes glaring, and cheeks bloated with intoxication. Hear those dreadful oaths and curses at every word belching from his stammering lips. Look at the wretch—lost! a very beast. Appalling sight! Turn from the loathsome object, and enter yon temple of the Lord, and there behold the striking contrast. An aged pilgrim presiding at a prayer-meeting, giving out the hymns with a pathos and solemnity that bespeak a heart full of adoration, thanksgiving, and love to the Redeemer. Listen to the glowing effusion of his soul in prayer, all on fire for God, confessing the enormity of his past sins, yet humbly exulting and glorying in the sanctifying influences of the Holy Spirit to prepare his heart for the reception of the ever blessed Son of God, that he may there ever live and reign, a million, million times welcome guest, the joy of his soul, the daily increasing delight of his life. But who is this aged pilgrim with silver hair, so full of heavenly fire?

Who is he? Listen, O earth, and you, ye angels of
God, who rejoice over a penitent sinner turned from
the error of his ways. Listen, ye angels, listen!
Who is he? Why, the aged silvery-haired pilgrim
is no other than the once poor blaspheming rebel
whom you saw prostrate on the ground, in all the
horrors of intoxication, covered with filth. Yes,
praise to the tender mercy of God, this is the very
wretch whom Jesus saw weltering in his blood, bade
him live as the lost whom he came to save, and then
put on him a new robe, and made him the author of
'The Sinner's Friend.' Is any thing too hard for
the Lord? This is the proof of the power of changing grace." Merciful God! O God of wonders!
Well may this poor man sing,

> "Through all eternity to thee
>   A joyful song I'll raise,
> But Oh, eternity's too short
>   To utter all thy praise."

Is it any wonder then that when I speak of Christ
I am all in a blaze? Why, the very stones would
rise up against me were I to be silent one single
moment. The Lord Jesus is always in my thoughts,
my heart, my tongue, and I can no more help or cease
speaking of him than I can live without breathing.

OCT. 10. The natural birthday of my dear, dear
wife, dearer than ever, dearer than when she completed her nineteenth year as my wife. Now she
has lived to see the returns of her birthday forty
times since we have been united in the bonds of
increasing love, a numerous offspring, and our children's children, with mercies on every side. Oh

what reason to call upon our souls and every power within us to bless and praise the Lord. We had a happy family party. After dinner we united heart and voice in singing, "Praise God, from whom all blessings flow." After tea we repeated hymns, and I took the opportunity to address my dear children, entreating them to make the Lord their trust, and then they would find him to be as kind to them as he had been to their father. When I am dead and gone perhaps they will think of this. Oh may the Lord fix it upon their souls.

"MAY 26, 1846. I take up my pen to write you in the midst of tears. 'But why should my father shed tears?' I'll tell you, dear Newman. I have just been reading the thrilling tale of Joseph and his brethren, and although I have read it so often, yet it is ever exciting to the highest degree, and I cannot help it, old fool as I am. Talk of romance or tales of imagination; why, nothing in the world exceeds this simple unvarnished truth. And then I began to think of the mercy of God to myself in an almost similar but far different respect, because I was not ruler of all Egypt; but God had raised me up to nourish a dear mother who had been by misfortune reduced from respectability and plenty to poverty; and then God sent me into a strange land—Worcester—unknown to any one, and without a shilling of my own; and there God gave me power and money, and a heart of love to my poor parent, whose letters to me were often commenced, 'My dear Joseph in Egypt, the meal is almost gone,' and then through the Lord's mercy I was enabled most will-

ingly to supply all her wants until she entered
heaven; her last words, for two hours, invoking
blessings upon her son. The recollection of all this
made me weep again, as I now do, to think of the
goodness of God towards me; and then to give
me such a wife, and to load me with temporal and
spiritual blessings till my heart is overwhelmed with
joy and sorrow, sorrow of the deepest kind at the
remembrance of my past ingratitude to my forgiving God. And then, again, to think of the excess of
his goodness in making me a herald of salvation to
hundreds of thousands of sinners in every part of
the world. Oh, it is too much. The Lord preserve
me from pride or self-complacency. But Oh, how
I do love the Lord, his ways, his people, and how
my heart does rejoice when I can speak a word for
his holy name.

"Poor Okill is yet alive, but I think to-morrow may be his last; he is now a wonder to all
his family—so changed. They see it with overwhelming gratitude. He appears to have no doubt
of acceptance with God. This trophy of divine
grace, once a tiger in temper, is now as a lamb, so
patient, so thankful, and is often heard to ejaculate, 'Blessed Lord, blessed Lord!' · I was once
obliged to discharge him because his blasphemies
were not to be endured. I am with him every day,
always invited by him to engage in prayer, and
then he holds my hand in his own, and with a convulsive squeeze endeavors thus to express the grateful feelings of his heart. God be praised. Marvellous mercy! What a change too in M——. One

of his fellow-workmen, who works close beside him
in an apartment where there are thirty dissipated
men, among whom M—— was the worst, informed
me that he stands his ground before them all, man-
ifesting the power of changing grace; that they all
wonder, but do not follow him. M——, with a heavy
sigh, told me that he used to pay a man to sing profane songs. The kingdom of God is full of wonders.

"Nov. 14. When a single string of the body
is out of tune we begin to utter discordant notes.
How much worse is it when the soul becomes dis-
ordered, when carelessness or indifference obscures
our view of that celestial light which is intended to
warm our affections into a glow of heavenly ardor,
blazing, burning with love to God. Nothing but a
close union with Christ can possibly keep this light
from becoming dim; therefore how needful for
every believer to strive for a closer walk with God.
I feel it, dear Newman, more and more every hour,
and I pray to be ever on my guard that Satan may
not get an advantage of me in my old age, and thus
bring my silvered hairs with shame and sorrow to
the grave. It is one of the greatest absurdities in
the world for a professor to think himself safe because he is old. Oh no, Satan will worry the saints
throughout their whole pilgrimage, even to the very
gates of heaven; but blessed be God, he cannot get
in after them. Why, the cunning old chap is always at me exhibiting a black catalogue of sins,
black as hell itself, which would obliterate even a
glimpse of hope, were it not for that reviving and
encouraging declaration, "The blood of Christ

cleanseth from all sin;" and when I say, "Satan,
look at that," he assumes a horrible grin, expands
his wings, and away he goes to frighten some poor
wretch who has never been at the foot of the cross
and taken shelter under the Rock of ages. What
should I have done had it not been for the blood of
Christ? We want something more than a mere
change of life—we want an indwelling Spirit, to be
full of love of the most exquisite degree, ever panting after God, every thing within us new; then it
is that we shall not only possess hope, but implicit
confidence in Christ, and peace and joy. We have
procured Bunyan's 'Jerusalem Sinner,' and also
Dr. Robinson's 'Biblical Researches in Palestine,'
3 vols., which, with Horne's 'Critical Study of
the Scriptures,' will quite occupy our little time.
Horne's work was exceedingly instructive to me a
few years ago while I was daily rioting in 'Scott's
Commentary.' Had I not received so much benefit to my own soul by the study of 'Scott's Commentary,' 'The Sinner's Friend' would never, in
all probability, have made its appearance; but the
comfort which I myself had enjoyed created a sigh
that others might also enjoy the same blessings, but
which they would not be likely to do from want of
time or the means of purchasing such expensive
books, and this led me to a feeling of pity that the
truths of the gospel could not be reduced into a nut-
shell, that people might see them in a moment without the labor of study.

"I shut my Bible, and on my knees entreated
the Lord that if it were his pleasure that I should

compile or write something to direct sinners to seek salvation, he would be pleased to instruct me what to say and what to write. My mind was directed to produce 'The Sinner's Friend,' which has been made a blessing in every quarter of the world, thus proving that from apparently very small causes great effects arise.

"On looking into the pages of Bunyan's 'Jerusalem Sinner,' the thought occurred to me that in the class of sinners, Bunyan, Newton, and your poor father, might be named together, only in that class your poor father taking the lead; but in the class of saints your father must be at an immense distance behind either of them, and yet not separated from the Saviour. Oh no, for I am sure, and all the arguments in the world could not convince me to the contrary, that Jesus ever lives in my heart a most welcome guest, dearly loved, my soul's unceasing joy. Yes, he is my never ceasing joy, although I never cease to mourn for sin, sins forgiven. This expression may appear very paradoxical to those who do not understand the subject; but I mourn because of my past ingratitude, that in the midst of an ocean of mercy I rebelled against the hand whence all my blessings came; but this does not in the least interrupt my confidence in pardon purchased by a Saviour's blood. What infinite mercy, dear Newman, that you as a minister for Christ are placed in a position to preach this blessed doctrine, forgiveness of sins that are past to a lost and ruined world, and that not even the most abandoned shall be rejected—coming to Christ.

May almighty grace bless and preserve you in
every step you take, that you may be kept humble
and watchful, especially against the temptation of
popularity. Take care; be watchful. Dr. Gordon's conversion I pray for."

MARCH 20, 1847. This day the Tract Society
published a new edition of "The Sinner's Friend"
in Italian, and I received the first copy. I took it
into my hand, and on my knees entreated the Lord
to accept and accompany it with his blessing for
Christ's sake.

DEATH OF COL. H——. Edinburgh. This dear
redeemed sinner passed from earth to heaven March
6. He had maintained the Christian conflict nine
years, giving a bright evidence to all around of the
great change which had been effected in his soul:
once a profane swearer, turned to a man of fervent
prayer—ever praising God. He told the Rev. J.
B—— that "The Sinner's Friend" had been the
saving of his soul, by directing him to Christ the
sinner's true Friend.

JUNE 24. This evening we had a most delightful
prayer-meeting in our house of about forty. We
esteemed it a great mercy to be allowed and disposed to open a place in our house for prayer. Oh
what especial mercy to hear M—— and S—— pour
out their hearts in praise and prayer, two men who,
five years ago, were drunkards and most profane
blasphemers. But these dear men were not so depraved as John Vine Hall, yet the Lord has made
him a praying man for the last thirty years.

My dear son Newman visited Dr. Malan of Geneva, at his own residence, on the 16th of August. He took a letter and a copy of "The Sinner's Friend" from me. He says, "On entering the enclosure, we saw through an open window a comfortable party at tea, one an old man with grey hairs in curly luxuriance flowing over his shoulders. On our entering the door, he came forward, and without asking my business, introduction, or any thing else, drew us both to the table and made us sit down. I said to him, 'But you do n't know who I am;' to which the doctor replied, 'Oh, but I know if you did not love Jesus, you would not take the trouble to come and see me.'"

SEPT. 7. This day I most unexpectedly received a copy of "The Sinner's Friend" in the Dutch language. On my knees I presented the copy before the Lord. I was quite overwhelmed by such an unexpected favor, as I had not known of "The Sinner's Friend" having been translated into the Dutch language.

OCT. 21. This morning I received from St. Petersburg copies of two editions of "The Sinner's Friend," in two different languages spoken in the Russian empire. I was quite overwhelmed with gratitude that it has pleased God in infinite mercy to clear the way for the circulation of "The Sinner's Friend" in Russia. I immediately on my knees presented copies to the Lord, earnestly praying that his blessing may accompany every copy circulated in Russia.

"DECEMBER, 1847. Dear Arthur, your poor father has experienced the bitterness of sin, though through the mercy of God he has found the antidote, the precious blood of Christ. Read that beautiful chapter, second of Ephesians, 'You hath he quickened who were dead, dead in sin.' Dead—not mere natural death; then there would be no resistance to the divine will; but it is spiritual death. Think of the power, but think much more of the love of God to obdurate sinners. Dead in sins, without Christ! Perhaps it may have been so even with us, dear Arthur. Without Christ! Misery complete. No hope, nothing but fearful apprehension of all evil for ever. But now through Christ made nigh, nigh to God. But do we think what the blood of Christ implies? What suffering to bring us nigh! Do we lay these things to heart, dear Arthur? The eye runs over the words, 'The blood of Christ,' but is the heart impressed? Oh the cost of that precious blood! The efficacy also of that blood: peace to those who were at enmity with God; peace also from the great anxieties of life—anxieties in every station, even among the rich, for they often have far more anxieties than the poorest of the poor. Access to the Father; what an honor! 'Fellow-citizens with the saints, and of the household of God.' Household of God! His family, his children! What felicity, what security against harm; safe from every foe. Household of God! 'Habitation of God!' God resides in the human heart, in those hearts once in rebellion against him? Matchless grace! How careful then we ought to be not to allow any other occupant to engross the heart created anew and quickened for the habitation of

God in the person of his beloved Son. All our salvation depends on Christ; all blessings in, by, and through Christ; all our blessings in him. To him we owe all our deliverance in times of danger. Your deliverance from blindness or death when you fell on the steps in the tower at Tintern Abbey. I fear I may be tiresome to you, dear Arthur, but my mind was so deeply impressed with the beauty and the vital importance of the second chapter of Ephesians, that I could not refrain from writing you a few of my thoughts thereon. May the grace of God ever be with you, to keep you from all evil either in thought, word, or deed, that you may never have to grieve as your father does over the sins of early days."

MARCH 14, 1848. I enter my seventy-fifth year in perfect bodily health, my soul panting for the living God. I rely solely on the atonement of Christ for acceptance with God, and for the pardon of all my dreadful sins. Blessed be the Lord, he hath given me plenty of this world's goods, more than enough, to which he has bountifully added a bank-note of eternal life. "None shall pluck you out of my hands." Oh marvellous mercy!

MAY 9. "Come to Jesus." This little work was published this day, the production of my dear son Newman. I took several in my hand, and on my knees held them up before the Lord, entreating his blessing to accompany them in the same successful manner as "The Sinner's Friend." Oh what mercy that father and son are each engaged in calling sinners to the Saviour.

MAY 26. This day I had the blessing of giving the fifty-thousandth gratuitous copy of "The Sinner's Friend" to a poor shoemaker. What infinite mercy to have been thus spared in life, and to have had the power, the means, and the will to disperse these messengers of mercy gratuitously, in addition to many thousands for which I obtained the money from pious Christians by begging the same for the sake of my dear Redeemer.

Nov. 2. Dr. Gordon, Hull. A letter from Newman, with intelligence of the increasing illness of this excellent man, this kind and generous friend, suffering excruciating inward pain, which he tries to conceal from his friends, but all in vain. He is reduced to a skeleton, yet patient in the extreme.

Nov. 14. Kent Auxiliary Bible Society. Annual Meeting. Court Hall, Maidstone. While presiding at this meeting, I put up a silent prayer to the Lord to accept my thanks for the great honor bestowed upon me, entreating him to keep me humble, that I might not be lifted up with pride. Oh the blessed change, that I who once in the very same room, in the days of my youth, had sported in the giddy dance, the most conceited coxcomb upon earth, and had mingled also in convivial drinking parties under the very same roof—that I should be now presiding at a Bible meeting, praising God. Oh it was a great change indeed.

DEC. 7. "The Wonderful Escape," my speech at Exeter Hall, May, 1836. This day received a letter from Mr. Hallock of the New York Tract Society, stating that they had printed 322,267 copies of that

speech. Who would ever have ventured to conjec-
ture it?

Jan. 22, 1849. Wrote dear Dr. Gordon a long
note of gratitude and praise for the mercy of the
Lord towards him, and encouraged him to trust
implicitly for the continuance of grace until the
end.

Sent two copies of "The Sinner's Friend" to the
Queen and the Prince. Reply from the Secretary
of the Privy Purse:

"Buckingham Palace, Jan. 16, 1849.

"Sir—I am directed to express to you the Queen's and the
Prince's thanks for the copies of your tract, which her Majesty and
his Royal Highness have most graciously received. You must allow
me, sir, to bear my humble testimony to the practical usefulness
of your little work, several cases of which have come under my own
personal observation. There is no tract which I have more pleasure in distributing than that whose title and text refer to 'The
Sinner's Friend.' I have the honor to be, sir, your obedient servant,' etc.

Jan. 30. Dr. Gordon still lingers on earth, rejoicing with ecstacy in redeeming love. His new birth
has unlocked his heart and loosened his tongue, so
that he is now full of rapture in speaking boldly of
Christ. He preaches the gospel affectionately to
every one who visits him, and openly tells what
great things the Lord hath done for him. He is
indeed "a wonder unto many," but especially to
those about his bed, who have long been the followers of our gracious Lord and Saviour. He is sinking gradually to the tomb, awaiting the approach of
death without a particle of fear, but rather rejoicing
in the prospect before him. He is lovely in his
meekness and temper, confessing himself a sinner

with implicit confidence in the righteousness of Christ alone for the salvation of his soul. His sayings are of the most exquisite kind—so genuine, so truly the teaching of the Holy Spirit as to preclude every doubt of his acceptance with God.

FEB. 3. Journey to Hull. We were very soon at the bedside of the dying saint. But what a meeting! No language can possibly describe it. The joy of Dr. Gordon surpassed all imagination. His look of love spoke unutterable things while he told us the great things Christ had done for him. We remained with him till near midnight. His testimony of what Christ had done for his soul was of the most thrilling description. The beautiful hymn, "There is a happy land," was sung in his chamber by his wish, and I was requested to offer prayer. My heart was full. It was the gate of heaven.

SABBATH, FEB. 4. Dr. Gordon much worse this morning. We came to Hull just in time. Newman's text, "Lord, now lettest thou thy servant depart in peace, according to thy word, for mine eyes have seen thy salvation." Had some delightful conversation with dear Dr. Gordon. He wished me continually to speak of Christ, as he was never tired of hearing. He kept his hand in mine with warm pressure of affection. It was worth a thousand journeys of two hundred miles to see and hear him, so splendid a monument of redeeming love. Told him how great pleasure I received from speaking to him of Christ, because he now understood me—that he now knew experimentally the love of God. Dr.

Gordon is the most interesting evidence of the power and love of God I ever beheld. In the afternoon the Lord's supper was administered in his room; the hymn, "There is a land of pure delight," was sung. Oh what a dying scene! May my latter end be like his.

May 2. Pleasing incident. "Cast thy bread upon the waters, and thou shalt find it again after many days." This day Mrs. A—— addressed me as follows: "About six years ago, sir, you were travelling with me in an omnibus, when you gave the passengers copies of 'The Sinner's Friend.' On reading the words, 'Sinner, this little book is for you,' I felt offended, because I then thought myself to be a Christian; but on reading the little book I discovered my mistake, which led me to seek the kingdom of God in right earnest, and ultimately to unite myself with the church of Christ." On my knees I returned thanks to the Lord for this new instance of his mercy. What encouragement to sow the seed of the kingdom of heaven on every opportunity.

July 6. Scott's Commentary on the Bible. Began the New Testament again with an increased appetite for this blessed book, which I had previously read six times throughout, making large extracts from the same. I had previously occupied seventeen years in the study of Scott's Commentary on the Old and New Testament with unspeakable delight and satisfaction. It has been my great happiness to have now been in the daily study of the word of God thirty-four years, never ceasing to feel delight therein, with earnest prayer for the teaching of the Holy Spirit. I began in right earnest in 1815.

OCT. 10. Your dear mother's birthday. What mercy to have her continued to us so many years, yet so soon gone. But there is a state where *time* will be unknown, and we shall enjoy felicity *for ever*. I have been in an agony of joy this morning—feelings which God alone can understand—the results of his own splendid mercy. This morning brought me a supply of contributions to the full extent of my prayers for answering a call to procure Malagasy translations of "The Sinner's Friend" and "Come to Jesus." I knelt before the Lord almost suffocated with gratitude; being alone, I wept aloud for joy that the Lord has never forsaken me when my heart has been directed to his glory. I pray daily that "Come to Jesus" and "The Sinner's Friend" may run together calling sinners to Christ. What mercy, what cause for humility that father and son should be allowed to be God's instruments in directing sinners to the Saviour! The nearer I approach the end of my course, the more deeply I feel my own dreadful sinfulness; and I should derive very little comfort from a change of heart, were it not that "the blood of Jesus Christ cleanseth from all sin." Let him that thinketh he standeth, take heed. Take heed.

1849. Honor thy father and thy mother. No forms, notions, subscriptions to charities, building chapels, or any thing else which looks like faith, zeal, or piety, can prove that man to be a true

Christian who neglects to honor his father and mother, or to supply their wants according to his ability. Matt. 15 : 1-9. The blessing of the Lord always attends the observance of this duty. I know it by experience. The Lord mercifully gave me the opportunity, ability, and practice to my dear mother, which he has blessed a thousand-fold.

FEB. 14, 1850. .Scott's Commentary on the Bible. Blessed be God, I have now purchased eight copies of this invaluable work for my dear children, a copy for each. Oh may this book be made as great a blessing to my beloved children as it has been to their father, who has with intense earnestness and prayer read the whole of the Old Testament and notes four times, and the New Testament six times, making many extracts.

MARCH 14. Blessed be God, my first waking thoughts early this morning went up to him with grateful praises that he had brought me to the commencement of my seventy-seventh year in perfect health, surrounded with every temporal comfort. But I grieve in my soul on account of my dreadful sins. Yet, had they been a million times worse, they are not beyond the cleansing sacrifice of my precious Redeemer. Thirty-eight years ago on this day, March 14, 1812, the Lord sent his arrow of conviction into my heart to bring me to that precious blood which cleanseth from all sin, even my sins. Oh what a monument of mercy am I!

MARCH 16. To his daughter Eleanor. "As I suppose you have received Scott's Bible, I pray that

our gracious God may make the reading of this
splendid Commentary as great a blessing to your
soul as it has been to the soul of your now poor old
father. It has been an especial mercy that I have
been enabled to present a copy of this work to
every one of my eight children, to whom I trust a
large portion of the grace of the Holy Spirit will be
poured out, that they may be indeed the children of
the Most High. What pleasure does it impart to
us that your dear husband preaches the gospel in
all its fulness, purity, and truth. The Lord bless
him in all his ways. What a blessing to have Jesus
always in the heart. Under every trial or perplex-
ity we thus have a Rock to rest upon that nothing
can possibly remove. He is never unwilling to do
his people good ultimately, though the blessing
sometimes seems retarded almost beyond our
strength, to try our faith whether we can really trust
him or not under every circumstance. Ah, dear
child, this does indeed require great strength of
faith, only to be had at the Fountain; but that
Fountain is always open and always free for every
thirsty seeking soul. May you find it, dear Nora,
and rejoice in it also. May Christ, our dear, dear
Lord, be ever the welcome occupant of your dear
affectionate heart. Amen."

SEPT. 1. Visited Mrs. S—— at the almshouse.
Found her ill in bed. Spoke to her of Christ, the
only way to heaven. She wept exceedingly, and
for some time could not speak distinctly, sobbing,
"What shall I do?" Directed her to look to the
Lord Jesus Christ as the eternal Son of God, whose

blood cleanseth from all sin, and that none who come to God by him shall be rejected. She had known me from the time I was twelve years of age, and had witnessed the follies of my youth. We had often danced together at balls and private parties, at which time it was not at all probable that I should ever come to speak to her about salvation. She had been for many years a professed Unitarian, therefore it was trying work to speak to her of Christ as the only way to God. Told her of what God had done for my own soul, and that he had sent me to tell her the way of acceptance by his only begotten Son—no other way. Oh may the Lord make my visit useful to her soul.

SEPT. 22. This day commences the thirty-fifth year of my great emancipation from wine and spirituous liquor, and also my separation from the world and worldly company. Christ has been my constant companion and my greatest joy. It has been my supreme delight and the very ecstasy of my soul to speak of him and his mercy to poor sinners. Hundreds of delicious opportunities have I been permitted to enjoy of this kind during the last thirty-five years, to testify by voice and life that I am not ashamed of the gospel of Christ, for I know by happy experience that it is the power of God unto salvation—salvation in the hour of temptation. Oh what horrid temptations have been spread in my path, frequently, suddenly, into some of which I might have fallen had it not been for the grace of God, and all my prospects and usefulness would have for ever been destroyed. A voice, seemingly from heaven, said to me one day in a moment of great temptation, "Flee." I ran away in a moment and escaped the net. Psa. 25:15.

DEC. 11. This morning, between six and seven o'clock, I repeated fifteen psalms, twenty hymns, and the fifty-fifth and fifty-eighth chapters of Isaiah, and the second chapter of Ephesians and part of chapter six, from verse 10 to 20, praising God for a retentive memory and for the pleasure of retaining heavenly things. Oh it is indeed good to praise the Lord sleeping and waking.

MARCH 8, 1852. This afternoon my beloved wife and self took possession of our sweet cottage at Penenden Heath. We dedicated ourselves and the house in prayer to our gracious God, with thankfulness and praise for so sweet a retirement in our old age.

MARCH 16. Dear Arthur and Warren. These dear, affectionate, assiduous sons have been most persevering in getting all the accounts posted up to the last hour of my retirement from business. They have been the great comfort of my life, attending to business with so much cheerfulness and untiring perseverance.

MAY 6. A delightful day at the summer-house on Boxley Hill, from eleven in the morning till seven in the evening. A large family party, including dear Newman and C——, dined and had tea at the summer-house. Nightingales singing sweetly, and we sang several hymns praising God for his great mercies.

OCT. 6. This morning in my walk into Maid-

stone, I repeated the following Psalms: 23, 25, 27,
30, 34, 51, 86, 91, 103, 116, 121, 130, 139, 143, 145.
Oct. 7. This morning, in my walk into Maidstone,
I repeated twenty-one hymns, which occupied me
till I reached the bottom of Brewer-street. These
exercises keep the soul active. I bless the Lord for
the pleasure thus afforded.

CHAPTER XI.

SERENE AGE.

1853 TO 1860—AGE 79-86.

JANUARY 1, 1853. Through the infinite mercy of God, my beloved wife and self are brought in comfort to the commencement of another year. We are now, as it were, alone; our dear children all separated from us: Edward in Maidstone, M—— E—— at Tovil, Newman at Hull, E—— at Eyam, Arthur and William at Camden Town, S—— in China, and Vine at Calcutta. But we are not alone, for the Lord is ever with us, the life of our souls. The lines also are fallen to us in very pleasant places, and we have a goodly heritage. Through the kind providence of God we are favored in our old age with more than sufficient for all our wants, and plenty for the poor and for the service of God, and above all, our love for each other is warmer than ever. Praised be the Lord.

MARCH 14. This day, by the mercy of God, I commence my eightieth year, in full bodily health and vigor of mind, surrounded by every comfort. Long before the dawning of the day my heart was lifted up to God with praise. In my dream I had been praising God with most rapturous feelings. I was quite overwhelmed with ecstasy at his mercy towards me. My tenderly beloved wife was also spared to me in increasing love, if possible, and we praised God that he had preserved us together in happy union upwards of forty-six years, our hearts mutually united to the Lord Jesus Christ, whom we dearly love as our only hope and trust, with whom we desire ever to live and reign. He is indeed to us "the Chief among ten thousand, and the altogether lovely."

APRIL 18. I was honored this morning by the kindness of the pious Archbishop of Canterbury, at his palace at Lambeth. His lordship met me in the kindest manner, putting forth his hand with expressions of real pleasure on seeing me. I opened my whole heart to him, and spoke warmly on the love of Christ. In speaking of my dear son's little work, "Come to Jesus," he said it contained evangelical truths without going round about; and when I spoke of my little work, "The Sinner's Friend," he emphatically said, "Not a little book. I call it a great book, for it has done great good in the world."

MAY 20. A day ever to be remembered; for this day 1804, forty-nine years ago, was the first time of my speaking to my dear Mary, of whose name and residence I was perfectly ignorant. I had only watched her coming and going to Angel-street chapel, Worcester, with an elderly lady, and I myself was engaged in the same manner, with my dear mother leaning on my arm, and the similarity of our situation awakened my sympathies, so that I fell in love with this young stranger, determined to find her out, and endeavor to win her affections. She had not then reached her seventeenth year. A gentleman, who saw me apparently in conversation

with her, asked me the next day how long I had
been acquainted with Miss Teverill, the cleverest
girl in all Worcester. Thus I learnt her name and
address. The next day I was introduced to the family, and thus commenced a courtship which has
proved the greatest bliss of my life. We have loved
each other most ardently forty-nine years, and I
think, I am sure, our love to each other is now more
warm than when we were first united on Tuesday,
August 26, 1806.

JULY 27. I do trust that my heart pants after
God, although deeply laden with sin. I am surrounded with mercy upon mercy, a paradise to dwell
in, all the free gift of God. My dear, dear wife is
to me next to heaven itself. I bless the Lord with
every breath for the gift of such a wife, who has
been the dear object of my affection more than forty-
nine years, and I love her now better than ever.
She is the joy of my life. We shall soon, soon be
separated on earth, only to be reunited in eternal
glory with him whom we both so dearly love. Praised be his dear name. He has long been the welcome occupant of each of our hearts. May he be
the same to each of our dear children and their children, that we may all meet together to praise God
for ever and ever.

OCT. 5. My heart increasingly mourning on
account of past sins. I awake praying the Lord
for pardon. I walk in my garden praying earnestly
to the Lord. I take off my hat, and looking earnestly up to heaven, I pray the Lord Jesus to look upon
the purchase of his precious blood, and come and

take full possession of my heart, that heart so greatly changed by sovereign grace and almighty love.
My heart is ever yearning after the Lord Jesus.

My dear son S—— has had "Come to Jesus"
translated into Chinese, and printed at Ningpo, at
his own expense.

JANUARY 20, 1854. A feeling of deep heartfelt
sorrow for sin came upon me this day. Sins of
youth, sins of age all crowd upon me and cause my
soul to grieve before God. I cry for mercy, mercy
treasured up in Christ Jesus. O what should I do
without Christ? I have no other refuge. He is my
all in all. I do love him dearly. It is the greatest
delight of my life to tell of his wondrous mercy to
my own soul, and to declare boldly what he will do
for all who come to God by him. It is a comfort
that "a broken and a contrite heart, O God, thou
wilt not despise."

JAN. 22. Visited the schools and classes in Albion
chapel. Addressed a class of young men, about thirty. Then addressed a class of females, about thirty.
Then addressed another class of church-members,
and concluded by addressing about thirty candidates
for church-fellowship.

FEB. 22. This day a copy of "The Sinner's
Friend," in modern Greek, was sent me from Athens.
My heart beat high and warm while on my knees I
presented the copy to the Lord, praying his blessing to accompany "The Sinner's Friend" in Greece.

MARCH 14. This morning, by the mercy of God,
I commenced my eighty-first year in sound bodily
.health, mental vigor, my soul devoted to God. I

have no words wherewith to praise the Lord according to my feelings of his wondrous goodness in providence and grace: in providence, a goodly heritage, lines in pleasant places; in grace, a penitent heart, deep sorrow for sin, trusting alone in the blood and righteousness of Christ for salvation, the Lord Jesus my only refuge as the Saviour of the lost.

MARCH 28. To his son Newman. "How shall I begin to praise the Lord for his great mercy in the bestowment of a son to sound forth salvation in the very pulpit where Rowland Hill called sinners to repentance? No words can express what I feel for the goodness of God to us for so great a blessing. After pouring forth our heartfelt thanks, our prayer was for humility, and to be kept where only we are safe, at the foot of the cross. But we have to pray also for our dear son, that *he* may not be lifted up above measure, but be kept in a constant holy spiritual frame, looking momentarily to the Lord, to enable him to discharge his responsible duties to the glory of God. It might appear out of place that a mere *disciple* should venture to admonish a *minister;* but when that disciple is the minister's *father*, *he* may be allowed to remind his dear son that angels are looking upon him, that the Christian world is looking upon him, desirous that he should not only perform the duties of his station, but that his lamp should be always burning with a clear, unmistakable light, evidencing that the grace of the Lord Jesus occupies his heart to the very full. My dear Newman will pardon his aged father, not dictating,.

but most affectionately admonishing a greater watch-fulness than ever, seeing that the honor of Christ himself is closely united with the walk and conversation of his disciples in the midst of a glowing profession and an ensnaring world. I will only add, may the Lord bless you, dear Newman, in all your ways, for Christ's sake. Amen."

JUNE 19. At a meeting of deacons I resigned my deaconship, after holding it twenty-four years. What infinite mercy that I, once an unbeliever, should ever have been unanimously elected by the church to become an officer in the service of God. Praised be the Lord that he has kept me all these years in the hollow of his hand, and not allowed me to bring any disrepute upon the name of Christ. Oh that my heart may ever be the abode of my blessed Lord.

JULY 2. Sabbath-day at Surrey chapel. Dear Newman commenced his pastorate this day. At the door we were welcomed by our dear Edward, and were soon joined by our dear Arthur. In the evening we all sat in the same pew, exactly opposite the pulpit, praising God. Newman's morning text, "Who is sufficient," etc., and, "Brethren, pray for us." Evening, "Other foundation can no man lay than that is laid, which is Christ Jesus." A prayer-meeting was held in the vestry the previous evening by the elders and trustees. Newman and self present.

JULY 17. To his son. "I am not insensible to the mercy of God in your transition to the pulpit of the sainted Rowland Hill. It is not only a great change but a great responsibility, pregnant with events of

the most important kind. Woe to the ambassador,
if he be not faithful to the charge! He may well
exclaim, 'Who is sufficient for these things?' Yet,
his feet firmly on the Rock of ages, he may boldly
express his confidence that 'other foundation can
no man lay than that is laid.' The prayers of hundreds, nay, thousands, have been offered for you, but
by none more earnestly and affectionately than by
your father and mother. We are now agitated with
much anxiety on account of our own projected re-
moval to London, that we may all as a family be
united in the service of our gracious God. The
time will very soon arrive when we shall be again
separate, only for a short time, to be reunited in a
kingdom of never-ending holiness and bliss. If there
is one thing in the world which I long and pray for
more than any other, it is a holy, contrite, believing
heart, full, overfull of love to my gracious Lord and
Saviour, who has purchased me with his precious
blood. To him be endless praises. Amen."

SABBATH, SEPT. 3. To-day my beloved wife and
self renewed our vows to our Lord at Week-street
chapel, probably the last time. Our dear pastor in
a most feeling manner spoke of our expected departure. After the celebration of the Lord's supper,
I addressed the communicants, commending them
to that gracious God from whom we had experienced such great mercies during nearly forty years'
membership at Week-street, and during which time
I had been twenty-four years a deacon.

SEPT. 12. This morning we bade farewell to
Maidstone, and were heartily welcomed by our

dear sons Arthur and Warren at Camden Town, near London.

SEPT. 20. This evening my dear sons Newman and Arthur were engaged in open-air preaching near the Obelisk, Blackfriars road, to about four hundred persons, all attentive and respectful. ' Oh what mercy that dear Arthur should have thus been engaged with his brother in speaking for the Saviour. Praises ten thousand times to our gracious God.

SEPT. 22. This evening my beloved wife and self took possession of our new dwelling, Heath Cottage, Kentish Town. We on our knees consecrated our dwelling and ourselves anew to our gracious God, with thankfulness and praise. N——, C——, A——, and W——, came to supper, and we closed the evening with prayer and chanting the twenty-third Psalm. What infinite mercy that all my children are seeking the Lord.

OCT. 27. Saw a poor old negro, and on conversing with him found that he was a servant of the Lord Jesus. He had been a slave from Africa, but his master had given him his freedom. My heart praised the Lord for this great treat in meeting a poor black follower of Jesus. When, with a few pence, I put a copy of "Come to Jesus" into his hand, he looked at the title and pathetically exclaimed, "Jesus! ah, he has been with me many years. Yes, he is my strength and my support." On asking him how he came to know all this, he said his master had taught him, and he hoped he was in heaven, for he was a good master. I hope to see this **black Christian** again.

DEC. 21. At the request of my son Newman, I addressed nearly one hundred persons in the school-room of Surrey chapel, on the love of Christ, his willingness to take possession of every heart. I was exceedingly warm in exhortation and encouragement to all to come to Jesus. The people were excessively kind, very many of them stretching forth their hands to take hold of mine, expressing their thanks.

CHRISTMAS DAY. I drove dear Mary to Surrey chapel, a large congregation. Family party to dinner. No wine. Sang and praised God.

DEC. 27. Saw the poor negro sweeping the footpath near the model prison. Gave him a shilling for Jesus' sake. The poor man looked on the money with a smile and said, "Ah, my Massa sent me dis." Special prayer-meeting this evening, Kentish Town Congregational church, for the influence of the Holy Spirit. Mr. Fleming very faithful in addressing the congregation, as to what progress they had made in the ways of God during the last fifty-two weeks. If I inquire of myself, how have I been making progress during the last year, I think I can answer sincerely, I love the Lord more than ever; I repent of sin more than ever; I hate sin more than ever; I pant after holiness more than ever; I trust entirely in the sacrifice of Christ more than ever for the salvation of my soul; I feel gratitude to God for his mercies to myself, my dear wife, and my children more than ever; I love my dear wife more than ever; I feel an earnestness, a warmth in prayer more than ever; I exercise and enjoy mental and ejaculatory prayer more than ever; the Lord Jesus is **ever** in my heart, my exceeding joy and my supreme delight, more than ever. Praised be his dear name. I believe that what I have here written is the very. breath of my soul, the truth.

Dec. 31. Watch-night. I drove my dear Mary and Eleanor to Surrey chapel this morning, and in the evening we went again to be present at the watch-night service. The chapel literally crammed. Many persons could not obtain admission. About 2,500 present.

January 16, 1855. The Rev. W. C. Milne sent me the first copy of "The Sinner's Friend," translated by him into Chinese. On my knees I presented this copy to the Lord, with praise that he had spared my life to behold this little work printed in Chinese. What mercy that I should have been spared to witness the publication of two hundred and ninety editions of the tract, in twenty-three languages, comprised in 1,268,000 copies. All praise to the Lord, for it is entirely his own work in putting it into my heart to write this apparently mere trifle, which the Lord has so greatly accompanied with his blessing to poor sinners.

May 2. I attended the meeting of the Bible Society at Exeter Hall. 3. Attended meeting of the London City Mission. Dear Newman spoke. 4. Tract Society meeting, Exeter Hall. I was prevented attending this meeting by a cold—much disappointed. Mr. Gill, from Rarotonga, spoke warmly of " The Sinner's Friend," as the fourth publication in the native language. 9. London missionary sermon at Surrey chapel. Dr. Raffles preached one

hour and a half. W—— and self held collecting
boxes at the doors. 10. Attended the anniversary
of the London Missionary Society. Went at eight
o'clock. The chair was taken by Lord Shaftesbury
at ten o'clock. Concluded at three.

JUNE 28. I visited a man named C—— near
Surrey chapel, confined to his bed several years
Mr. C—— had known me in Maidstone, from 1806
to 1803, having been one of my early companions
He had heard of my conversion forty years ago, and
was so rejoiced at it that he told it to Mr. K——
one of my old companions, who on hearing it said
he should not wonder now at any thing. At his request I prayed with him. He knew me when I was
a poor blasphemer. Mrs. C—— also knew me at
that time. O what a change does she now see.
Now we knelt together at the footstool of divine
mercy. Praised be the Lord. What a glorious
manifestation of his saving power. Conducted the
inquirers' prayer-meeting at Surrey chapel. Spoke
very warmly from the words, "The Lord will abundantly pardon." I felt very warm indeed towards
these dear people, young and old, about forty of
whom came up to shake me kindly by the hand.
The Lord be praised for any good which may arise.
Oh for a humble heart.

JULY 1. Arthur preached in the open air this
evening in a field. Newman preached in the open
air at the Obelisk, after evening service at Surrey
chapel. Oh what infinite mercy that my two dear
sons are thus engaged in calling sinners to seek the
Lord.

Aug. 26. Wedding day. Forty-nine years ago my beloved Mary and self were united in matrimony. I think we love each other better than ever, praising the Lord for his great mercy in having brought us together, and preserved us in health and comfort to the present time. I drove my dear Mary and Newman to Surrey chapel this morning.

Sept. 10. Wonder, love, and praise. What great things hath the Lord done for me, once an infidel, blasphemer, and every thing evil, to have the heart so completely changed to love the Lord Jesus Christ with sincerity of soul, and to have been raised up to become twenty-two years a deacon in the church of Christ at Maidstone, and now invited to become one of the elders in the church of Christ in Surrey chapel, and my dear son Newman the pastor of the said church. Praised be the Lord. Oh for a humble heart and a watchful spirit, that I may never forget the hole of the pit whence I have been digged. May I set the Lord always before me.

Oct. 16. From Rev. Richard Knill. "DEAR OLD SAINT—I bless God that you were ever born, and that you were born again, and that you have written for the glory of God and for the good of souls. And now dear Newman and Arthur are following their father's steps. Please give my love to dear Mrs. Hall and your beloved children. While I was preparing to preach in the fields at Tintworth I ruptured a bloodvessel, and was nearly drowned in my own blood. God has been very gracious to me, so that I am able to preach once a week again, but I have lost my youthful buoyancy, and wish to stand

in a waiting posture every day to obey the summons
to depart and to be with Christ. I hope to see you
coming after me, if I go first; and what a meeting
we shall have! Shall I sing louder than you? I
should like to do so. Farewell till we meet in glory."

OCT. 16. This day T—— A—— and myself visited the archbishop at Addington. His grace met
me at the door of his study, and put forth his hand
with a hearty shake, expressing great pleasure at
seeing me again. On making some excuse for my
warmth of feeling, he said he was glad to see it, for
there was apt to be too much coldness. And on my
expressing thankfulness for his kindness, he said he
should not expect anybody to be unkind to the
author of "The Sinner's Friend." He said he thought
that much of its usefulness might be attributed
to its containing gospel truths without going round
about. I was all in a blaze in speaking of the Lord
Jesus, the love of God in each of our hearts. There
appeared no difference between us. Who would
ever have thought, fifty years ago, that poor J. V.
H., then engulfed in misery and sin, should become
a welcome visitor to the Archbishop of Canterbury,
to unite with him in praises to God? Also to have
been chosen an elder of Surrey chapel. To God
alone be all, all the glory.

OCT. 22. This evening Mr. Webb and myself
were publicly acknowledged and received as elders
of Surrey chapel. Newman announced this interesting setting apart in the most touching manner,
alluding to his own early introduction to acquaintance with holy things by his dear mother, who was

present, having directed his mind that way by reading "Bunyan's Pilgrim's Progress," and comment-
ing thereon. The school-room was literally crammed; a most solemn, holy occasion. Oh bless the
Lord, my soul, for this especial mercy in having delivered my soul from death, and raised me up to be
numbered with his people in prayer and praise. Is
any thing too hard for the Lord?

Dec. 16. I desire to bless the Lord that I am
brought to rest all my hopes of eternal bliss upon
Jesus Christ alone. I have been greatly tried by
looking to my past dreadful sins, of which I deeply
repent every moment, daily praying the fifty-first
Psalm.

Dec. 31. Present at the prayer-meeting and the
watch-night. J. V. H. engaged in prayer. At half-
past ten the watch-night service commenced; a
most glorious assemblage of upwards of 2,500 persons. The prayer-meeting was indeed a meeting of
solemn and heartfelt prayer, with warm thankfulness
to God for his mercy during the past year. Rev. E.
Cecil first gave a lecture on the past; Rev. W. Brock
on the present; dear Newman on the future. A
watch-night service was also held at Kentish Town.
Our dear Arthur presided. They had a glorious
meeting. Oh what infinite mercy, my dear children,
with father and mother, all engaged and delighting
in the service of the Lord. Praised be his holy name.
Amen and Amen.

February 9, 1856. Dear Newman and my dear
wife quite scold me for mourning so much on account of my past sins. Ah, they little think of the

nature and filth of the sins of my youth. I have indeed sunk in deep mire, and although I have been snatched as it were from the very centre of hell, and have been preserved nearly forty years, yet I cannot forget my vileness, nor cease to grieve from the heart with the deepest sorrow for sin. I mourn in agony and pain. Still I would endeavor to trust in that precious blood shed for all manner of sin.

FEB. 17. Teloogoo edition of "The Sinner's Friend" presented me this day from the Tract Society. Prayed the Lord to accept my thanks.

MARCH 4. B——, gardener, here at work, sober. Spoke encouragingly to him not to be out of heart, but make use of prayer for strength to resist his besetting sin, once my own, but God has delivered me. Why not deliver B——? Lord, have mercy upon him, and deliver him for Christ's sake.

JUNE 17. I feel my soul more quieted by reposing entirely upon the sacrifice of Christ. If I perish, I perish at the foot of the cross. O Lord increase my faith. I am looking to Christ every hour. He is all in all to me. If I did not believe his word I should sink into utter despair. Neither repentance nor amendment of life, nothing but the payment of my debt by the sacrifice of Christ, can possibly save me from eternal ruin. But, blessed be God, the blood of Christ was shed for the sins of the whole world, for every one who believes in him. Praised be the Lord for such magnificent mercy. This morning I called on the archbishop at Lambeth Palace. He welcomed me as a brother in Jesus, and was pleased to say that I had done much for

his cause, intimating by "The Sinner's Friend."
His grace presented me with a small Bible, on a
blank leaf of which he wrote, " J. B. Cantuar, to the
author of 'The Sinner's Friend.'" He said, " You
are very warm-hearted, Mr. Hall;" to which I replied, " Yes, my lord, it is because Jesus Christ ever
occupies my heart, and this it is which keeps me ever
in a glow of warmth when speaking of him."

JULY 19. Praised be the Lord, this day completes
thirty-eight years since porter, ale, or malt liquor
has ever passed my tongue. My heart full of gratitude to God, yet full of sorrow on account of past
sins. But I cast my whole soul upon the sacrifice
of Christ for the sins of the world.

JULY 21. Trip to Wales, Liverpool and the Isle
of Man. This morning dear Mary, Newman, and
self set off to the Welsh mountains. We flew by
express to Bangor. We found dear Arthur at Bangor, where he had obtained lodgings at a temperance
hotel. Dear Mary and self knelt before the Lord
with thanks for his protecting care. Mountains far
and near, leading the heart to him who made them
all. In the evening we drove to the tubular and
suspension bridges. Wonders of art beyond all
description. 22. By train to Carnarvon. where we
inspected the ancient castle. My dear Mary as-
cended to the top of the very highest tower. Gave
Welsh "Sinner's Friend" to the guide of the castle.
By car to Beddgelert. Heard a language that we
understood not. Shoes and stockings seemed to
have been dispensed with by boys, girls, and women.
Gave two Welsh "Sinner's Friend" to two female

19

cottagers. 23. Snowdon. This morning my **dear**
Mary and self on ponies, with Newman and **Arthur**,
reached the summit in two hours and a half. A
cloud on the top prevented a prospect, but the various views in our ascent were sublime. Near the
top is a narrow path three yards wide, called "the
Saddle," 3,000 feet high, with a precipice on each
side a thousand feet. Over this frightful place we
rode with perfect safety, but not without some little
thought as to the fatal result if the horses should
stumble. We found several travellers on the top,
where were three coffee-houses, and we were soon
supplied with broiled ham and good coffee. Gave
three "Sinner's Friend," Welsh, to three Welshmen.
I rode all the way from the top of Snowdon to
Beddgelert, where, as soon as we arrived, my dear
Mary and self knelt before the Lord with thankfulness. Below the summit of the mountain all was
fine and clear. Eight and a half hours occupied in
this excursion. I would not undertake it again upon
any representation, although the whole prospect is
of the most exciting description, a world of wonders.
Three men at the top sang some anthems most de-
lightfully. Newman and Arthur in vain attempted
to persuade me to approach the edge of a precipice
over a most frightful abyss, but my dear Mary had
more courage and she ventured nearer than I dared
to do. What mercy that no dizziness came upon
her. I had prayed the Lord to protect her. She
walked down the dreadful declivity of "the Saddle,"
Newman and Arthur close by her side. Arthur had
placed my mackintosh cape on the ground for his

dear mother to sit upon, but he forgot to take it up again, therefore it was lost, though it may prove a welcome prize to some poor traveller.

AUG. 26. Wedding day. Fifty years have now been completed since I was united to my beloved wife, still continued to me in good health by the abounding mercy of an ever gracious God. Blessings upon blessings have attended us all our days. We are both in the enjoyment of good health, surrounded by every comfort, affectionate children, and above all Jesus Christ in our hearts. God be praised for the unspeakable gift of his beloved Son.

SEPT. 22. On the 22d of September, 1816, forty years ago, I was enabled, by divine grace and mercy, to abandon entirely the use of wine of any kind and spirituous liquor, not a drop of either having passed the surface of my tongue during all those forty years. God be praised. And what is almost miraculous, not the slightest desire after them has ever haunted me; but on the contrary, the most positive disgust has occupied my mind at the very smell. Having been many years the slave of strong drink, I might have been tempted to return to it, but God in tender mercy changed the whole of my nature, and enabled me to triumph over my once besetting sin, in his strength and in that alone. Also he has caused the love of Christ to occupy my soul, making it my supreme delight to promote his glory. "I'm lost in wonder, love, and praise," when I consider what God has done for me in providence as well as grace. Beginning life without a shilling, He raised me up to be a Joseph in Egypt to my poor mother and my two brothers, all long since gone the way of all flesh. My poor mother, in writing me for pecuniary aid, addressed me, "My dear Joseph in Egypt, the corn is almost gone, and I look to you again to supply my need." It pleased God so to prosper me, that I was able to supply all her temporal wants. She died praying for her then prodigal son. The Lord gave me the disposition and opportunity to help many others, to the grateful rejoicing of my heart. In adition to a vast number of various tracts, I have enjoyed the privilege of distributing gratuitously upwards of 57,800 copies of "The Sinner's Friend." But it is all of the Lord. He put it into my heart to write "The Sinner's Friend," which he has followed with his blessing. "Oh that men would praise the Lord for his goodness."

Nov. 3. Death of Rev. Edmund Jenkins. This faithful servant of the Lord had been forty years the beloved pastor over the Independent church at Maidstone, esteemed by all who knew him. He had been to us a most faithful friend in every trial.

Nov. 8. I have loved Christ dearly many, many years, and all his people of every denomination, and I do love them still, and the Lord Jesus more and more, and this causes increasing pain that I have sinned so deeply against him. I mourn hourly on account of sin; still I dare hope for mercy through the sacrifice of Christ. This day attended the funeral of our late pastor. Newman gave an impressive address. A large number of ministers and many friends proceeded to the Wesleyan burying-ground amid heavy rain. Kindly greeted by several of our old acquaintances. The street was lined with spectators up to the grave.

FEB. 26. This evening my dear Mary and self, with Newman and C——, went to the House of Commons to hear the debate on China. Newman and self sat in the speaker's gallery; my dear Mary and C—— in the ladies' gallery. The debate was most animated. The house rose at twenty minutes past twelve. Mr. F. C—— was exceedingly courteous, found his way to C—— and Mary, and gave them ices and tea, and then brought us oranges. He afterwards conducted us into various parts of the magnificent building.

MARCH 14. The Lord has spared me to enter my eighty-fourth year in full health of body and mind, but a sinful heart. The Lord in my own person has verified the truth of the ninety-first psalm: "With long life will I satisfy him;" the Lord has also "delivered me and honored me" in various ways, by giving me the friendship and love of so many dear Christian friends. Dined at Newman's. Received congratulatory letters from several of my children.

JULY 23. Frightful mutiny of native troops in India. Forty Europeans, men, women, and children, murdered at Delhi, which city is in possession of the rebels, who amount to many thousands. The *Golden Fleece*, commanded by dear Vine, chartered to take troops. Aug. 3. Delhi still in possession of the rebels. Forty of the rebels blown away from

the mouths of guns. These troubles in India are
a retribution for our unjust attack on China.

Aug. 27. Took the chair at temperance meeting
at Surrey chapel. Rev. T. Cuyler, from New York,
gave a lecture. Rev. Hugh Allen proposed a vote
of thanks to Mr. Cuyler. Eighteen hundred persons present. I commenced the meeting by a short
address, as follows:

"Allow me, my friends, to introduce myself to
you as an old teetotaller, probably the oldest in this
assembly. When it pleased God, many years ago,
to call me by his grace, I felt it necessary to forego
the use of wine and strong drink, lest at an unguarded moment I might abuse the use of the same,
and bring dishonor upon the name of Christ. I
prayed God to give me strength to resist every
temptation to evil. The Lord mercifully answered
that prayer. This was more than forty years ago,
and from that time to the present hour, blessed be
God, not so much as a single drop of wine or spirituous liquor has ever passed the surface of my
tongue. I never drink any thing stronger than tea
or coffee, and although the enemies of temperance
may insinuate that such simple beverages will never
give strength, yet I stand here a witness to the contrary; for although a few years have passed since
my eightieth birthday, I am, through the mercy of
God, full of health and strength, the love of God
cheering my soul, and the Lord Jesus ever dwelling
in my heart a welcome guest, my only hope of glory.
I am so convinced by happy experience of the blessings of total abstinence, that I would not depart

from it in the smallest instance for all the wealth in the world. I would sooner die. I do not make these resolutions in my own strength, but in the strength of that merciful God who has delivered my soul from death, mine eyes from tears, and my feet from falling; therefore with humble gratitude I would say, Not unto me, O Lord, not unto me, but to thy name be all the praise. I think temperance, accompanied by the grace of God, is the greatest blessing in the world."

At the conclusion of the meeting, I entreated the people not to depend entirely on the pledge, but to get the love of Christ in their hearts, as the best security against the temptations to indulge in strong drink.

DEC. 9. Dear Newman's new volume of hymns, with a dedication to his dear mother. What mercy to have been spared to our dear children, to witness their respectful and tender affection on every occasion. Praised be the Lord.

"MOTHER, to thee, of right, this book belongs;
    For, seated on thy knee, an infant weak,
    With lisping tongue, I learnt from thee to speak
'In psalms and hymns and spiritual songs.'
    Oft didst thou stroke my head and kiss my cheek,
And weep for joy to hear thy child repeat
    How the good Shepherd came from heaven to seek
His wandering lambs, and how his hands and feet
    Were pierced with nails ; while he, the sufferer meek,
Prayed for his foes, then mounted to his throne.
With themes like these my years have still upgrown,
    Through thy persuasive teaching, tender care,
    Thine and a loving father's life of prayer.
The book I offer thee is thus thine own."

Dec. 21. Prayer-meeting at Surrey chapel. Was requested to offer the first prayer, previous to which I gave the congregation a solemn admonition. 22. Tea-meeting of members. Newman called on me to speak first. I felt all on fire to open my mouth to tell of the mercy of the Lord. Blessed be his name.

Christmas day. Family Christmas meeting, seventeen in all. After dinner sang, "Praise God." Arthur entertained us with microscope and magic-lantern. We had abundant cause to be thankful for this happy meeting.

Jan. 23, 1858. Walked from Camden Town to St. John's Wood, then walked in Regent's Park, and from thence walked all the way to Heath Cottage—a great feat. 24. This day, seventy-two years ago, I first entered the old house, Maidstone, as a little errand-boy.

Feb. 8. Prayer-meeting this evening at Surrey chapel. Offered the first prayer; not in a spiritual frame. After prayer-meeting went with Newman to Exeter Hall to hear Mr. Gough.

Feb. 22. Prayer-meeting. A temperance-meeting afterwards in Surrey chapel. I took the chair. About fifteen hundred persons present. Dear Arthur made a most impressive speech, detailing his own experience and the way in which he had been brought to sign the pledge; also the mercy of God in having rescued him from infidelity, and brought him to seek the Lord and become a minister for Christ. Arthur alluded in the most touching manner to his dear mother's teaching in his youth. Dear Newman also confirmed Arthur's testimony of his dear mother's teaching and example of a consistent walk as a Christian.

MARCH 14. My birthday. Completed my eighty-fourth year. How great has been the mercy of God throughout the whole of my long life! But my heart aches with the deepest sorrow that I have so deeply offended against so good a God. Have mercy upon me, O Lord.

MARCH 22. Went to Surrey chapel prayer-meeting. Remained afterwards at the temperance-meeting. About seventeen hundred present. At the close, I told the people to begin their temperance life at the foot of the cross, to seek to have Christ in the heart, then they would have strength to resist temptation to evil.

MAY 18. Wedding ring. My dear Mary's first wedding ring being completely worn asunder, I presented her with a new one this day, which I placed on her finger with a heartfelt kiss of love and gratitude to Almighty God for his great mercy in having continued us to each other so many years as husband and wife, with love to each other more than ever. Married fifty-one years, eight months, and three weeks.

JUNE 17. Praised be the Lord, I have him for my defence—Christ the occupant of my heart. Rev. Dr. Legge, from China, called this afternoon and cheered our hearts respecting our son Stephen.

JUNE 19. I feel it quite time to be prepared to meet my God; but Oh the meeting—a holy God and an unholy rebellious sinner. Nothing but the sacrifice of Christ can possibly deliver me from the lowest hell. I look to Christ at once for deliverance and salvation. My eyes, my heart, my soul are up to thee, O Jesus, my rock and my defence, my everlasting hope.

Aug. 9. The Lord's prayer. Mr. T—— referred to the simplicity of its language, yet the weight of its meaning. It breathed a filial spirit, "Father;" a catholic spirit, "Our;" a reverential spirit, "Hallowed;" a missionary spirit, "Thy kingdom come;" an obedient spirit, "Thy will be done;" a dependent spirit, "Give us this day our daily bread;" a forgiving spirit, "As we forgive," etc.; an adoring spirit, "Thine is the kingdom," etc.

Oct. 10. My dear Mary's birthday. What infinite mercy the Lord has bestowed upon us during the last fifty years, through many a cloudy day, crowning us with loving-kindness and tender mercy. Blessed be his name. In the afternoon dear Mary and self united in prayer and thanksgiving, each offering praises and prayer to our gracious God.

Oct. 13. This afternoon dear Mary and self set out to visit Edward at Oxford. Found Edward waiting for us at the station. Dear Mary and self knelt before the Lord with thankfulness for safety in our journey. 14. Inspected the University Press; a wonderful stock of Bibles. Gave a "Sinner's Friend" to the foreman, who had been there forty years.

Nov. 14. Enjoyed a private prayer-meeting; self and dear Mary both engaged in prayer. Heartily thanked the Lord for the blessing of a praying wife. I pray the fifty-first psalm every morning, beseeching the Lord to give me a humble contrite spirit, soul-sorrow for sin, with humble yet implicit confidence in that precious blood which cleanseth from all sin. I believe that I do indeed love the Lord most sincerely, with the most earnest desire to live to his praise in thought, word, and deed, that every power within me may be devoted to his blessed service.

Nov. 19. Anniversary. God be praised for his great mercy in giving me grace, on the 19th of November, 1818, to give up entirely the use of strong drink of any description whatever. During the whole of the forty years which have now passed away I have never had the slightest temptation to take either wine or spirituous liquor or malt liquor of any description whatever, but on the contrary have shuddered even at the smell of strong drink of any kind. Marvellous mercy! Praised be the Lord. The Lord has also mercifully sustained me during forty years as his servant, Jesus Christ ever in my heart, my only hope of salvation. The Lord has preserved me from bringing any disrepute upon his holy name, and has given me many opportunities of exhorting sinners to seek his face. Blessed be his dear name, dear to my heart.

Nov. 27. I not only with grief confess to the Lord that I have sinned deeply, but I enumerate my dreadful sins, praying the Lord to give me soul-felt repentance and implicit confidence in his dear Son.

Dec. 30. This evening attended the watch-night at Surrey chapel. Upwards of two thousand pres-

ent. Home at 1.15. The Lord has mercifully
brought us through another year with much comfort, bestowing upon us grace to feel our sinfulness
and his mercy. Before quitting Heath Cottage for
Surrey chapel, dear Mary finished reading the
psalms, last chapters of Malachi and Revelation.
Afterwards we knelt and prayed, each of us, with
gratitude and praise. Our mercies and blessings
unspeakably great. Thank the Lord for such a
dear wife.

NEW-YEAR'S DAY, 1859. Praised be the Lord for
health to commence the new year under the shadow
of the Almighty, Jesus Christ the million times welcome occupant of each of our hearts.

MARCH 7. Blessed be the Lord, "The Sinner's
Friend" has been the instrument of leading a man
eighty years of age to the Saviour. This is recorded in the "Religious Tract Society's Reporter" for
the present month. The poor sinner was once a
wealthy solicitor, an infidel, reduced to poverty by
intemperance. Had led a godless life till then.
Why was it not my own case? It would have been
so but for the grace of God.

MARCH 14. This day I enter my eighty-sixth
year in perfect bodily health, through the abounding mercy of God, to whom my soul pants with
gratitude and praise. Six children and a grand-
child breakfasted with us.

APRIL 28. I want, I sigh, I pray for my heart to
be free from sin. Praised be the Lord, my bodily
health is perfectly good. "Oh for a closer walk
with God."

JUNE 11. I called on Rev. Henry Townley. Affectionately received. Mr. Townley had been very unwell. Gave a workman "Sinner's Friend" and "Come to Jesus." Praised be the Lord, I have now circulated gratuitously upwards of sixty thou-sand copies of "The Sinner's Friend" in various parts of the world.

JUNE 21. My heart mourns on account of sin, but the blood of Jesus cleanseth all. Once I was the most miserable wretch upon earth, but I have been restored by the grace of God. Once a dirty, wicked boy, cursing, swearing, mingling with the lowest scum of society, no friend to counsel or help me, and yet raised up by especial grace to be a dea-con in the house of God and author of "The Sin-ner's Friend." God be praised for ever and ever Amen.

JUNE 27. I conducted the prayer-meeting and spoke warmly, then attended the temperance meet-ing and gave the first speech.

JULY 1. Arthur's departure for Luddenden Foot to preach the gospel of our blessed Lord. O may the Lord be ever with him, and make him faithful and useful. 17. Dear Mary and self had a private prayer-meeting for Arthur and Newman. Aug. 14. Prevented enjoyment of the sanctuary, but the Lord was with us in our cottage, and we united in praise and prayer, alternately pouring out our hearts be-fore him.

AUG. 26. Excursion to Luddenden Foot. At Wakefield Arthur was waiting for us. Arrived at Luddenden, we all knelt before the Lord with thankfulness. We attended Arthur's new church; the first time we had ever heard him preach. A most searching sermon. What abundant cause for us to bless the Lord for having so evidently called Arthur to the ministry. Sept. 6. Dear Newman walked from Halifax. My beloved Mary, Newman, and self each engaged in prayer for dear Arthur. His ordination took place this evening. He gave a most exciting statement of the way in which the Lord had led him to the ministry. Newman gave the charge in a most impressive manner. My dear Mary and self had abundant reason to bless the Lord for the public testimony of Newman and Arthur to the consistency of their father and mother as professed followers of the Lord Jesus. 7. I am so overwhelmed with gratitude for the mercy of God, that I am ready to burst forth with songs of joy for his great benefits—a dear wife to cheer my declining years with her precious love, also for affectionate children. God be praised for so many choice and precious gifts.

SEPT. 11. Sabbath. A most exciting day. Newman and Arthur conducted the service this morning. In the afternoon Newman preached again. Two or three hundred people following Arthur from open-air preaching to the church, singing the praises of God. Newman preached again in the evening. Hundreds could not gain admittance. Arthur took them into the school-room and preached to them there. To witness both our sons engaged in the service of the sanctuary was most exciting to us. Praised be the Lord. 22. Mercy upon mercy. This day forty-three years ago I discontinued the use of wine and spirituous liquors. Not a drop of either has ever passed the surface of my tongue during the whole of those years. All praise to the Lord.

OCT. 10. My dear Mary's birthday. Praised be God for his great mercy in having spared her to me during so many years, and that we love each other more than ever, the Lord Jesus the welcome occupant of each of our hearts. 11. Knelt together in thanksgiving to our gracious God for his mercy during seven weeks and five days that we had been with dear Arthur. Found Edward, Newman, and Warren waiting to welcome us home. Knelt before the Lord with thankfulness.

OCT. 31. Arthur's birthday. Praised be the Lord that he is now an ordained minister of Christ. Nov. 3. Walked to and from Highgate hill, Andrew Marvell's cottage, and dined with Newman and C——. Attended Surrey chapel in the evening. 25. Body perfectly well, but my sin is ever before me. I pray God daily, hourly, to give me sincere repentance and humble confidence in that precious blood which cleanseth from all sin.

Nov. 26. Disappointment. Eight times I have gone round by the railway arch to see the poor blind man, a Christian, to give him copies of "Come to Jesus" and "The Sinner's Friend," and sometimes a shilling for Christ's sake. This morning I went again on purpose; he was not there. I have often conversed with this poor man about the love of Christ. He reads the Scriptures by means of raised letters for the blind. I have given him many

copies of "Come to Jesus" and "Sinner's Friend"
for sale for his own benefit, intimating to him that
I did so for the love of Christ. Mr. Freeman, Mrs.
F——, and J—— called on me. We passed an hour
in spiritual converse. Mr. Freeman engaged in
prayer. It was a delicious meeting. 28. Went to
the railway arch to see the poor blind man. He was
not there—the ninth time I have sought him. Gave
"Come to Jesus" and "Sinner's Friend" to various
persons on the pavement.

DEC. 8. Dear Mary and self attended a prayer-
meeting at the Sunday School Union. 14. Prayer-
meeting at Crosby Hall. 30. Crosby Hall. A full
attendance. Ten persons prayed. 31. This evening dear Mary and self kept New-year's eve at
home. We prayed alternately, and at two minutes
before midnight we knelt in silent prayer while 1859
was making place for 1860. We of all people had
most abundant reason to praise the Lord for innumerable mercies heaped upon us during the past
year: Arthur become a minister for Christ; Newman continued useful in the Lord; yet I have a
constant heartache on account of sin. I have also
a foreboding of some evil. This is very weak and
foolish, if not sinful, doubting the mercy of that
gracious God who has never left us even under the
most trying circumstances. Oh for more faith!

JAN. 1, 1860. Dear Mary and self united with the
disciples of the Lord this day in commemorating
his dying love. It was a blessed time. Newman's
text, "Redeemed with the precious blood of Christ."
12. Dear Mary and self, with Newman, attended a

communion service at eleven o'clock at Poultry chapel; very many ministers present. Afterwards we attended a prayer-meeting in Exeter Hall. Afterwards we took tea with the old women at Rowland Hill's almshouses. Afterwards attended ser vice at Surrey chapel. A superb day.

FEB. 7. A blessed spiritual day. Dear Mary and self attended prayer-meetings at Crosby Hall and Exeter Hall. Lord Shaftesbury presided. Afterwards enjoyed a most delightful interview with Lord Roden. A day to be remembered with gratitude. 9. Crosby Hall prayer-meeting. I offered fifth prayer. In the evening we attended Surrey chapel. Then dear Newman persuaded us to go to Exeter Hall to hear Gough conclude a lecture on temperance. A great treat of good things.

MARCH 1. This day, 1816, Dr. Day was consulted on my propensity for strong drink, against which he gave a prescription, which I took daily until the end of September following, from which time to the present hour, forty-three years, I have never taken even so much as a single drop of wine or spirituous liquor of any kind. Praised be the Lord.

MARCH 13. The Lord is very merciful and gracious towards me in preservation so many years. This evening, 1811, I was delivered from the lowest hell. I was lying in intoxication at the edge of a canal, on a dark night, near Brierly hill. A stone lay in the way, by the mercy of God, to prevent my rolling into the canal. One turn more and I should have been lost for ever. "Bless the Lord, O my soul, who hath redeemed my life from destruction,

and crowned me with loving-kindness and tender
mercy." Oh may I never forget his benefits. 14.
My birthday; enter my eighty-seventh year this
day. Praise the Lord.

APRIL 6. To his son Arthur. "When you see a
poor vile sinner evincing the smallest desire to return from the error of his way, half afraid to trust
in the promises, let the case of your once lost father
lead you to give him encouragement to trust in that
gracious God who is not willing that any, even the
vilest, should perish; for there is no one too bad for
Christ, whose precious blood is sufficient for all.
You will forgive my preaching to you, dear Arthur,
an ordained minister, and believe me ever," etc.

APRIL 20. Sent a parcel of "Sinner's Friend" to
Miss Marsh, Beckenham; also to St. Pancras workhouse. Sent them with prayer. Vine was this day
appointed to command the Great Eastern on account of his skill as a sailor. He had no patronage.

MAY 1. This day our son Warren was married
by his brother Newman. After breakfast, prayer
was offered by Rev. Francis Tucker. It was a
deeply interesting service, and we had abundant
reason to bless the Lord. 2. Newman accompanied
us to a public meeting of Field-lane Ragged School.
Lord Shaftesbury in the chair. The Bishop of Ri-
pon made the first speech, succeeded by our Newman. 6. A glorious Sabbath, to be remembered
with praise. Dear Mary and self, after the morning service and sacrament, remained in the vestry
with dear Newman, and dined off sandwiches and
tea. In the afternoon we accompanied him to St.

James' Hall, where he preached to a very large congregation. Afterwards we returned to Surrey chapel, and attended evening service, which was overcrowded. Our hearts were full of gratitude to the Lord for giving us so much enjoyment.

MAY 8. To meeting of Band of Hope. Exeter Hall crammed to suffocation.

MAY 13. At Surrey chapel. Mr. Brownlow North gave a most energetic address. 15. Warren with his bride returned to his new dwelling, where we were waiting to receive them. After tea, prayer was offered that the Lord would bless them and dwell ever in their hearts.

MAY 22. Newman's birthday. Most lovely morning. Nightingales singing while I lay in bed. We all went to Leith hill in an open van. A fall. Ladder gave way with myself, by which I was thrown to the ground, with a severe bruise on my right leg. Mercy that no bones were broken nor hurt on my back, but pain very severe. Praise the Lord.

MAY 23. Arose with great difficulty, assisted by my dear Mary. Leg painful, but better. Resolved to go home this day. 24. Dear Mary so kind. 26. Shaved myself. Praise the Lord that, except the bruise, which is black all round, my bodily health is good. Oh that my soul were in an equally comfortable state. I mourn on account of sin, but I pray the Lord almost hourly to forgive my sins, and give me more faith in the blood shed on Calvary. 27. Swelling very bad; must have patience two or three weeks. 30. Dr. Carlill encouraged me about my leg, but says it will take many weeks for recovery. 31. Three doctors, Dr. Carlill, Dr. Hillier, Mr. Quain; favorable opinion, but patience.

JUNE 1. N——, C——, M——, and H——- gone to dine with their brother Vine on board the Great Eastern. 3. Sabbath. Newman called with C—— on the way to Surrey chapel, and prayed. After they had gone, Mary and self prayed alternately for Newman and Arthur as ministers of the gospel. The large print Testament and Psalms presented to me, very useful at the present time; my daily companions. My beloved wife so tender and kind. Praise God for such a wife. 4. Newman called. Yesterday he asked the communicants at the Lord's supper to pray for me. 5. The patience and kindness of my dear Mary. Praise the Lord for so dear a wife. 6. Need of more patience. Lord, be pleased to grant it. 8. On my bed. New Testament and Psalms great comfort; they cheer my heart. Dr. Hillier thinks the swelling smaller. Walked round the bed; praise the Lord. Newman called; brought strawberries; prayed. 9. My soul looking to the Lord. My dear Mary so kind; my comfort and joy. Walked round the bed, going and return-. ing from the sofa, praising God. Sent twenty-five "Sinner's Friend" to E——. 10. Sabbath. Dear Mary read the Scriptures; we repeated hymns and prayed together. Praise the Lord. 11. Swelling not reduced. Doctor recommends opening. 13. In doubt respecting operation; I fear pain. I am perfectly well in health. Praise the Lord.

JUNE 14. Operation. Vast quantity of black blood poured out. 16. Leg better. My dear Mary

so untiring; in good health, praised be the Lord.
18. Dear Henry Townley called; prayed with us;
wept with tenderness; kissed hands. Arthur came.
20. Leg no better; want more humility and patience.
Arthur is a great comfort. 23. Praise the Lord, I
am a little better. Twenty-five thousand volunteers
reviewed in Hyde park. Newman called and prayed. 24. E—— came to see us, and repeated hymns
with us.

MONDAY, JUNE 25. My beloved Mary so active,
so kind; full of health, praise the Lord.

The entry of June 25th is the last.

For some time he progressed favorably, his general health being unimpaired. A slight operation
was followed by erysipelas, and this, combined with
an attack of congestion of the lungs, threatened to
terminate his life within a few hours. The doctors
recommended wine. My mother at once said the
proposal was useless. Then it was suggested that
beer might be less objectionable. My father, who
had been lying in a state of great weakness, apparently unaware of what was said, emphatically
groaned out, *Never, never!* Though wine was
thought essential, and only twenty-four hours were
given as the limit of life, to the astonishment of all,
he rallied so as to leave his bed and go out in a
Bath-chair.

It was my great privilege to be with him very
much during his illness. I was reminded of the
similar honor and happiness I enjoyed in the case
of my dear friend and father-in-law, Dr. Gordon.
He, during eleven years "grown familiar with the

skies," was now waiting to welcome the aged pilgrim who had so often prayed for him and affectionately spoken to him of the Friend of sinners.
For a short time the enemy strove to darken my
father's mind with doubts as to whether he had
ever been truly a child of God. I told him I could
not remember the time when he was not habitually
walking with God. "Ah, but at a great distance."
Then after a pause, "But he has plucked my feet
out of the net, and established my goings." "What
would be your answer if Christ were now to say,
Lovest thou me?" He replied fervently, "Lord,
thou knowest that I love thee." I read the following words of Rowland Hill on his death-bed: "Modest words before God become us best. Strong expressions of personal interest may do for some, but
not for all. I can see more of the Saviour's glory
than of my interest in him. God is letting me down
gently into the grave, and I shall creep into heaven
through some crevice of the door. I have no rapturous joys, but peace, a good hope through grace—
all through grace." He replied, "Yes, I've peace,
I hope."

He said on different occasions, "If this should
carry me off, I've nothing to fear, nothing to ask
for. This is not the experience of an hour, or a
day, or a month, but of forty years. I've been
travelling to that home many years. To think of
laying down this shabby tabernacle and having one
all of white! Nothing to soil it; without spot or
wrinkle, or any such thing. No, nothing shall separate from the love of Christ." I said, "What a

difference between what we were and what we shall
be." He responded, "Yes, and what we *are!*"
"All things are overruled; this accident to bring
me nearer to Christ, and it may be to bring me
home." "You'll kiss this hand when I sha'n't feel
it." "But we shall meet again. Yes, we're on the
same road. Glory, glory, glory! I've no rapturous joy, but I've a humble dependence on the
Lord Jesus Christ."

Reminding him of our motto for the year, "Redeemed with the precious blood of Christ," he said,
"I have prayed every day for many years that he
would come and take possession of the heart he
purchased with his blood." I referred to his having been always ready to speak of Christ. "Because the subject was always nearest my heart." It
was said that many who had been led to heaven by
"The Sinner's Friend" were waiting to give him a
triumphal entry. "Oh, if I can but crawl in on
my hands and knees, I shall be very well satisfied.
Lord, have mercy upon me a sinner; this is my
prayer every day, and many times a day. I so
grieve that I have so little grief for my sins. I've
been a great sinner, and I need a great Saviour."
On Sunday morning he said to me, "Preach about
Christ and his salvation; I've proved it. It's not
less valuable after forty years. Better than ever;
I've proved it."

His thankfulness of spirit was continually exhibited. He regretted giving what he called so much
trouble to those who felt it the greatest privilege
to minister to him. One day, while being fed, he

lifted up his hand. When asked if it was a sign that he declined any more, he answered, "To praise God." I read a letter to him from a lady, who spoke of the usefulness of the Portuguese edition of "The Sinner's Friend." He lifted up his hands solemnly, saying, "Praise the Lord! praise the Lord! praise the Lord!" Hearing of some instances of useful ness, he said, "Praise the Lord; he makes me to bring forth fruit in old age. How wonderful that I should make known Christ. There was a good woman who was told that I had gone to pray with a sick man. 'What,' said she, 'Mr. Vine Hall? Then I shall never despair of any one.'"

He still endeavored to be useful to others. Within a very few days of his death he gave orders for various parcels of his little book to be sent for distribution to Christian friends whom he named. To his barber he said, "You'll not have to shave me much oftener. Here's a little book. I wrote it years ago. It has been blessed to thousands. I hope it will be blessed to you. Follow its directions. Seek Christ with your whole heart. I hope to meet you in heaven." He sent affectionate messages to absent members of the family, enjoining them to meet him above. To his son Vine he sent word: "Tell him that, while captain of the Great Eastern, he must not forget that God placed him there. He must have Christ for *his* Captain, and then he can smile at the storm." To his son Stephen at Hong Kong, who had been abroad upwards of thirty years, and had often expressed his intention of returning to England to see his parents once more, "Tell him how I love him—how glad I should have been to see him; but he must meet me in heaven."

SEPT. 15. He was evidently much weaker. I said, "You are not so well, dear father, to-day." He replied, "I wish the last were here." "The promise of long life has been fulfilled." "Yes, long ago." "Your only plea is Jesus." "Nothing else." On Sunday morning, September 16th, I asked him if he had any message for the congregation. He replied, "Give my Christian love to them, and thank them for all their affection towards me." After this he almost entirely lost the power of speech, but in the afternoon he turned his eyes towards my mother and myself as we were standing at the foot of the bed, and said, "God bless you both." We felt it a patriarchal and a parting benediction.

On Tuesday morning he looked affectionately towards his sorrowing wife and several times uttered her name with considerable distinctness, "Mary! Mary! Mary!" A few hours after, having suffered much from difficulty of breathing, he again made a successful effort to speak, and said with great earnestness, "*Jesus! Jesus! Jesus!*" It was very touching and very characteristic, this mention of the two names most dear to him—expressive of his earthly and his heavenly love. For upwards of fifty years his heart had been linked with that of his wife by ties never surpassed in strength and tenderness. For upwards of forty years the name of Jesus had been music to his soul. These two passions absorbed his whole being. He enjoyed all pleasures, performed all duties, loved all relations and friends, in connection with them. He had no aim, no affection apart.

On Thursday morning he endeavored in vain to speak to us so that we could understand him. These words alone were distinguished: "Passing away, passing away." Then, "Jesus! Jesus!" Then, "He is! he is!" I suggested, "He is here, he is precious." He nodded assent, and we caught the word "Pray." We knelt round his bed in supplication that Jesus would speedily release his dear servant, and take him to join the great congregation of the saints made perfect. He earnestly responded, "Amen!" lifting up his hands as if eager to be gone. Then after putting his arm once more round my mother's neck, he gradually sank into a state of stupor, out of which, on Saturday morning, September 22d, at twenty minutes past five, he awoke in the immediate presence of "The Sinner's Friend."

What welcomes greeted him: from many dear friends gone before, with whose hearts his own had beaten in warm response as they spoke together of Jesus; from hundreds, perhaps thousands of ransomed souls who had been guided to heaven by his instrumentality; from the angels to whom he had been the means of giving so much blissful work in their "rejoicing over one sinner that repenteth;" above all, from Him whose name had so long been music to his ears, the thought of whom had so long ravished his heart.

He had told my mother where to find a letter for her to read after his decease. After many expressions of the most fervent love to herself, the letter closes thus: "Grieve not, dearest, that your ever tenderly loved husband is taken from you, only to be *restored* in the Lord's time; but rather *rejoice* that his soul is relieved from its tenement of clay, to be *for ever* with the Lord. Yes, *for ever* with the *Lord.* I hope there may be no presumption in this assertion, nothing rash, irreverent, or bold; nothing unbecoming a poor redeemed sinner, in whose heart the Lord Jesus has held occupation so many years, ever a million million times WELCOME Guest, always the *delight* of my life, the *joy* of my soul.

"Our blessed and merciful God will never leave you, never forsake you. We have *proved* and *experienced* his faithfulness.

"As my soul has long mourned over my sin with deep repentance, my God has forgiven it too, but I have never forgiven *myself,* nor have I ever ceased to feel the deepest sorrow. But God be praised, 'the precious blood of Christ cleanseth from *all* sin;' yes, even from *my* sins, crimson as they are. And oh what special mercy that I have long been delivered from all fear as to the article of *death* or the *act* of dying. Whether my body expire in agony, or in peace and gentleness, I know the Lord will give me *dying* grace, and I wish to know no other will than his. I love him too warmly to distrust him a single moment.

"AUGUST 24, 1858."

CHAPTER XI.

FILIAL REMINISCENCES BY THE EDITOR.

In this supplementary chapter I propose to lay before the reader a few additional facts illustrative of my father's history and character.

John Vine Hall was born at Diss, in Norfolk, March 14, 1774, just before the Americans drew the sword of independence, and sixteen years before the first French revolution. His father had accumulated considerable property in business, but lost it in speculation; so that "little Jack," as he was called, was sent at eleven years of age to earn his own bread, as related on page 11. He often used to speak of his early struggles and hard toil when a mere child.

Those who knew him only in old age will not be surprised to learn that, as a young man, his company was much valued. He was innately courteous, both in disposition and manners a "*gentleman*." He was a good musician. At fourscore he still played well on the flageolet, and drew from the flute a peculiarly rich tone; while the fine tenor voice he consecrated to "psalms and hymns and spiritual songs," must have been a great acquisition in the convivial circles of his earlier years. He was to the last witty and facetious, had a store of capital anecdotes, and could imitate to perfection the Scotch, Irish, and Welsh diction.

The physical manliness and courage he manifested in youth aided him when he became a good soldier of Jesus Christ. He was always ready to help the weak against the strong. He often related how, on hearing the shrieks of a woman in the market-place at Maidstone, he rushed to her assistance, and with one blow of his fist felled to the ground the ruffianly husband who was beating her, receiving for his reward a blow from the woman's patten, which left its mark on his forehead till the day of his death. He said that afterwards, whenever he saw a man and woman quarrelling, he moderated his indignation by saying to himself, "Remember the patten." He once pinioned a highwayman single handed, retaining him in his grasp till assistance came. On another occasion, returning home on horseback with a large sum of money, he saw a man apparently drunk rolling about a lonely part of the road. Suspecting a trick, he pulled up, drew his pistol and threatened to fire if the man did not instantly stand aside. The click of the trigger put the pretended drunkard to flight. On reaching home he found his pistol had no priming. When the first Napoleon was threatening to invade this country my father joined the Yeomanry Cavalry, and at a grand review before George III. was selected, as the best swordsman of his regiment, to go through the exercise before his majesty. It fell to his duty as a volunteer to form one of the escort who guarded the conspirators tried at Maidstone for complicity in the mutiny at the Nore, from Maidstone to Sheerness. A celebrated German swordsman was at that

time employed by government at the Maidstone
military dépôt to instruct the soldiers, and gave an
exhibition in the Town-hall before a large company
of the aristocracy and military. My father was
urged to accept his challenge with naked swords.
Using great caution, he parried all the cuts and
thrusts of his adversary, and then seizing his opportunity, ripped up the embroidered sleeve of the
German from wrist to elbow amid the plaudits of
the assembly.

As a man of business he was eminent for dili-
gence, punctuality, and caution. He made himself
master of every department, and was never ashamed of any thing which was necessary or expedient
for him to do. Whatever he did, however trivial,
he did thoroughly. He could not endure slovenli-
ness or waste in little things. He was exact in the
daily balance of cash, and kept a watchful eye to the
stock in trade. He was never idle. On commencing at Worcester, he had to restore the character of
the house. There was little genuine business, but
as it would be ruin to be idle he used to take down
reams of paper, count the quires, and tie them up
again; or he would rule paper hour after hour. One
day he overheard a laborer who was passing exclaim, "Hey, but that's a working chap, he's always
at it." "Go on, my good friend," said my father to
himself, "that's right, spread it over the city." He
frequently used to mention this in after-years as a
lesson to young men. He has been known to spend
weeks together without leaving the house except for
a place of worship, diligently engaged from morning

to night in carrying on an extensive and complicated business. Years would elapse without his having a week's holiday. He kept up this assiduity until he had worked off the chief portion of his heavy pecuniary obligations, and until his sons growing up rendered such close application less necessary.

He was punctuality itself. At seven in the morning he was regularly seated at Scott's Bible. At eight, to a minute, he rang for family worship. He never kept any one waiting for him a moment. He wrote with his watch open before him to secure exactness. When the time came, he would quit any occupation, however absorbing and pleasant, to keep the appointment of the hour. Nothing could draw him away from doing the right thing at the right time. From the business of the present moment he would let nothing deter him.

His punctuality in monetary transactions was not less remarkable. No traveller called twice for an account. Conversing once with a banker about the interest charged on overdrawn accounts, my father remarked, "You never charge me any." "No," said the banker, "you never give us a chance."

He used to relate the following incident as a caution not to make confidants of strangers. Coming once from London by the stage, a fellow-traveller became exceedingly communicative to the passengers respecting the business which was taking him to Maidstone. His object was to establish a county newspaper on a plan which would not fail of crushing all competitors: and he was good enough to explain in detail all the secrets of his intended diplomacy, to the immense amusement of my father and his fellow-townsmen. The talkative stranger concluded by asking Mr. Hall the names of the principal booksellers in the town, that he might enlist them in his cause. Mr. Hall included his own name in the list. The next morning he observed the would-be newspaper proprietor approaching his shop accompanied by a well-known friend, and immediately placed himself in a conspicuous position at the door. The talkative gentleman suddenly stopped, made some observation to his companion, turned on his heel, and nothing more was heard of him or his project, the secrets of which he had so prematurely disclosed.

The following were favorite business maxims: "Civility is cheap, and goes a great way." "Mind your business, and your business will mind you." "If you would have your business done, go; if not, send." "Watch your stock as you would watch a thief." "Take care of the pence, and the pounds will take care of themselves." "There's only one way to do business, and that is the right way." "If a thing's worth doing at all, it's worth doing well." "Never back a bill, even for your own brother or father, unless you can answer two questions: When due, can I pay it; and am I able and willing to lose it? Beware of the plea, 'It's only a form.'"

While by far the most diligent man in his house, he was never exacting towards others, nor indifferent to their infirmities. He was very unlike some employers, who seem only to calculate how much profit they can get out of their work-people, careless of the welfare of those who have helped them to prosperity. When he took the business at Maidstone, he found there an elderly man who had acted as foreman during many years, and who very soon fell ill. Nevertheless his weekly wages were paid him till he died, although he never came near the printing-office; the amount thus given to the old servant of a predecessor being upwards of £100.

As a deacon of the church he was as exemplary as in other relations. He ever cherished and manifested towards his minister sincere respect and affection. As treasurer he received and disbursed the pew-rents, and when the quarter came round, whatever might have been the delay in supplying his official treasury, there was never a day's delay in paying the ministerial stipend. He always supplied the pastor with books and stationery, receiving no payment and sending in no account. Whatever the claims of his business, he was always present at the prayer-meeting on Monday, and the weekly lecture on Wednesday, as well as at the deacons' meetings and church-meetings. Whoever might be absent, his pastor might always rely on him. His motto was, "God first, business next, pleasure last."

He was remarkably generous and unselfish. A striking instance of this was his transfer to the benefit of his employer of the offer of alderman Christopher Smith to advance him money when required to go into business. The alderman was surprised and pleased, advanced the £1,000, and renewed his promise to my father, which he afterwards nobly

11*

redeemed by lending him several thousand pounds
on his personal security. It was no difficulty to him
to do good to others, whether by speech or letter,
to instruct or console them, or by hand and purse
to relieve their sufferings. He could not deny street-
beggars even, though he might suspect the truth of
their tale. He used to say that, even if an imposter
should happen to get the money, it would not be
lost if given in the name of Christ. A "converted"
Jew called on him once with a letter of introduction,
and begged the loan of a few pounds, which were
promptly lent *in that Name.* The Jew promised repayment, "As sure as I am a Christian." My father
used to tell this with great effect, adding, " The Jew
kept his word, he did not pay." He often scolded
sturdy mendicants, but the scolding was an invari-
able antecedent to a gift. Accosted once by an
Irish beggar, he said, "Now you know, Pat, that if
I give you something you'll spend it in whiskey."
"No, your honor," replied Pat, "I've not had any
whiskey this three months." "That's only because
you have had no money to buy it," rejoined my father. "That's true, yer honor," said Pat, laughing
all over. An extra gift, of course, was the reward
of this reply, which my father often delighted to
repeat. When he gave tracts to the poor he wrap-
ped up pence in them, and after his death his coat-
pockets were found stored with this ammunition of
love, without which he never went out of the house.
Not only would he give generously from his purse,
but his heart yearned with kind sympathy to every
one. He was always ready to hear patiently any

tale of distress or anxiety. I have heard him groan
in sympathy with one; I have seen him weep with
another; and I have seen him in ecstacy of thankfulness with those who had good news to commu-
nicate, responding to their tale with, "Praise the
Lord." Thus literally fulfilling the injunction to
"rejoice with them that do rejoice, and weep with
them that weep."

He had a most tender spirit. Any tale of suffering or affliction brought tears to his eyes. There
were incidents in his own life which he had related
hundreds of times, but to which he could not refer
without choking with emotion in the attempt. This
was specially so when, in answer to our earnest request, he would sometimes tell us the tale of Dunk's
deliverance, or of his first acquaintance with my
mother. My earliest remembrance of him arises
partly from this feature of his character. My mother
was from home, and in the early morning I clam-
bered out of my little crib into his bed and begged
him to tell me a story. He told me about Joseph
in Egypt with such emotion that I felt as if he himself had witnessed the circumstances he so feelingly
described, especially Joseph's making himself known
to his brethren, an incident over which my father
wept perhaps as much as Joseph himself. Morning
after morning the request was repeated, "Tell me
again about Joseph," and morning after morning the
narrative was repeated with undiminished emotion.

His affection for his mother was very strong.
For many years she was supported by him, and when
his pecuniary resources were very small he loved to

minister to her necessities. He had sent at the usual
time, through the post-office, a £5 note which was
stolen. His mother anxiously waited till her resources were nearly exhausted. At length she wrote,
"My son Joseph in Egypt, the corn is nearly gone."
Great was his grief. Another note was promptly
posted in a letter, on the outside of which was written, "This letter contains a £5 note. The last was
stolen. Please let this pass; it is for a poor widow."
It arrived safely. Often have his children heard
him speak with choking utterance and streaming
eyes of how this mother died with these words on
her lips: "The Lord bless him, my Joseph in
Egypt; the Lord bless him, bless him, bless him."
Verily the prayer was answered, and the promise
literally fulfilled, "Thy days shall be long in the
land."

In the domestic circle he was all tenderness and
unselfishness, delighting to provide for the comfort
and enjoyment of his family, but seeking no separate
gratification for himself. I should think there have
been few whose personal expenses were so small as
compared with the measure of his outlay for others.
To his wife, as the journal abundantly testifies, he
ever showed the most tender and considerate affection; an ardent lover as well as a faithful husband
to the very last. He entered with all his heart into
the joys, sorrows, and projects of his elder children,
and delighted to romp with the younger. He treasured up with great interest specimens of our first
efforts in writing and drawing. His generosity of
heart led him to rejoice in the pleasures of others.

even though he could not share them. Many times when, through pressure of business, he was unable to join his family in their excursions of pleasure, he took the greatest interest in their comfort and enjoyment, tapping his barometer to see if the weather would be suitable, and parting with them at the door with the kindest expressions; then, on their return, meeting them so pleasantly, and hearing with evident delight and gratitude their accounts of a happy day. The family scene on a Sunday evening, when parents and children sat round the fire repeating hymns, will ever be fresh in the memory of us all. He always commenced, the child on his left hand following, and so on, round and round the circle, till it was time to break up for evening service. With what pathos would he repeat his special favorites, such as, "Oh for a heart to praise my God," "Guide me, O thou great Jehovah," etc. And sometimes, with peculiar solemnity, he would interrupt the repetition by urging on us to give our hearts entirely to God, so that we might all meet, a redeemed family in heaven. This hallowed exercise of speaking to one another in psalms and hymns and spiritual songs would then close by all uniting in singing,

"May the grace of Christ our Saviour,
  And the Father's boundless love,
With the Holy Spirit's favor,
  Rest upon us from above:

May we thus abide in union
  With each other and the Lord,
And possess in sweet communion
  Joys which earth cannot afford."

This "hymn-repeating" is continued by his children
to the third generation—a valuable incentive to personal piety by those at home, and a precious bond
of sympathy with those afar off. My brother Arthur, referring to these family gatherings, writes,
"Hallowed seasons these. Often, when tossed upon
the billows of the deep, or upon the still more dangerous depths of sin, has the returning Sabbath
evening hour of hymns and psalms been to my soul
like the sheet-anchor to a storm-tossed mariner.
'They are now engaged in repeating hymns, and I
in the service of the devil.' Often have tears started at the thought. Such were some of the cables
which bound our hearts to the family circle, and
held us in many a hurricane of temptation from
being driven upon the rocks of sin. It was the
holy, consistent life of my honored parents at home
that alone saved *me* from falling into the fearful
abyss of infidelity. I had joined an infidel club.
In my ignorance I deemed the arguments against
the Bible conclusive. I *wanted* to disbelieve what
marred my sinful pleasure. I began to inspect the
lives of professors, and tried to put them all down
as more or less deceived or deceivers, as hypocrites
and humbugs. But when I looked at home, I felt
that there at any rate were two whose lives were
daily evidences of the truthfulness of their profession. I believe it would have rejoiced me to have
detected a flaw in the religious consistency of my
parents; but I could not, and their *lives* upset all
the sophistry of the debating-room. I said to myself, 'Whatever others may be, I know that my

father and mother are sincere. Their holy lives persuade me there must be something in religion, after all.'"

It is worthy of remark that, whereas my father dated his conversion from March 14, 1812, it was not till November 19, 1818, that he was finally victorious over his besetting sin. During upwards of six years the conflict lasted, and often the flesh seemed to have gained complete victory over the spirit. Was he then insincere in his religious convictions during that period? None who read the original diary can think so; few who read the extracts given in this volume. My own full persuasion is that, from the 14th of March, 1812, my father became a real Christian, in spite of his lamentable failures while the stern struggle lasted with the evil habits by which he was "tied and bound." Surely his example teaches the duty of long-suffering forbearance towards all who manifest any desire for reformation, however numerous and distressing may be their temporary relapses. In this respect the conduct of the Methodists at Worcester well deserves praise and imitation. God's forbearance with us should make us forbearing with our fellow-sinners. The church should never sanction sin, but should never cease to bear with it patiently, and should never cast off its erring members so long as they have any compunction for their faults. Better to err on the side of charity than of sternness—to hold a fallen brother too long, so as to incur the charge of complicity, than to cast him off too soon, so as to plunge him into hopeless despair.

But how was it that the conflict lasted so long?
How came it to pass that, in spite of the grace of
God, the study of the Bible, the preaching of the
gospel, the holy sacraments, the society of Christians, and earnest prayer—how came it to pass that
again and again he fell so grievously, and often
seemed so nearly lost? Were all human means
used which were appropriate? In my father's case
habit had become a second nature. Moreover, the
occasional lust for wine had assumed the diseased
form known as *oinomania*. For him, entire abstinence was essential as a preventive of excess. There
were times when a single glass acted as a spark to
gunpowder. The spark might have been withheld;
but when applied, the explosion was unavoidable.
But this thought did not occur to his anxious and
distressed friends. Still they placed wine and spirits on their tables, partaking of those beverages in
his presence, and encouraging him to join them,
only with the advice to be moderate—advice inap-
plicable to him. At length medical treatment was
resorted to and medicine prescribed. But that
medicine failed till abstinence was practised. My
opinion is, that it may render total abstinence less
difficult; but that total abstinence without the medicine will be successful, while the medicine without
total abstinence will only encourage vain hopes,
and do more harm than good.

Had my father abstained altogether, from March
14, 1812, all that conflict, disgrace, agóny, and peril
had been spared. Would it have been unphilosoph-
ical or unscriptural if his friends had said, " Broth-

er, your safety requires you to relinquish these beverages entirely. It is especially difficult for you,
with habits so inveterate and a morbid craving so
strong, to give them up. It is scarcely possible for
you to do this if to your other difficulties is super-
added that of standing alone, and being remarked
in every society. It is easy for us who have not
your infirmity. For your sake then we will join
you in a resolution of abstinence. We will not hold
before your eyes, and praise in your hearing, and
enjoy in your presence that which we know you
cannot safely drink yourself. We will not place
before you a temptation too strong for you to resist.
And so to encourage you in what is for you absolutely necessary, we will agree with you totally to
discontinue the use of these drinks as beverages."
Who can doubt that, with my father's deep convictions, earnest resolutions, and the help of divine
grace so evidently imparted to him, this course
would have been successful from the first?

But as with many other useful discoveries, the
thing which is simple when known, was not then
conceived of. But it is different now. The simple
method of cure by abstinence, the application to
this special case of our Saviour's precept, "See that
ye *enter not* into temptation," is well known, and is
the means of rescuing thousands of drunkards annually. I am almost weekly applied to for advice by
persons in the upper classes of society on behalf of
some friend whose besetting sin is intemperance.
Beyond the general advice which every Christian
would give, I have but one reply: The person thus

ensnared must abstain, and his friends must show
their sincerity on his behalf by abstaining too, in
order to render it easier for him. I venture to ask
whether such a course would be opposed to that
Christianity which says, "Unless a man take up his
cross and deny himself, he cannot be my disciple.
Let no man place a stumbling-block, or an occasion
to fall, in his brother's way. It is good neither to
eat flesh, nor to drink wine, nor any thing whereby
thy brother stumbleth, is offended, or made weak."

Bending over these memorials, was it fanatical
if my brother Arthur and myself resolved, by the
help of God, more fervently than ever to wage war
against those pernicious drinking customs which
annually destroy so many thousands of precious
souls, and to which our honored father so nearly
fell a victim? Had he not been rescued, how useful a life, how bright an example would have been
lost to the church; how precious a jewel would have
been missing from the Saviour's crown! And what
would his children have become?

My father's strong faith in the power of prayer
was aided by several remarkable instances in his
own history. On March 14, 1812, when he seemed
to hear a voice saying, "If thou wilt forsake thy
sins they shall be forgiven thee," a day which he
always regarded as that of his spiritual as well as
his natural birth, my mother had been more than
ordinarily earnest in prayer, in consequence of the
sad condition into which at that time he had fallen.
Having, in the last extremity, implored some special
succor when, without an almost miraculous interver-

tion, utter ruin seemed inevitable, she went out on some domestic affairs; and when she returned found my father, as above described, "a new creature."

My brother Arthur says, "One department of his business at Maidstone was an extensive wine trade, handed down from his predecessor. Though an abstainer from wine from personal considerations, he did not then see any impropriety in the traffic, as he did not supply public-houses, but only the nobility and gentry of the neighborhood. The formation of Total Abstinence Societies led to the discussion of the traffic question. At that time I despised teetotalism, and expressed my determination that when I had a share of the business I would push the wine department. When circumstances had led me to London for a time, my father saw the danger to which I should be exposed on my return, and in my absence determined to give up the trade, refusing to sell it as such, at a premium, and simply making over the stock at a valuation to another wine-merchant. He earnestly prayed that the opposition I should certainly make to his act might be removed. That prayer was answered. Unknown to my parents, I had at the same time, in London, become convinced of the importance of teetotalism as an agent of physical, political, and moral good, not then seeing its vast importance in a religious point of view. I determined to go home and sign the pledge in my native town, where I was well known as an enemy of total abstinence. I sent word that I was coming, but did not explain my

object. Before entering the house I went to **the**
secretary of the society and signed the pledge.
This detained me some little while. Well do I remember that night. My father had given me up,
as the omnibus had passed the door several minutes, and he was pleasurably astonished to see me
enter. 'What makes you so late?' said he.
'I've been to sign the pledge,' I replied. My parents looked at each other speechless, my father's
arms upraised in gratitude and astonishment. Their
prayer had been answered. That night was a
memorable one in my history. Signing that pledge
was the first step to the cross of Christ, though I
knew it not then. As with thousands, so with me,
it was my stepping stone to salvation."

His religion exhibited a remarkable combination
of personal strictness, with charitable consideration
of others. He had no relish for general society, or
for amusements which some devout people regard
as unobjectionable. But he never made his own
conduct a rule for others, or questioned the sincerity of those who differed from himself in reference
to what was not absolutely condemned by the word
of God. He would never tolerate conversation which
had even the appearance of backbiting or slander.
Nor could he endure any approach to angry alterca-
tion. He has often quietly left the room, when even
a pleasant argument has been carried on, as he
thought, too warmly. His was the charity that "en-
vieth not, is not puffed up, is not easily provoked,
thinketh no evil," but "hopeth all things and endureth all things."

The modest character of his Christian confidence and joy is illustrated by the following conversation, which he frequently quoted, between the Rev. Rowland Hill and himself. On the second visit of this eminent preacher, my father, in reply to an inquiry after his welfare, said, "I am just where you left me." "What," said Mr. Hill, "got no further?" "No," said my father, "not a step." "Where was it then?" inquired Mr. Hill. "Rejoicing with trembling," was the reply. "Be sure and stop there," eagerly responded the venerable evangelist, "do n't try to go a step beyond. I 've met sometimes with people who got further than that, and when I have asked about them they had got away out of sight altogether. My old book says, 'Blessed is the man that feareth always.'"

I never met with any Christian who was so constantly bearing witness to the love of Christ. He was indeed "instant in season and out of season." For many years he regularly visited the prison, and conducted a religious service weekly in the workhouse. But his chief labors were with individuals. It was scarcely possible to be in his company a few minutes without hearing from his lips some testimony for God. He used to delight in placing in the hedges copies of "The Sinner's Friend" open at the page, "Sinner, this little book is for you." Being reminded of this during his illness, he said, "Yes; and I always stuck them up with a prayer." In coaches, steam-boats, by the roadside, it was his habit to present a religious tract to young and old, rich and poor, and generally to enter into conversa-

tion with them. That which would have been felt
intrusive in most people, did not seem so in him. So
impressive yet so benevolent and courteous was his
manner, that even when the theme was uncongenial
he himself was listened to with interest. However
busy he might be he was always ready to speak of
Christ, and to engage in religious exercises. I have
often seen him, when immersed in cares and labors,
lay down his pen on the entrance of a Christian
friend, speak to him for a few minutes with the utmost spiritual ardor on heavenly subjects, and then
resume his work as if there had been no interrup-
tion. He often said he was like a bottle containing
water and oil; when shaken, the oil is mixed with
the water, but the moment the bottle is at rest, the
oil mounts to the surface. Fervent love to God in
Christ, to a living, personal, divine Saviour and
Friend, was habitually the dominant emotion in his
soul, and out of the abundance of his heart his mouth
spoke.

He concerned himself very little with abstruse
theological questions. His all-absorbing thought
was this, "God is love. Jesus is the Friend of sinners. He has saved me, even me. He is able to
save to the uttermost all who come unto God by
him. He is able and willing to save you." This
was the burden of his speech for nearly fifty years.
This was the message which he sent all over the
world by his little tract. And I feel I cannot close
this sketch in a manner more pleasing to himself
than by quoting his appeal on the first page of that
tract:

"Sinner, this little book is for you: to give you hope and comfort, joy and peace.

"Only believe in the *willingness* of God to forgive *every* PENITENT sinner, and pray earnestly to him for mercy, and rest assured that if you are truly penitent, NOT ELSE, he *will* pardon you, yes, even *you*, for the sake of his beloved SON.

"REMEMBER, 'the Lord *waiteth* to be gracious' unto you, therefore put away the temptations of Satan, who would have you distrust the mercies of God, and persuade you to believe that your sins are *too great* to be pardoned. This is *impossible;* and the reason is, because *the blood of* CHRIST *cleanseth* US from ALL sin. 1 John 1:7.

> " 'Let not conscience make you linger,
> Nor of fitness madly dream ;
> The only fitness HE requireth,
> Is to *feel your need* of HIM.'

" *Secret*, earnest *prayer*, is the *never failing* method of obtaining relief and comfort in seasons of the deepest distress.

" A tender, broken, contrite heart; a humble consciousness of having merited condemnation; an earnest application for mercy—these are things which accompany salvation, and *will always be received* by our gracious GOD.

" The reader of this little book must remember, that, of *himself*, he can do nothing to *merit* the favor of God; but he need not be discouraged, for God is willing to bestow his Holy Spirit on *every* one who asketh; and also to give repentance, faith, and the spirit of prayer to every seeking soul; *none denied.*"

The mortal remains of Mr. J. V. Hall were interred in Abney Park cemetery, on September 26, 1860.

His true monument, "The Sinner's Friend," is in every land. His tombstone in the cemetery bears this inscription:

In Memory

OF

JOHN VINE HALL,

THE BELOVED AND HONORED AUTHOR OF "THE SINNER'S FRIEND,

WHO ENTERED INTO THE JOY OF HIS LORD,

SEPTEMBER 22, 1860,

IN HIS EIGHTY-SEVENTH YEAR.

"REDEEMED WITH THE PRECIOUS BLOOD OF CHRIST."